FIRST LOVE, LAST LOVE

FIRST LOVE, LAST LOVE

Rosemary Anne Sisson

Severn House Large Print
London & New York

This first large print edition published in Great Britain 2002 by
SEVERN HOUSE LARGE PRINT BOOKS LTD of
9-15, High Street, Sutton, Surrey, SM1 1DF.
First world regular print edition published 2002 by
Severn House Publishers, London and New York.
This first large print edition published in the USA 2003 by
SEVERN HOUSE PUBLISHERS INC., of
595 Madison Avenue, New York, NY 10022

British Library Cataloguing in Publication Data

Sisson, Rosemary Anne, 1923 -
  First love, last love. - Large print ed.
  1. Love stories
  2. Large type books
  I. Title
  823.9'14 [F]

ISBN 0-7278-7181-1

Printed and bound in Great Britain by
MPG Books Ltd, Bodmin, Cornwall.

To my long-time friend and agent,
Anne Dewe,
who gives care and encouragement
to all her writers, young and old,
with affectionate gratitude.

This story takes place some time before 1971 and about ten years after the arrival of the *Windrush* bringing the first immigrants from the Caribbean, so the author trusts that Norman and friends will forgive her – and Miss Pollock – for telling it as it was.

One

'Don't you understand, Miss Pollock?' said Mr Simmonds.

'No,' said Miss Pollock. 'I don't.'

Mr Simmonds sighed. It was nearly six o'clock. He had come out of office hours to try to make things clear to Miss Pollock, and after twenty minutes by the wheezing old clock on the mantelpiece, he was no nearer than when he had begun. He took a deep breath.

'As I say, the houses on each side of yours are going to be pulled down.'

'I don't mind what you do with them,' said Miss Pollock. 'I don't never hardly see any of the neighbours, anyway.'

'But, Miss Pollock,' exclaimed Mr Simmonds, 'you haven't any neighbours. All the other houses are empty. Didn't you know?'

'I never took much notice,' said Miss Pollock.

This was not quite true. Ever since the bombing, when one of the houses was destroyed, the two on each side of it had been

9

empty, propped up with timbers, their windows boarded up. One by one, others had fallen silently into vacancy, curtains disappearing from the windows, weeds creeping over the tiny front gardens. One morning, Miss Pollock, peering between her own lace curtains, had seen that the people from the house next door were moving out. When she went out to do her shopping, she counted and found that only two other houses besides her own were still occupied. She felt a panic then. Suppose the other two houses should fall empty? It would be like living in a graveyard. Oh well, she thought, remembering what her mother used to say, *What can't be cured must be endured.* And then, thrusting the panic away from her, *Best not to think about it.* So ever since, she had walked along the street with her head bent down, careful not to look at the other houses. But if she hadn't noticed when the last one had become empty, it had been because she was determined not to do so.

'It's not very pleasant for you,' said Mr Simmonds, 'living here alone.'

'I'm used to it,' said Miss Pollock.

She looked at the clock. It was nearly time for her tea. About now her father used to come home from work, and he always looked in the door on his way to the scullery to wash.

'Got the kettle on?' he used to say. 'Or

aren't we having tea today?'

And her mother would look up from laying the white tablecloth on the red plush cover. 'Get along with you!' she would say. 'It'll be ready as soon as you are.'

Tea had always been the favourite meal in their house, and even now Miss Pollock looked forward to her bit of potted meat on toast in the winter, and bread and marge in the summer. She wished Mr Simmonds would go away.

Mr Simmonds suddenly rose to his feet.

'Miss Pollock,' he said, 'I'm very sorry, but you've got to go!'

'Go?' said Miss Pollock. She wasn't alarmed so much as indignant. '*Where*?'

'Well,' said Mr Simmonds, 'as I think I told you in my last letter...' He paused. Miss Pollock looked mulishly blank. Mr Simmonds glanced at the buff envelopes stuck up behind the clock. He cleared his throat. 'A place has been found for you in an old people's home.'

'A *home*?' exclaimed Miss Pollock, astonished. 'You won't get me into no home!'

'A ... an *old people's* home,' said Mr Simmonds, faintly. 'You'd find it very ... Most people are only too anxious to ... It's very difficult to get a place in an old people's home!'

'I'm not old,' said Miss Pollock. 'I don't want to go to one of them places.'

'You'd be well looked after there,' said Mr Simmonds.

This was the final insult. 'Looked after', as if she was 'wanting'!

'I don't want looking after!' she said, furiously. 'I've always done for myself and I always will!'

Mr Simmonds was suddenly desperately tired. He had a headache, too. He moved towards the door and paused, looking back.

'Miss Pollock,' he said, 'this house is scheduled for demolition. You will have to leave. We ... we might be able to find you a room somewhere if you feel that you—'

'A room!' cried Miss Pollock. 'I don't want a room! I've got a house!'

'But you can't stay *here*.'

'Why not?' Miss Pollock demanded. 'I pay my rent. The landlord can't turn me out if I pay my rent.'

'It isn't a landlord. It is the Council.'

'Don't make no difference,' said Miss Pollock obstinately. 'They can't turn me out if I pay my rent.'

Mr Simmonds glanced at the clock, hesitated, and then came back into the room. Miss Pollock's expression was not encouraging. She set her small lips and looked up at him suspiciously out of round blue eyes. He decided to make one last effort to explain to her what was really so simple and commonplace.

'The Council bought this property, Miss Pollock, two years ago, and you've been paying rent to them ever since.' He paused. 'Didn't the Council rent collector explain this to you?'

'Oh, I noticed there was a different chap come to collect the rent,' said Miss Pollock. 'Didn't make no difference to me. I always had it ready for him just the same.'

'But we wrote to you to tell you...' He looked at the envelopes behind the clock, stopped, and started again. 'Didn't the Council rent collector tell you that the Council had bought these houses for demolition?'

She looked blank.

'In order to pull them down,' said Mr Simmonds.

'Oh,' said Miss Pollock. 'He said something about it. I never took much notice. I didn't think he meant *this* house.'

'They are all going to come down,' said Mr Simmonds, 'so that new houses can be built.'

'I don't want no new house,' said Miss Pollock, decidedly. 'I'll stay here.'

Mr Simmonds found himself back where he had started. A feeling of hopelessness overcame him. He stared at Miss Pollock and she looked back at him with all the single-minded tenacity of childhood or old age.

'Miss Pollock,' said Mr Simmonds very

gently, 'you can't stay here. You will have to go.'

Miss Pollock stood up. Mr Simmonds was not a tall man, but even so he towered over her as she stood on the hearthrug, gazing up at him defiantly.

'I won't!' said Miss Pollock.

Two

It was raining when Mr Simmonds left Miss Pollock's house, and the wind blowing from the sea was at once blustery and cold. He had come out without his raincoat, and even before he reached his car, his tweed jacket and grey flannel trousers were wet through. When he arrived home, he found that no one had opened the garage doors. As he struggled with them in the wind and rain, he found himself thinking that if he hadn't gone to visit Miss Pollock, he would have got home in the dry.

'Oh, you're soaking!' cried his wife as he went breathlessly inside. 'And you're late for your tea,' she added, reproachfully.

'Yes,' said Mr Simmonds, 'I know.'

He had been thinking about it all the way home. His wife always had tea at half past four with the children, and he had his on a tray in the sitting room – his own little pot of tea, with bread and butter and a slice of home-made cake. With the children up in their bedrooms doing their homework, and his wife busy in the kitchen, that half-hour alone in front of the fire with the evening paper was the very best time of the day for him. But tonight, since he was late, the children had finished their homework. They were bouncing about on the sofa and insisted on having the television on – some horrible, noisy American comedy series – and he felt tired and old and irritable, and when his wife brought the supper in at nine o'clock, he couldn't enjoy it.

'There!' she said. 'And mixed grill, too! Your favourite! That's because you had your tea too late!'

It was quite true. If he had his tea after six o'clock, he never could enjoy his supper. And Mrs Simmonds didn't like to have supper later than nine o'clock, because then there was so little time to sit down before they went to bed.

'What were you doing?' she asked. 'What made you so late?'

'Oh, I had to go and see an old lady, a Council tenant. Her house is due for demolition and she won't get out.'

'Couldn't you write to her?'

'I've tried that, but she doesn't seem to read the letters, or else she doesn't take them in. She's really a problem.'

'I don't see why *you* have to go and see her.'

'Oh, well...' said Mr Simmonds.

'You're too kind-hearted,' said Mrs Simmonds.

It was true, she thought. He was much too kind-hearted. Of course, that was what had first made her love him. It didn't sound very romantic. Women were supposed to love men who were masterful and ruthless. But she didn't. She loved Billy because he was so kind. Only, people did take advantage of it, and that annoyed her.

'Next time,' she said, 'you write her a letter!'

Three

'By the way, Bill,' said Mr Harper, 'what's the situation with Hampton Row? There's a tenant, isn't there?'

'Yes,' replied Mr Simmonds, 'an old lady.'

'Oh yes, that's right,' said Mr Harper. 'I thought she might die, but of course these old people never do when you want them to. We've found alternative accommodation?'

'Er ... yes, but ... She says she won't go.'

16

'Won't go?' exclaimed Mr Harper, bracingly. 'Nonsense! She's got to go. What steps have you taken?'

'Well, I've notified her that the houses are coming down and that her tenancy will be terminated. And I went and saw her yesterday and tried to explain it to her, but—'

'One of these obstinate ones, is she?' said Mr Harper. 'Well, it's no good arguing. I should just send an official notification that unless she's out by ... When did we say?'

'October the sixteenth.'

'Yes, that's right. Unless she's out by October the sixteenth, we shall be forced to evict. I'll get in touch with the Old People's Welfare. All right?'

'Yes ... er ... Tom. All right.'

Mr Harper was housing manager, and although he had told Mr Simmonds to call him Tom, Mr Simmonds could never do it without a slight qualm. Mr Harper reminded him so very much of his old colonel in the War. Mr Simmonds himself had never risen above a lance corporal, but he knew that Mr Harper had been a squadron leader in the RAF, and when he stood by the door and barked, 'All right?' it was all Mr Simmonds could do not to come to attention, salute and say, 'Yes, Sir!'

'I'm making my report to the Council next week, you know,' said Mr Harper. 'I can give them a completion date for the newly-wed

17

flats. That'll go down well, especially with the Press. But I'd like to give them Hampton Row as a follow-up scheme, and we want it all neat and tidy before then. Don't want the old lady going to one of the local papers saying she won't get out and starting a row. I should get that letter off to her today. Show her she's got no alternative. Kindest way in the long run. All right?'

'Yes, S– ... er ... Yes, Tom,' said Mr Simmonds.

'I'm going down to the club for a drink before lunch,' said Mr Harper.

Mr Simmonds sat and gazed at the closed door. Mr Harper always made everything so clear. You couldn't help admiring him. And he was quite right, of course. The sooner Miss Pollock realised that she had to go, the better it would be for her and everyone else. That had always been one of his faults, thought Mr Simmonds, refusing to face the inevitable. And another, he knew, was not being able to see the wood for the trees. He worried too much about individuals instead of looking at the wider good. It certainly wasn't a kindness to let dozens of people stay homeless, just so that one obstinate old lady – she was obstinate, she really was! – could stay in a slum dwelling. Although he had so far faithfully fulfilled all the procedures meticulously, and had only delayed the final eviction notice by one day, Mr Simmonds somehow felt that he had been weak and faltering – a lance corporal instead of a squadron leader, a housing officer instead of a housing manager. He would get that letter off to Miss Pollock at once!

Four

'The usual, please, Harry,' said Mr Harper.

Standing there with his foot on the rail, he could almost imagine that he was back in the officer's mess. He had never been Operational, of course. His maths wasn't good enough for flying. But within two years of joining up as a clerk in the Local Government Office, he had been posted to Admin and had risen to be a squadron leader in a training wing in a rather remote Welsh town. How he had enjoyed it – and his wife, too! 'Squadron Leader and Mrs T.O. Harper, At Home, No. 1 Squadron, Marine Hotel.' The parades, the salutes, his office on the first floor (formerly the best bedroom) looking out over the harbour, and those happy hours in the anteroom. And then, although he had in his charge the welfare of two hundred cadets ('my men', he used to call them proudly) somehow it was all so easy. Everything was laid down in KRs and ACIs. You didn't have to take decisions and formulate policies.

Like with those newly-wed flats. Of course, they weren't entirely his responsibility. He had only sat on the committee. But everyone knew he had been enthusiastic. It had sounded such a good idea from the public relations angle – and he had learned in the RAF how important that was. It would read so well in the local paper: 'The only council which is really tackling the problem of housing newly-weds!' 'No more living with in-laws!' Only, the truth was that during those first years when they had no children, young couples could manage in furnished rooms. It was later, when they had two or three children, that they really needed the Council's help, and that waiting list was getting longer every day. His 'newly-wed flats' were useless to help that. Still, Hampton Row was going to be replaced with new, small family houses. It was only a drop in the bucket, but it would look good. Mr Harper hoped it would look good. He desperately wanted to make a success of this job, so that he might perhaps move on to a London Borough. His wife would like that, too. Until you'd been in a London Borough, you hadn't really arrived. It seemed to Mr Harper that ever since he left the RAF he had been struggling to arrive at a status which he knew in his heart was gone for ever.

'Another pink gin, Harry,' he said in his squadron leader's voice.

By the time he got back to his office, he had quite forgotten Miss Pollock and telephoning the Old People's Welfare.

Five

Miss Pollock always got up at the same time – seven o'clock, winter and summer. When her father was alive, they used to get up at six o'clock, but after his death, they became, as her mother said, 'a little bit lazy'. And seven o'clock was really soon enough now. Miss Pollock always came down in her nightdress and dressing gown to light the fire and put the kettle on. She didn't have a gas stove or an electric kettle or any of that nonsense. They just swung the kettle over the kitchen grate and there it was. By the time she was dressed, the kettle was boiling and she could sit down and have a cup of tea and a piece of toast before getting on with the housework.

She was just spreading the marmalade on her toast when she heard the letter come under the door. She didn't get many letters. In fact, well, she didn't really get any. They never used to have very many even in the old days – just one or two a year from Auntie Maud or Uncle Alfie. But after Auntie Maud and Uncle Alfie died, well, there really wasn't anyone else to write. Uncle Alfie died while her mother was still alive, and they went up to his funeral. He had a coal business in Enfield, and it was a very nice funeral, but they never had liked his wife, and she didn't make them at all welcome, and as they came back in the train, Miss Pollock's mother said, 'Well, if I never see *her* again, it'll be too soon for me!' and they never did. Auntie Maud lived all alone in Wandsworth, so the first Miss Pollock knew of her death was when the hospital sent her a ring and a brooch and said she was gone. It was a dreadful thing, thought Miss Pollock, for Auntie Maud to die in a hospital – almost as bad as dying in a home.

She looked down at the buff envelope lying on the faded linoleum in the hall. She had never liked opening letters like that because her mother had always said that 'business' was 'best left to the men'. Her mother always opened the 'family' letters, and her father opened the others – although before the War they never used to get many of those, and when they came they always meant trouble. Miss Pollock picked up Mr Simmonds' letter and took it back with her into the sitting room.

Mr Simmonds was quite right in thinking

that Miss Pollock hadn't read his previous letters. She had in fact opened them, but to read them she needed her spectacles, and when she had held the letters at arm's length and seen the heading 'Brightlesea Borough Council Housing Department', she didn't bother. She had a house. She didn't want any more. But Mr Simmonds was not right in thinking that his visit had made no impression on her. It had frightened her quite a lot. She hadn't really understood what he was saying because she didn't want to, but one thing she couldn't even pretend not to understand was that they were trying to take her house away from her. She found her spectacles on the mantelpiece under her pension book, took the letter out of the envelope and sat down to read it.

They were not, strictly speaking, *her* spectacles. They had originally been her father's, and then her mother used them, and now Miss Pollock did. They certainly made the letters bigger, but they blurred them slightly, too, and that made Miss Pollock's reading rather slow, especially of the longer words. This letter was mostly composed of long words, and Miss Pollock's mind slid across them without any real understanding – 'slum clearance scheme', 'termination of tenancy', 'refusal to comply will result in eviction', 'alternative accommodation has been arranged'. She came to rest upon the final

23

words in that paragraph – 'in Brightlesea Old People's Home'. She never read the last paragraph, which invited her to go to the Housing Department for further advice and information. She didn't even try to read the letter again to make more sense of it. She folded it up and put it back in the envelope and put the envelope down on the table and sat looking at it. They were going to take her away to a home, just like old Mrs Briggs next door.

Miss Pollock had been only ten when Mrs Briggs was taken away, but she remembered it as if it were yesterday. Miss Pollock's mother had said it was wicked of Mrs Briggs' daughter and son-in-law to let her go, but Mr Pollock had said, what else could they do when she kept getting after them with the bread knife? So the relieving officer came and dragged her away, with all the neighbours standing outside their doors watching, and poor old Mrs Briggs screaming that she didn't want to go. She had died quite soon after, in the home, but even now, more than sixty years later, Miss Pollock felt the same horror and disgust that she had known as a child of ten, peering out from behind the curtain in her blue serge suit and buttoned boots. And now it was going to happen to her.

Whatever would my mother say? thought Miss Pollock.

She sat there quite still, staring at the envelope, her little hands clasped in her lap, and
conscious thought fell away from her. She
became from head to foot one silent, frantic
cry for help. And then she heard the
milkman outside the door.

Six

The trouble with a milk round was that it left
so much time for thinking. That was
one thing John Weatherfield had always
rather liked about it – that and having his
evenings free – but now it was different. He
got out the half-pint of milk and his book.
It was ridiculous really having to drag all
the way down Hampton Row just to sell
old Miss Pollock half a pint of milk a day.
Time they pulled these rubbishy old houses
down and built some new ones. But that was
the Council all over. They were very big on
illuminations and champagne all round for
the councillors and their wives, but when it
came to doing something for the working
man ... Would things have been different, he
thought, if he and his wife had had a house
instead of living in one room with the kids?
Would she have stayed at home then, instead
of...?

He knocked at the door with his knuckles, but the action was purely automatic. He wasn't thinking about Miss Pollock, but of getting home to find Johnny and Eileen hanging round the steps like a couple of slum kids, and of going up to their room at the top of the staircase and finding his wife out, and of sitting down to wait for her to come in, knowing that she was with another man.

Miss Pollock opened the door with her purse in one hand and an envelope in the other.

'Good morning,' said John Weatherfield.

Miss Pollock had never asked for help from a stranger in her life. Even when she went to the post office to fetch her pension, she was quite annoyed if the clerk tried to help her fill in the form, and any bus conductor who helped her off and said, 'There we are, Mum!' got a very chilly look for his pains. Miss Pollock had always kept herself to herself, and expected other people to do the same. But now something had happened which she couldn't manage by herself, and her father was dead, and Uncle Alfie, and she didn't know anyone else except the milk-man and the rent collector. The milkman had always said a few words to pass the time of day, like, 'Nasty wind!' or 'Hot enough for you?' or 'Looks like rain.' She felt that she knew him, at least.

She said, 'They say they're going to pull these houses down.'

'Oh yes?' said John Weatherfield. ' 'Bout time, too. Time they cleared all these slums.'

'They say I've got to get out,' said Miss Pollock.

'Well, I expect you will, if they're pulling them down,' said John Weatherfield, looking in his book, though the sum never varied from week to week. 'Seven halves – two and sevenpence ha'penny, please.'

Miss Pollock fumbled in her purse.

'They'll have to find you somewhere else to live, you know,' said John Weatherfield.

One by one she brought out a two-shilling piece and a sixpence and a penny and a halfpenny and gave them to him, gazing up at him with round blue eyes.

'They say they'll send me to a home,' she said.

'Oh well, you'll be all right, then,' said John Weatherfield.

He gave her the half-pint of milk, picked up the small, empty bottle from the doorstep and turned and went.

Who was she going with? he was thinking. How could he find out? He slammed the empty bottle in the wire basket, put the book in his pocket, got into the electric cart and moved away down the silent street.

Miss Pollock closed the door.

Seven

Miss Pollock found that she didn't fancy the piece of toast now. She threw it out into the back yard for the birds, and poured the cold tea down the drain. 'Waste not, want not,' her mother used to say, and she didn't think she had ever thrown away so much food in her life before. It increased her feeling of a crumbling world.

As she carried the little earthenware teapot inside again – the one she and her mother had used ever since her father died – she was thinking about something the milkman had said. 'All these slums.' And she remembered that the letter had mentioned 'slum clearance'. But this wasn't a slum! It had always been a respectable neighbourhood, and as for the house, it was just the same as when they had come there from the country. She looked round the kitchen. Even the pictures on the walls were the same – the photograph of her father in uniform from the first war, and the picture of the little girl in the sun-bonnet called *Little Sweetheart*, which her mother's mistress had given to her when she left service to get married. On the mantelpiece was the mug which she had got at Sunday school for the coronation of King Edward VII, beside the donkey with a basket on its back which had once held an Easter egg, and the jug with 'A present from Southend' on it, which Uncle Alfie had given them and in which they had always kept tacks and drawing pins. There was the black grate, with the little oven beside it – lovely for baking scones and lardy-cakes – and they had electric light, too, put in when the rent went up to seven shillings a week, just before the War. Of course, there was only a cold tap in the scullery, but you kept the kettle boiling, and you'd got the copper for washing. You could heat the water for a bath in that, too. The tin bath hung where it always had, against the 'outside'. You had to go outside, of course, and it was a bit cold in the winter, especially at night, but if you were used to it, you didn't think anything of it. A slum, thought Miss Pollock. How could it be a slum? It was their house!

She went upstairs to make her bed. In the old days, they had always turned the mat-tresses every day without fail. But towards the end, when her mother was a bit poorly, they didn't always manage it, and now that Miss Pollock was on her own, she found it such hard work – being so small, and the mattress on its iron bedstead rather high – that she only did it once a week on Mondays, when she put on clean sheets. But of course she stripped the bed every day, and put all the blankets back one by one, and all the time she did it this morning, she was thinking about the house and puzzling over why they should suddenly want to pull it down now, after all these years.

She was still puzzling over it when she put on her coat and hat, took her purse and the black shopping bag, and went along to Bickstead's on the corner to get her rations.

Of course, now the War was over, they weren't really 'rations' any more, but it came to the same thing for Miss Pollock. She always got the same. Four ounces of streaky bacon, three small eggs, four ounces of butter, four ounces of marge, a quarter of tea, a small white loaf, and a cabbage. Then, every so often, she got a pound of sugar and a bit of flour and a pot of strawberry jam or salmon and shrimp paste and a few potatoes. And she always bought it all at Bickstead's. Very often she got a knuckle of ham for boiling, too, so she didn't even go into the butcher's. She got everything at Bickstead's, just as they used to when the shop belonged to old Mr Dewsbury, and she was sent along by her mother with sixpence clutched in her hand and was told to bring the change safely back. You could still see the name Dewsbury faintly showing behind the 'Bickstead' over the door, but Mrs Bickstead had been there ten years now, and Miss Pollock almost felt that she knew her. In a way, since all the houses in between were empty, she was Miss Pollock's nearest neighbour.

Miss Pollock pushed the door open and went in.

Eight

Saturday was always a busy day in Bickstead's. Mrs Bickstead often wondered why people like old Miss Pollock, who didn't go to work, couldn't do their shopping some other morning. But no, it had to be Saturday! They were so slow, too, these old ladies. Fumble, fumble, fumble. Oh dear, it drove you mad! Still, poor old things, they couldn't help it.

Mrs Bickstead was a Londoner, and after all these years she still found people slow round here and wished herself back in the bustle of the Fulham Road. She wondered if her husband was still living in Fulham with that woman. As soon as she'd found out that he was deceiving her, she'd taken Donald and walked out. She came to Brightlesea to live with her father, and when he died and left her a bit of money, she bought the shop from old Mr Dewsbury. Everyone here

31

thought that she was a widow. Even Donald thought so. She sometimes worried about not having told him, but ... After all, for all she knew, her husband *was* dead. And Donald had got through his eleven plus, and was at grammar school now, and doing so well. She didn't want him to know about his father, ever. He was helping her in the shop this morning, as it was a Saturday, and that gave her a chance to get the orders up. She was beginning to get some of the better customers now, from Nash Terrace. If she could only build up the business a bit more – if the Council rebuilt Hampton Row, smartened the neighbourhood up a bit. Supposing Donald went to university – she must be sure that Donald didn't suffer from her having walked out, leaving him without a father.

Miss Pollock opened the door and came in, the little bell tinkling over her head.

Oh, bother! thought Mrs Bickstead, weighing cheese.

But Donald had moved forward to the counter.

Donald didn't mind working in the shop on Saturday mornings, as long as his mother paid him. He knew his way round the stock pretty well, and didn't have to think much as he fetched things from the shelves and noted the prices down on a bit of paper. As a matter of fact, he didn't often think about anything just now, except records. He kept the *Musical Express* on the counter and read it in between customers, or even while they made up their minds what they wanted next. He didn't smile at them or say anything except 'Yes?' or 'Which one d'you want?' or 'Seven and a penny, please.'

He was saving up for the new Cliff Richard LP and was going through the songs in his mind, first one side and then the other.

Miss Pollock hesitated by the counter, glancing at Mrs Bickstead. Mrs Bickstead had always seemed so kind, so competent. Managing a shop, she was ... she might...

'Can I help you?' said Donald.

'Oh, just the usual, please,' said Miss Pollock.

Nine

Miss Pollock was always sorry when Saturday morning's shopping was over. It made what her mother would have called 'a bit of life', and the rest of the day dragged rather. She listened to the wireless a lot – her father had bought it from the Cuthbertsons when they moved away – but on Saturday afternoon there seemed to be nothing but football. She sat and listened to the frenzied screams of the commentator and the roars of the crowd, and tried to feel that she was joining in it, that she understood it. But really it only made her feel lonely. So did the jazz and most of the record programmes. They never seemed to play the good old songs now, or have nice plays on a Saturday night like they used to.

She went to bed early, with the hot-water bottle she bought at Boots when her father was so ill. She had made it a purple knitted cover with red buttons, and she still thought of it as a luxury. She lay in bed listening to the Saturday night traffic, and the noise from the Lord Nelson on the corner of the London Road, but she couldn't sleep. She didn't know what to do.

Then it came to her that tomorrow was Sunday, and she would go to church.

Miss Pollock's mother had been brought up Congregational, but she sent her daughter to the Methodist Sunday school because they had better outings. Mr Pollock was Church of England, although he didn't, in fact, ever go to church. However, they had been married in a village church twenty miles away, and Mrs Pollock felt that gave the Church of England a certain claim on her. When they came to Brightlesea, she used to go to evensong at St James's with her friend Mrs Cuthbertson, but after the Cuthbertsons moved away, she didn't like to come home in the dark alone. Later on, she and Miss Pollock went to morning service now and then, but they never really enjoyed it. They felt it was, as Mrs Pollock said, 'a posh people's service'. Everyone had their own pew and said 'Good morning' to the churchwarden, and if you didn't, you felt a bit out of it. It made Sunday dinner so late, too. So bit by bit they got into the way of listening to the service on the wireless, and that was what Miss Pollock usually did now. Just occasionally, on Christmas Day, or if it was very fine, she'd fancy going along to St James's, but somehow or other – she didn't know why – when the service was over, she usually felt disappointed.

She set out this morning soon after twenty to eleven. The church was ten minutes' walk away, and she didn't want to be late. She had on her best coat and the felt hat with the orange feather in the hatband, and she walked along quite briskly, with the feeling that at last she was going to be all right.

Ten

It was very quiet in the vestry as the vicar robed himself for the service. Heavy wine-coloured curtains divided the inner room from the larger area where the choir gathered, and now that the choir consisted, not of twenty giggling, shoving boys, but of four teenage girls, two women and three elderly men, their assembly caused only a subdued murmur. The vicar smiled a little. He was remembering the day when, as a young curate, he had prepared to take morning service alone for the first time. He had been so overcome with a sense of his own unworthiness that he had dropped on his knees halfway into his surplice, and the Verger, coming in unexpectedly, had been very much embarrassed.

Well, thought the vicar, no one could possibly worry about being worthy to take a service at St James's. It must be the most moribund parish in England. The two former incumbents had been very old – the first infirm and the second lazy – and in two years' hard work, he was only just beginning to make some headway against the general apathy and indifference. The trouble with the modern state, he thought, was that it robbed the Church of its most dramatic functions – healing the sick and tending the destitute. He visited parishioners, of course, though he often wondered whether his offer of spiritual consolation was not accepted chiefly to alleviate the monotony of their lives. And for the rest – there was the National Health Service, the National Insurance scheme, and all the machinery of the welfare state, in the face of which Christian charity seemed superfluous. Even his work as Hospital Chaplain was not exactly challenging. He had been less conscious of this in his former parish in a poor quarter of Liverpool, where people did, in fact, come knocking on his door for help day and night.

But here, in this seaside resort ... They still knocked at his door, but what was it for? To arrange Mothers' Union services or the Christmas Bazaar, or any of the other affairs with which the middle-aged ladies busied themselves – chiefly, he often thought, to give themselves a feeling of importance. No wonder his son refused to come to church. He had never tried to influence him, of course. He had always said he wouldn't force religion down his son's throat. And if, thought Mr Fanshaw, Alec chose to march to Aldermaston or attend political meetings instead of coming to morning service, well, it wasn't such a bad thing. In fact, Alec had widened his own outlook, made him realise that to young people the teachings of the Church might seem outworn and lifeless, lacking in political awareness.

The vicar glanced round his congregation as he took his place and waited for the organist to allow the last sour note to die away. Much the same as usual, he thought. A number of elderly ladies who came out of habit, and some married couples who came because it was 'the thing to do'. There were just a few young people, though. That was a good sign. He would like to see a congregation in which young people outnumbered the old ones. Then he would know he had succeeded. He wondered whether a church skiffle group might not be a good idea. Perhaps Alec might organise it. He played the guitar, and they could start, perhaps, with purely secular songs.

Thinking of this, the vicar was almost surprised to find that the prayers and psalms were over, and that the hymn before the sermon was to be announced. In the third verse he knelt down and prayed that his words might lead his hearers – especially the older members – to an understanding of the need for a wider view of world affairs, less engrossment in themselves. The hymn ended, and he went up into the pulpit. He had a resonant voice and was glad to know that he could use it in the service of God. He gazed at his congregation with kindly severity.

'We are all members,' he said, 'one of another.'

Then he began his carefully prepared sermon on the World Council of Churches.

Miss Pollock had been surprised to see Mr Fanshaw at first. She had expected to see kind old Mr Treadgold with his silver hair and his hearing aid. Then she remembered that this young man had taken the Christmas Service. He had a lovely voice, she thought. You could hear every word, even from the back pew. When he went up into the pulpit, she fixed her eyes on him with a feeling almost like hope. She didn't quite know what she hoped for. Perhaps it was ... guidance. Her mother sometimes used to talk about praying for guidance.

But soon Miss Pollock found that she wasn't listening to the sermon. Sitting here so quiet, with nothing to occupy her hands and take her mind off it, she seemed to realise for the first time what Mr Simmonds had told her. She would soon have no house to live in. Somehow, she had lived there so long that she had come to think of it as *her* house, but it wasn't. If they said she had got to get out, then she had got to get out. But what could she do? Where would she go? How did you live if you hadn't got a house?

Waves of terror swept through her small body as she sat perfectly still, her woollen-gloved hands in her lap, her eyes on the vicar's face.

The vicar paused and several people, realising that the sermon was nearly over, began clinking coins in their search for collection money. His discourse had ranged over world affairs, the evils of apartheid, the perils of the hydrogen bomb, and the essential quality of the brotherhood of man. He waited until the slight rustle was over and then spoke impressively.

'We are all members one of another,' he said.

Miss Pollock's hands trembled as she fished sixpence out of her purse with clumsy woollen fingertips and her heart seemed to beat in a hollow. She held the hymn book open at the wrong page, and moved her lips as though she was singing. Although she was in the last pew, it took her so long to pick up her handbag and put the hassock straight and gather herself together that when she finally moved out, she was surrounded by the main body of the congregation also shuffling towards the door. The vicar stood outside, shaking hands with some, smiling at others. Miss Pollock moved uncertainly towards him. As she met his eyes, she paused. He smiled.

'Nice to have you with us,' he said. Then

his eyes went past her. 'Ah, Pete!' he cried. 'Good morning! Glad you could come!'

Miss Pollock took a few more steps, hesitated, and glanced back. The vicar was shaking hands with a tall young man in a duffle coat and talking to him eagerly. Miss Pollock went through the iron gates. Several people were getting into cars and offering each other lifts. Others stood in little groups, chatting. No one spoke to Miss Pollock.

She passed through them, turned the corner into a deserted Sunday street, and walked home alone.

Eleven

'Ah, and what about Hampton Row?' asked Mr Harper, pausing at the door.

'Well, I wrote to Miss Pollock,' replied Mr Simmonds.

'Miss...?'

'The tenant.'

'Oh yes.'

'She hasn't been in to see us,' said Mr Simmonds. 'I don't know if the Welfare people have been there...'

'Oh,' said Mr Harper. 'Yes. Er ... well...'

Mr Simmonds knew at once what had happened.

'Did you ... um...?' he enquired casually.

'Completely forgot!' said Mr Harper, with a cheerful resilience which Mr Simmonds envied enormously. 'Never mind. I'll get on to them at once. Plenty of time.'

'Would you like me to ring them?' asked Mr Simmonds.

'No, I may as well drop in,' said Mr Harper. 'I might just catch Miss Waterlow before she goes to lunch.'

The Old People's Welfare weren't in the Council Offices, but occupied the ground floor of a Georgian house just off the seafront. As Mr Harper strode along, smelling the sea air, he could almost imagine himself heading for the anteroom, acknowledging salutes from airmen and WAAFs. When he came to think of it, Miss Waterlow was rather like that WAAF driver of his. By Jove, she was a grand girl! Everyone used to joke about it, even his wife. 'Tom's Redhead', they used to call her. It had never gone further than a few kisses and a bit of a cuddle in a pub, but the funny thing was, he hardly thought his wife would have minded if it had. Everything was so easy then, so uncomplicated. He entered the house and knocked at Miss Waterlow's door.

'Anyone home?' he said, cheerfully.

Ann Waterlow had seen Mr Harper passing the window, and her lip curled in disgust as she waited for him to come in, waited for that awful, hearty voice and that phoney travelling-salesman smile. Miss Waterlow was dark and pleasant-looking. She knew that other women said to each other, 'I'm surprised she's never married.' She was surprised herself. Perhaps it was because her mother was a widow. They never *met* anyone. They lived in a little, domestic, woman's world, just the two of them. It wasn't that her mother didn't want her to marry. It made it worse that she always talked of 'when you get married', and never seemed to realise that a girl who spent every day in an office dealing with the affairs of old people and every evening watching television with her mother was never likely to get married. Whom would she marry? Dr Kildare?

But somewhere far behind was an uneasier thought. Miss Waterlow did sometimes meet young men. There were some who worked in the Council Offices. There had been others at the technical college. Only, they never seemed to notice Miss Waterlow. Older men did. They found her very attractive. They flirted with her and gazed at her admiringly. It was disgusting. And most disgusting of all was Mr Harper. Somehow, Ann Waterlow always thought of him in connection with shabby hotel bedrooms and signing the wrong name in the register and dirty weekends. He had an awful wife, too, with dyed blonde hair which somehow made him

43

more nauseating. And all the time his exaggerated admiration nagged at her failure with younger men. If he had devised a course of insulting behaviour, he could not have offended her more.

She took care to be writing when he came into the room, drafting a report in her round, plain handwriting. She looked up with obvious reluctance. That awful bristly moustache, and the faint hint of watery pinkness in the stupid blue eyes!

'Well, well, well!' he said. 'How's my favourite Welfare officer, eh?'

He was like a dreadful caricature, thought Miss Waterlow. Or like a very bad actor playing the part of an RAF type.

'Good morning, Mr Harper,' she said.

He sat on the edge of her desk, which, annoyingly, brought him nearer to her and sent an unpleasant whiff of stale cigarette smoke in her direction from his thick tweed jacket.

'How's the world treating you?' he enquired, jovially.

Miss Waterlow sighed in a long-suffering way.

'Did you want something?' she asked.

'I always want something!' cried Mr Harper, with a grin which was more like a leer.

'I'm rather busy,' said Miss Waterlow. 'If there is something you—'

'Ah,' said Mr Harper. He leaned down

closer, confidential, a fellow worker and therefore claiming intimacy. 'Well, I'll tell you what it is. There's an old lady we're trying to get rid of.'

'Get rid of?'

Mr Harper shouted with laughter.

'We're not going to poison her!' he roared. 'At least, not unless we have to! No, I'll tell you what the problem is. She's in Hampton Row.'

'Oh yes?' said Miss Waterlow.

'Scheduled for demolition,' explained Mr Harper. 'She's got to get out. We've got a place for her in a home, but will she get out? No, she bloody well won't!'

Miss Waterlow frowned. If he thought that swearing made him seem like a jolly, up-to-the-minute young man...!

'What do you want me to do?' she enquired, picking up a pencil and drawing a sheet of paper towards her to show that there was no informal helpfulness in her attitude.

'Well, I thought if you could go and see her...'

'I'm very busy,' said Miss Waterlow, coldly. 'Can't you write to her?'

'We've done that. Been to see her. Everything. I thought if *you* went to see her ... You've got such a way with you' – another leer – 'if you don't mind my saying so.'

'Well,' said Miss Waterlow, in the tone of a hospital matron who has just found a dirty bedpan under the bed, 'what's her name?'

'Name!' cried Mr Harper, and hit his red shiny forehead with his fist. 'Oh, God! I've forgotten it. Hang on. Hang on.' There was a fearsome playfulness about him, as though he was saying, What a bad boy I am, but I know you love me for it!

'I'm afraid that if you don't know her name,' said Miss Waterlow, 'there's not much I can do, is there?'

'Got it!' he shouted triumphantly, as though she had some how joined in his teasing game. 'Pollock, that's it. Miss Ellen Pollock. Number Six, Hampton Row. Pop along this afternoon, will you? There's a dear.'

'This afternoon?' exclaimed Miss Waterlow. 'I can't possibly go this afternoon. I'm much too busy.'

'It's rather urgent.'

'I'm sorry,' she said, decidedly – more decidedly because of that insinuating note in his voice. 'You should have let me know sooner. I'll try to go tomorrow.'

'Oh, that's jolly good of you!' said Mr Harper. He got up, beaming at her. 'I always know I can depend on you!' He set off for the door and then paused. 'How about nipping along for a little drink before lunch, eh?'

'Thank you very much,' said Miss Water-low, in a tone like snapping dog fleas between finger and thumb. 'But I'm afraid I haven't time.'

'Oh, come on!' cried Mr Harper. 'Nothing like a little snifter to pep up the working girl.'

'No doubt,' said Miss Waterlow. 'But *I* have some work to do.'

'Oh well,' said Mr Harper, 'another time, perhaps, eh?'

Miss Waterlow didn't answer. She had picked up her pen and was writing again.

'Well, cheerio!' said Mr Harper.

Miss Waterlow glanced up with a tight, insultingly brief smile. Mr Harper went out.

I don't know why I bother, thought Ann Waterlow. He's so thick-skinned, you could spit in his face and he probably wouldn't even notice.

This wasn't quite true. Mr Harper had no idea how she really felt about him, but as he walked along the front, he felt depressed. His shoulders drooped a little. No imaginary airmen saluted him as he passed. If he had been a squadron leader, he thought, Ann Waterlow would have treated him very differently. She would have gazed up at him admiringly, hoped for an invitation to the anteroom or to the squadron dance. Instead he ... It was almost as though she...

Mr Harper turned into the club. He stood with one foot on the rail, drinking the bitter drink of bygone days. A profound gloom overtook him. What *was* he, after all? Just a potty little Borough Council official, married to a woman who dyed her hair. He used to be so proud of being married to a beautiful blonde. The first day he saw those dark roots was like the end of illusion, the end of hope. Her dark roots, his uniform packed away in mothballs...

'Another pink gin, Harry,' he said, and forgot to sound like a squadron leader.

After lunch, Miss Waterlow came out of her office and paused. She had a visit which must be made that day, but there would, in fact, be time to go to Hampton Row as well. She took a few steps, and paused again. She thought of Mr Harper. He would ring up next morning and say, 'Did you go? Just to please *me*? Oh, *good!*' Miss Waterlow turned and walked briskly away in the opposite direction.

Twelve

Miss Pollock could not sleep on Sunday night. She lay staring at the rim of grey light at the top of the blind and listening to the church clock striking the quarters, but the familiar room, the familiar night sounds had a terror in them, a threat and strangeness. In the morning, it was as though an earthquake had destroyed the house during the night and she stepped out into rubble. She crept downstairs and went like a conspirator to get her spectacles and the letter from the mantelpiece. She sat down, shivering, by the empty grate and read the letter through very carefully, word by word. When she had finished, she understood at last. They were going to pull down the house, and they wanted to put her in a home.

I would rather die! thought Miss Pollock.

As she sat there, trembling, the thought actually came to her that some people did kill themselves. But she knew she wouldn't do that. It was wrong. Her mother would say so, and her father. Her mother had been dead for years now, and her father even

49

longer, but they had all been so happy to-gether – hardly an angry word in all their lives – that what they had felt and thought was what Miss Pollock now felt and thought. Somehow, doing what they thought was right was still a way of showing her love for them. Miss Pollock couldn't kill herself. Besides, how would she do it? She bought the local paper every week, so she knew that some people gassed themselves, but, of course, there was no gas in Hampton Row. Still, she thought, it would have been a way of escape.

The word caught at her mind, and held. Escape. The house which had for so long been a refuge was now like a trap. Miss Pollock remembered a film she had seen as a girl in which a woman waited alone in a dark room while a murderer crept towards her. It had haunted her for years, and she had always thought that if it had been her, she wouldn't have waited. She would have run out into the street.

Miss Pollock lit the fire and went upstairs to get dressed. Although she never settled down to make a precise plan of action, yet everything she did from that moment on was directed towards escape. *She* would not wait until they came and dragged her away like poor old Mrs Briggs to the horrible and shameful home. She would go away where they could not find her, and she would do it that very day.

Miss Pollock put clean sheets on the bed. It was partly in the same spirit in which one put on clean underclothes before going to hospital for 'them' to see. But also, far away in the back of her mind was the notion that if they couldn't put her in a home, then the other half of the plan might fall through as well, and they wouldn't demolish the house after all. In a little while, when they couldn't find her, they would go away, and she would be able to come back. She wouldn't want to come back to dirty sheets.

Miss Pollock didn't do the washing, however. For the first time in sixty years the copper remained unlit on a Monday morning. Instead, she got her father's big brown fibre suitcase down from the top of her mother's wardrobe and put it on the bed.

The case hadn't been opened since her father's death and it was full of his clothes, carefully packed away in newspaper and mothballs. It gave Miss Pollock a funny feeling to look at them, and to remember her mother's plump, capable hands laying in, one by one, the flannel shirts, the combinations, the long woollen socks, and to remember, too, the watering eyes, the damp handkerchief of her mother's grief. Now they were both dead, and Miss Pollock was ... old? Was she really old? The little girl who had walked with a hand in each of her

51

parents' hands was as real to her now as were those parents in all the vigour of their middle age, in all the warmth and security of their love. As time slipped and shivered beneath her feet, Miss Pollock felt so dizzy that she had to sit down. Were they both dead? Or had her mother's death united them, and brought them back to life? And when Miss Pollock left the house, would they die then at last?

It took a long time to pack. All her father's clothes had to be carefully laid away in the chest of drawers from which her own clothes were taken, the little, childish chest of drawers which her father bought at a sale and gave her for her very own when she was ten – the same year that old Mrs Briggs was taken away to the home. Then Miss Pollock had to try to decide what she should take with her. She couldn't take everything. She had four complete sets of underclothes and nightdresses, two for winter and two for summer, with woollen stockings for winter and lisle for summer. Then she had two cotton dresses and a woollen dress for everyday, and a silk dress for best which had belonged to her mother. There were gloves, one woollen pair, one cotton pair, and one white silk crocheted pair, with scarves, woollen and silk, and three hats, one navy-blue straw, one navy-blue felt, and her best one. Miss Pollock stood there despairingly in the midst of a vast richness of possessions. To leave any of them behind was like cutting off a part of herself. And yet it must be done.

In the end, she took only her winter things, but, since this included her silk dress, she weakened so far as to put in her mother's navy-blue edge-to-edge coat with the rickrack round the collar. That had always been her 'best' summer coat and she couldn't bring herself to leave it behind. Luckily, all her jewellery went in one large square box, including the gold locket which Uncle Alfie had given her and her mother's amber-coloured beads – too valuable to be worn, but often taken out and admired. She decided to wear her best winter coat – bought in the War when the moths got into her other one – and her best felt hat, but she packed her best shoes and wore her old ones, in case she had to do a lot of walking.

Miss Pollock was dismayed to find how heavy the case was as she took it downstairs. And there were still some more things to go into it. She left the coronation mug and, very regretfully, the *Little Sweetheart* picture, because the frame was too wide for the case. But her father's photograph went in, of course, and the donkey with the basket on its back, and Uncle Alfie's 'A present from Southend', and the crocheted throw which had always hung over the back of the big armchair and which her mother used to put over her knees in cold weather. What with all these things and her warm dressing gown, the case was now bulging, and Miss Pollock had a struggle to fasten it, which left her panting and alarmed. What would she have done if she couldn't get it fastened? She was all alone. Her father was gone, and her mother, and Uncle Alfie. There was no one to help her. She was alone.

(It was about now that Miss Waterlow hesitated, standing in the October sunshine outside her office, before walking briskly away.)

Miss Pollock had her bit of dinner as usual, a slice of ham off the piece she had boiled for Sunday and some cold boiled potatoes. She sat and ate it with her coat and hat on and the suitcase standing by the door, and the empty, fluttering feeling in her stomach made it all unreal, as though she were feeding a doll or a dummy. When she had finished, she washed everything up and then carefully packed the remaining food in the green and black checked leather shopping bag. She put a quarter of tea in, too, and the pound bag of sugar which she hadn't yet opened, and the half-pint of milk, and the heel of the loaf and a bit of butter.

Finally, she got her pension book and post office savings book out of the dresser drawer and put them in her handbag. She made sure that the back door was locked and the downstairs windows fastened, and then she put her gloves on, took the suitcase and shopping bag outside, shut and locked the front door and put the key carefully away in her purse.

Miss Pollock saw the empty half-pint bottle which she had automatically put out on the doorstep. She should have left a note for the milkman. One always did that when one went away. *But no!* she thought. No one must know that she was going. If they knew, they would come and get her and drag her back to a home.

She looked quickly up and down the empty street. There was no one in sight. Miss Pollock picked up her suitcase and the shopping bag, went down the garden path, closed the low wooden gate behind her, and walked slowly but firmly away.

Thirteen

Miss Pollock was not so silly as to leave home without any idea of where she was going. Brightlesea was full of bed and breakfast places, and she would stay at one of them. It had better not be too close to Hampton Row, she thought, or they might find her. Anyway, most of the places would be nearer to the sea.

Although she had lived there nearly all her life, Miss Pollock didn't really know Brightlesea very well. In fact, in all those years, she had probably only been to the sea a dozen or so times. Her father had taken them to the concert party in the pavilion now and then, and once to a fireworks display. Or they would occasionally occupy a fine afternoon in walking to the sea and strolling down the promenade and back, sometimes even buying ice creams. As for sitting on the beach in a crowd of people and having to pay for a deckchair, the Pollocks would never have even thought of it, although on particularly hot summer days, they sometimes took chairs out in the back yard on an old piece of carpet and had tea there. That was quite enough. Miss Pollock had never bathed in her life, and never wanted to.

She found now that it was even further to the seafront than she had thought. The case was dreadfully heavy, and when she changed it to her other hand, the shopping bag felt very heavy, too. Also, something was worrying her. She remembered quite well that when they used to walk to the sea in the old days, it was past row after row of bed and breakfast signs. Now she had been walking for twenty minutes and hadn't seen even one. It was extraordinary, Miss Pollock thought. Where had they all gone?

She smelled the sea at last, and put her case down to rest. She was in a quiet street of terraced houses, made strange to her by the cars parked end to end down each side of the road. There was only one more street, she knew, before she came to the seafront. If she was going to find somewhere to stay, it must be now. She looked up and down the houses where bed and breakfast signs had once flourished in profusion, like aspidistras, with the additional decoration of 'Vacancy' or 'No Vacancy' cards in the front windows. Now, in the entire street, she saw only two boards. One said 'Bed and Breakfast'. The other, below a more imposing wooden board announcing the 'Pavilion Hotel', read 'Board Residence'. Miss Pollock hesitated. The Pavilion Hotel looked more attractive, with geraniums blooming in the window box and the outer door set invitingly open. On the other hand, it looked more expensive, too. Besides, the bed and breakfast house was nearer, and had a more familiar look about it. Several of her mother's acquaintances in the old days kept boarding houses which looked very much like this one.

Miss Pollock picked up her suitcase. She walked along the quiet, lonely street, climbed the five steep steps, and knocked at the door of Crestview.

Fourteen

Miss Pollock could not possibly regret the passing of the old days as much as Mrs Harrison did. Mrs Harrison, too, could remember when every house had its lace curtains and its china dogs, and when every outer door stood open, with wooden spades and shrimping nets and red tin buckets in the entry, and with nurses setting off down the steps each morning wheeling their prams, with babies in sunhats and little boys in white flannel shorts and little girls in cotton frocks, their mackintosh paddlers carefully stowed away with the bathing costumes and the striped beach towels in a waterproof bag. Mrs Harrison had once been one of those nurses herself.

Of course, Mrs Harrison's lady had not lodged in a back street. No, certainly not. They had always lodged in Sea View on the front, where Madam had the first-floor room and a drawing room, and nanny and the children had the top floor to themselves. But when she got married, her people helped Mrs Harrison to set up in Crestview. 'Her people', of course, were not her parents, because Mrs Harrison was an orphan. Her people were the Master and Madam. They even gave her all the bedlinen as a wedding present and, sitting on the beach with the children, she had embroidered her initials on it, just like Madam's. She was still using it.

Mrs Harrison was a rather stern-featured, upstanding thirty-two-year-old when she married Mr Harrison, crying bitterly because she was so afraid that she would regret it. But the years which followed were very happy ones. In the winter, Mr Harrison followed his trade of self-employed plumber and Mrs Harrison scrubbed and polished the spotless house, carefully replacing dust covers and old bedspreads in the empty rooms. But in the summer, her life began again. Her people's immediate family continued to stay at Sea View, of course, which was only right, but their cousins and friends stayed at Crestview, and the children called her 'Nanny', and were always, as she said, 'in and out'. Mrs Harrison bullied them just as she used to in the old days, and knew that she still had her place in the world.

Then the War came, and when it was over, everything was changed. Master and Madam were both dead, and John and Jennifer, both married, didn't come to Brightlesea any more. Mrs Harrison quite understood. Their children liked to do different things. They went on boats on the Broads, or to the continent, or camping in Scotland. Anyway, Brightlesea had changed, too. It wouldn't be suitable for them to come there now, mingling with the type of person who did come. Mrs Harrison left her bed and breakfast sign out, but there weren't many bookings. Such visitors as there were seemed to be mostly casual overnighters, and really she was half afraid to open the door to some of them. Leather jackets and white helmets, and no luggage except a haversack strapped on the back of a motorcycle. Mrs Harrison didn't like to let them into her rooms. They just didn't know how to behave. And she didn't really need the money. She and Mr Harrison both had their pensions, and she'd saved a bit. The house was theirs, and they didn't eat much. It wasn't worth taking trouble to cook for *him*, anyway. He never noticed what he was eating. Not like the Master, who was always so particular, and would go out to the kitchen specially to thank Cook for any meal he'd really enjoyed.

When Miss Pollock knocked at the door, Mrs Harrison was working on Jennifer's birthday present, a set of embroidered guest towels. (You could never have too many, and young ladies weren't fitted up with linen now when they got married as they used to be in the old days.) She went along the passage, her black lace-up shoes, as polished as the linoleum, creaking a little. She opened the door and saw Miss Pollock.

At least, she never really saw Miss Pollock. She saw a dreadful, bent-brimmed felt hat with a tatty orange feather stuck in it, and a shabby coat. She saw a 'common' leather shopping bag and a nasty, bulging fibre suit-case. (Madam's luggage was always matching, with her initials on it.) And she saw a pair of cracked, dusty shoes. ('Always keep your shoes nice,' Madam used to say. 'A lady is known by her shoes.')

Miss Pollock saw a harsh-featured woman in a black woollen dress with a gold brooch pinned in the front. Her heart sank, and her face became obstinate and secretive.

'Good afternoon,' said Mrs Harrison, like a sentry demanding a password from an undoubted enemy.

'I wanted a room,' said Miss Pollock.

'Oh yes?' said Mrs Harrison. 'For how long?'

'Oh,' said Miss Pollock.

She looked helplessly at her suitcase. Mrs Harrison looked at it, too.

'I don't take lodgers, you know!' she said.

Miss Pollock looked up at the sign above her head.

' "Bed and Breakfast"!' cried Mrs Harrison. ' "Bed and Breakfast" it says!'

Her people would have recognised the familiar, harrying tones of their old nanny and laughed delightedly. Miss Pollock had never had a nanny, never been lovingly bullied. She didn't hear anything but rudeness and heartlessness.

'Oh,' she said again.

'Anyway,' said Mrs Harrison, 'the season's over. I'm afraid I don't take people after the end of September. Good afternoon.'

She shut the door and went back along the echoing passage. All about her were the rich, companionable, lost days, the wooden spades, the red tin buckets, the sand in the hall, the tiny crabs brought in for her to boil for tea. Mrs Harrison – or rather, Nanny, for that she would always be, and marrying him could never change it! – went into the back room. It maddened her to see him sitting there with his thin, grey hair and the cardigan which he *would* wear over his shirtsleeves no matter what she said.

62

'For goodness' sake, make yourself useful and put the kettle on!' she said. 'It's nearly teatime.'

She remembered nursery teas in London round the square table, with the big guard in front of the fire, and picnics on the beach, with strawberry jam sandwiches, and that one which always fell in the sand and had to be fed to the sparrows. Mr Harrison's aged shuffle as he went to put the kettle on sent a quick stab of irritation through her, and so did the thought of that shabby old woman at the door, both so far removed from the trim, brisk, white-aproned nanny, the fresh young children, the halcyon days of happiness.

Mrs Harrison bent over the embroidery. She would send the towels off next week, and Jennifer would write to thank her for them. She was always very good about that. And then, quite soon, it would be Christmas. She always heard from both the children at Christmas – a card from John, and a present from Jennifer, very often with photographs of her children. Mrs Harrison smiled. She still had something to look forward to. She wasn't quite alone.

Miss Pollock folded her lips stubbornly, picked up her suitcase and struggled with it down the steep, well-scrubbed steps. She had to turn the case sideways to get it between the parked cars, and as she set out across the road there was a terrifying screech of brakes. Miss Pollock stopped still, and saw in amazement a car's bonnet only a foot away from her and a man's face scowling at her and mouthing something. Her heart began to beat furiously, and her knees trembled. She could hardly walk the rest of the way to the Pavilion Hotel, but she managed it at last. She put the suitcase down and rested the shopping bag for a moment on the low stucco pillar of the entrance. Then she climbed the steps and pressed the gleaming brass bell beside the open door.

Fifteen

Betty Sparkes had not been in Brightlesea as long as Mrs Harrison. It was only three years, in fact, since she had bought Bayview. She changed the name at once, partly because it wasn't true – you could only catch a glimpse of the sea through the attic windows at the back! – and partly because Pavilion Hotel sounded superior and go-ahead, the sort of place which might have a cocktail bar and a barman in a white coat whom everyone called George. The Pavilion Hotel wasn't licensed yet, but Betty hoped it might be one day. Meanwhile, she tried to keep it looking cheerful. It was terribly important for a seaside hotel to look cheerful. People came to enjoy themselves. They didn't want the place to look depressing at the very start.

Betty remembered what Bayview had looked like when she bought it, or rather, when her father bought it for her – the drab, coffee-coloured paint, the dark hall and staircase, and all the old ladies creeping about clutching their shawls, each with her own table in the dining room with its bottle of medicine and its bottle of synthetic wine (marked each night with a pencil on the label so that the waitress shouldn't drink it) and each with her own table napkin in its ring. Betty's father had been bracing and cheery as they sat in the chilly, musty lounge, drinking appalling coffee.

'You'll make a go of it!' he said. 'Don't worry! You'll make a go of it!'

But Betty had wondered whether she would ever make a go of anything again. Now that the mess was over – she never thought of it as a marriage and a divorce, but as a nightmare time of confused unhappiness and failure – she only wanted to crawl away into a small dark room and die. It was her father who talked to her about the future and who saw the advertisement for a 'Private Hotel, going concern, excellent situation in attractive seaside town', and who drove her down in the car, sick and listless as she was, to see it and buy it and plan with her a new success to be laid across the entrance to that corrupting cave of failure, her marriage.

In the months which followed, Betty still wondered whether she had the strength to struggle through the difficulties which beset her. Dealing with the builders and decorators needed confidence, and confidence was what she had lost. Even deciding where to put the new bathroom (Bayview had only one!) was almost more than she could manage. And all the time, the former owner – poor, feeble Miss Harmon, with her bundle of grey hair and her rabbit teeth – kept burdening Betty with her own worries, of which the worst was getting the old ladies out of the place for the 'vacant possession' which Betty's father had insisted on. Betty, down for consultations with the builder, was dismayingly involved in these dreadful evictions, which took on the aspect of a peculiarly grim pest extermination. Bayview was the old ladies' home. They couldn't believe that Miss Harmon would really sell the place, sell their home. For years they had grumbled and sniffed and complained to Miss Harmon, tried to train the waitress to behave like a parlourmaid instead of a girl in a caff, and complained to Miss Harmon again when they failed. But still, she was like a mother to them. They couldn't believe that she would abandon them.

All these details Miss Harmon recounted to Betty over cups of tea in the little back room, and told how she had managed to get one old lady into the nursing home – it would take every penny of the old lady's income, but after all, she had nothing else to spend it on – and how she had persuaded a niece to come and fetch away another of them. Betty was there that time, and saw the niece and her husband desperately trying to keep an air of jolly kindness as they hauled the old lady out to the car, light but stiff-legged, like an oversized doll, and twittering about 'her dressing case' and 'her hatbox' and 'that little table is mine!' The husband returned and picked up the dressing case. It was made of leather, with gold initials on it, and was full of crystal bottles with silver tops and silver hairbrushes. The man felt its weight, looked at the hatbox and the table and the sunshade and the umbrella, and then at the figure sitting bolt upright in his car, fawn straw hat set on white hair, gloved hands gripping the door handle.

'Oh, God!' he said.

The last old lady had nowhere to go and no relatives and very little money, and she wasn't ill enough for a hospital. She was only old. In the end, Miss Harmon had to call on the Old People's Welfare. At first, the smart young lady who was called Miss Waterlow said that she could do nothing, but when Miss Harmon burst into tears – for, after all, she was old herself – Miss Waterlow said that she would try to help, and did manage to find a place in an old people's home. So at last Bayview belonged to Betty and became the Pavilion Hotel, and she was going to make a success of it. She *must* make a success of it.

The first year was terrible. All those empty rooms – more empty for being newly painted – and the few people who did come sitting around looking at each other uneasily. An empty hotel, like an empty theatre, however good it may be, is a confession of failure. The second year was a little better, a very little, although not many of the guests from the year before returned because they had found the emptiness so depressing. But during the third year, the year which had just gone by, she had felt that the hotel was really beginning to be a going concern.

'You're coming through!' her father had cried jubilantly when he came down last week to see the books. 'You're coming through!'

There were even some permanent residents – an engineer who was doing a job in Brightlesea and went home to London at the weekends, and a husband and wife, back from abroad, with a daughter who lived just outside the town.

'Good,' said her father. 'You want a few permanent residents – but not too many, now. And keep the price up. If you charge too little, you only fill the place with the wrong sort of people, and then you don't get the others.'

Her father was quite right, Betty thought. If only Joe had had his head for business! But then, if only Joe had been faithful, or a good provider, or given her children, or even been kind, instead of ... Her mind shied away, and she quickly bent over next season's brochure. At that moment, she heard the bell and went to answer the door.

In spite of the suitcase, Betty didn't guess why Miss Pollock was there. She merely thought the poor old thing was collecting for something.

'Good afternoon,' she said, with her professional hotelier's smile. 'Can I help you?'

'I want a room,' said Miss Pollock.

Betty looked at her, aghast. In Miss Pollock she saw the frightful spectre of a former Bayview resident, only poorer and shabbier and more impossible than all the others. She felt an almost superstitious dread, as if this tiny old woman was somehow capable of forcing her way in and taking possession of the Pavilion Hotel, dragging down into ruins all Betty's hard-won success. *But what shall I say to her?* thought Betty, despairingly. She would have simply replied that the season was over, but she was afraid that the husband and wife might come downstairs for tea at any moment. She didn't want to hurt the old lady's feelings.

'Er ... how much were you thinking of paying?' she said.

Miss Pollock had thought this out very carefully during the walk from Hampton Row. She had her pension, and she didn't need to buy anything – only a few sweets now and then.

She answered confidently, 'Thirty shillings a week.'

'Ah,' said Betty. 'I'm afraid a room here costs rather more than that. I'm very sorry.'

But, because her tone was kind, Miss Pollock still lingered, and Betty caught the look of desperation in her face.

'Haven't you anywhere to go?' she asked.

Miss Pollock was almost surprised. It seemed as though everyone ought to know.

'They're pulling down my house,' she said.

'Oh. I see. But ... you have some relatives?'

'No,' said Miss Pollock. 'I haven't.'

She added, Uncle Alfie's dead, and Aunt Maud, and there's only that lot at Enfield, and I don't want to go there, and, anyway, they may have moved. But she was so much used to being alone and silent that she added all this to herself, and missed Betty's next words altogether.

'I'm sure there must be someone who

could help you. You could go to the Welfare people at the Council Offices. They'd help, I'm sure.'

She saw the blank look on Miss Pollock's face and paused. A sudden, joyful inspiration came to her. She remembered the last old lady of Bayview, gathered into the beneficent arms of the welfare state.

'I dare say they could find a place for you in an old people's home,' she said.

Miss Pollock stiffened. A look of terror came into her face.

'No,' she said. 'No!'

She picked up the suitcase and the shopping bag. It was hard to get down the steps, agitated as she was, but she managed it somehow.

'No!' she said again, and set off down the street.

Betty gazed after her in dismay.

'Wait!' she called. 'Wait a minute!'

Miss Pollock had nearly reached the corner.

'If there's anything I can do to help...!' called Betty.

But Miss Pollock was gone. Betty didn't know whether to be glad or upset. She turned back slowly and shut the door. She, too, had known what it was to be in despair, to be homeless. She almost hated the plump, well-fed husband and wife plodding comfortably downstairs to their tea.

71

But, after all, thought Betty miserably, business was business. What else could she have done?

Sixteen

It was with her last strength that Miss Pollock crossed the road to the promenade. Cars roared to and fro, as they never used to in the old days, but at last she saw a gap and walked across very slowly, the case banging against her knee at every step. She had no idea where she was going. There seemed to be nowhere for her to go. What was the good of searching further, even if she could drag that case round the streets any more, when she couldn't afford the price of a room, anyway? There was nowhere for her to go. Nowhere.

She came up on to the pavement of the promenade. The wind caught at her hat and she had to put the case down to save it. The absolute impossibility of carrying her case and shopping bag and handbag, and of holding her hat on at the same time, was like the final onslaught of a relentless enemy. She stood there holding her hat, buffeted by the wind, hopeless, frightened and alone. Then she saw a square wood and glass erection nearby. It wasn't like the little green, open-fronted huts which used to be there, but Miss Pollock recognised it as a rather grander variety of 'shelter'. The word set off a course of action, like the word 'escape' earlier. Almost dragging the case along, and tilting her head sideways to protect her hat from the grasping wind, Miss Pollock set off for the shelter.

As she drew near, she saw that there was someone sitting on the bench of the nearest compartment. Normally she would have avoided the company of a stranger, but when she arrived in the lee, she could not bear to battle out round the windy corner into the next compartment. She put the case down with a gasp, lifted the shopping bag up on the bench, and sat down, her heart thudding wildly, in the corner farthest away from the old gentleman who puffed his pipe and gazed at the passing cars. As she sat down, he turned to look at her and took his pipe out of his mouth.

'Good afternoon,' said Mr Charrington.

Seventeen

Miss Pollock never spoke to strangers, and she didn't now. She looked at Mr Charrington, folded her lips, and nodded.

'Lovely day, i'n it?' he said. 'Best time o' the year, autumn.'

Now, this was something her father used to say.

'The days are drawing in,' her mother would remark, dolefully.

'Go on!' her father would reply, cheerfully. 'Best time of year, autumn! You going to make a bit of toast, then?'

The first toast of autumn, the pot of chrysanthemums in the window, the curtains drawn against the early dusk – Miss Pollock's cold, frightened heart warmed and steadied a little. She nodded again.

'You just off the train?' enquired Mr Charrington.

This shocked Miss Pollock into speech.

'No!' she said. 'I'm not!'

'Oh. You live here, then, do you?'

'I've lived here all my life!' cried Miss Pollock, indignantly.

'Get away!' said Mr Charrington. 'So have

I. Wouldn't live anywhere else. Not like my son. He can't bear it. Wouldn't have it at any price.'

Miss Pollock wanted to ask more about Mr Charrington's son, but she did not know how to. Her mother had always been the talker. She was the one who brought home those interesting bits of information which they all enjoyed so much.

'I met a woman in Dewsbury's,' she would say. 'She told me her husband tripped over the cat and fell right down the stairs last night. Broke two ribs, he did. Dreadful!' Or, 'You know that young Doctor Baines? A woman in the fishmonger's told me he was drunk last night. She happened to be out late because she'd been visiting her sister – she's expecting a baby – and this woman was coming home past the Doctor's house, and she said he was outside, and he couldn't get his key in the lock. Couldn't get his key in the lock!'

This gift of conversation opened up great ranges of acquaintanceship to the Pollocks. They might never see the woman whose husband fell downstairs, but his two ribs – and whether the cat was hurt – occupied pleasant moments of chat round the tea or supper table, together with Doctor Baines' excesses, and even the other woman's sister, and whether it would be a boy or a girl.

It was only when Mr Charrington mentioned his son that Miss Pollock realised what a lot of interesting events she had been missing in the world since her mother died. She braced herself, cleared her throat, and said rather hoarsely, 'Why doesn't he like it, then?'

'Eh?' said Mr Charrington.

He turned to look at her. She saw a pair of fine brown eyes with a twinkle in them, a white moustache, and a pleasantly ruddy countenance. He saw china-blue eyes and the look of a hedge sparrow who sees a crumb of bread on the path but is afraid to come near. He moved to the middle of the seat. He was rather deaf, and wasn't sure how loudly she had spoken.

'What, Brightlesea?' he said. 'Ooh, I don't know. Lot of nonsense! Do you know, he wouldn't come and live in my house? After my wife died, there was plenty of room, but no! He wouldn't.'

'Fancy,' said Miss Pollock, not sure what was required of her.

'He wouldn't go into my business, neither. I said to him, "What you want to do is to learn a trade," I says. "As long as you got a trade, you're all right." '

'That's what my father used to say!' exclaimed Miss Pollock, pleasantly struck.

'Oh, yes? What was he in, then?'

'He was a butcher.'

'Never!' cried Mr Charrington. 'Was he

really? That's what I was!'

They were both pleasurably astonished. They kept shaking their heads and smiling and saying, 'Well, I never!' for quite some time.

'I might have known him,' said Mr Charrington. 'What was his name, then, if you don't mind my asking?'

Miss Pollock hesitated. It seemed rather daring to give her name to a stranger.

'Er ... Pollock,' she said, uncertainly. 'He was Mr Pollock.'

'Pollock,' mused Mr Charrington. 'I don't think I ... Did he have his own business?'

'No, he worked for Mr Parker.'

'Parker. Oh, yes, I know. Shop in West Street, wasn't it? Yes, I remember Mr Parker! Old chap with waxed moustaches. Well, I never!'

They were both delighted all over again. Mr Parker had been dead for forty years, but to both of them he was a mutual acquaintance politely introducing them.

'I used to work in Busby's,' said Mr Charrington. 'Big place it was. I don't expect you'd know it. It was right the other end of town. We used to live in Eastern Avenue. Well, that's funny, isn't it? Your father worked in West Street and we used to live in Eastern Avenue. Well, I never! That's funny, isn't it?'

Miss Pollock nodded and almost smiled.

77

'Nice little house we had there,' Mr Charrington continued. 'My own, too! But my son wouldn't come to live there. I had to sell it. Got two hundred pounds for it. Two hundred pounds! Not bad, was it?'

'Very good!' said Miss Pollock.

She was glad to know that Mr Charrington was a man of substance. Somehow it made her feel safer, too. Besides, she had a notion that old men who sat alone on benches were apt to be tramps. It was a relief to discover that Mr Charrington wasn't a tramp but a property owner.

'Where do you live now, then?' she enquired.

Mr Charrington seemed to hesitate.

'Oh,' he said. 'Well ... er ... Well, my son asked me to go and live with him. One of them new housing estates. I'd rather have stayed where I was, in me own house, but he wouldn't go there. He said it hadn't got a bathroom. Well, I don't mind about a bathroom. A wash down in the sink or a tin bath in front of the fire, that's good enough for me!'

He gave a chuckle.

'Oh!' said Miss Pollock, and clicked her tongue. It was her way of laughing when she was a little bit shocked at the same time. One didn't really talk about having baths to complete strangers. There was something pleasantly daring in the fact that Mr Charrington *did*.

'These new estates,' said Mr Charrington, 'not like the old places. All pink and yeller doors, and no hedges or nothing. Just a bit of wire round yer garden, and everyone looking in. I like a bit of privacy myself.'

'Oh yes,' said Miss Pollock.

'I like my independence, too,' said Mr Charrington.

This was too difficult for Miss Pollock. She knew she liked to keep herself to herself, but...

A silence fell. Mr Charrington held his pipe in his hands, staring away into the distance. Miss Pollock knew that any moment now, he would get up and say, 'Good afternoon,' and walk away, back to his son, back to the house on the estate, back to safety, leaving Miss Pollock alone and frightened. She wanted to think of something to say to keep him there a little longer but she couldn't. If only she could 'make conversation' like her mother. But she never had been one for making conversation, and she couldn't do it now. She sat perfectly still, her lips tight, frowning a little, as though she hardly knew that Mr Charrington was there, and certainly didn't care whether he went or stayed.

Mr Charrington moved uneasily, and sniffed. Miss Pollock was aware of his restlessness, even without looking at him. In another second, he would get up, walk away and leave her. The momentary respite of his company gave the thought a new and terrifying loneliness. She clasped her hands tightly in her lap. Mr Charrington sniffed again, knocked out his pipe on the sole of his shoe and put it in his pocket. He turned to Miss Pollock.

'Would you like a cup of tea?' he said.

Instantly, Miss Pollock knew that a cup of tea was the one thing in the world she really wanted. After one quick glance at Mr Charrington, she frowned, looked away, and said severely, 'Oh, I ... I don't know.'

'Come on,' said Mr Charrington. 'There's a café just down there. Wouldn't take a moment.'

'Well...' said Miss Pollock.

'Oh, my name's Charrington, by the way. George Charrington. Like the beer!'

'Oh!' said Miss Pollock, and clicked her tongue again, and smiled a little. 'How do you do?' she said, politely.

'I'd feel all the better for a cup of tea,' said Mr Charrington, 'and so would you. Come along!'

He stood up. Miss Pollock looked longingly at the café, which she could see just across the road, and then at her case.

'Oh, I ... I couldn't leave my—'

'Like to bring it with you?' asked Mr Charrington. 'I'll carry it for you.'

'Oh, no, it's too heavy,' said Miss Pollock. 'Besides, I—'

'Tell you what!' cried Mr Charrington, suddenly. 'I'll go and get a couple of cups and bring them up here. Eh? What about that?'

'Oh, I—'

'Don't you move!' cried Mr Charrington. 'I won't be long!'

'Oh dear!' cried Miss Pollock, but it was an exclamation of excited delight. No one had ever before run about fetching her cups of tea. She felt suddenly tremendously important and – somehow – feminine. Her blue eyes sparkled as she watched Mr Charrington hurry across the promenade and down the path.

The cars were still roaring to and fro along the road, only rather more of them now than earlier. As Mr Charrington stood on the edge of the path, Miss Pollock began to feel some anxiety. He didn't move very quickly. What if one of them should get him? Suddenly, Mr Charrington's safety was the only thing in the whole world which mattered to Miss Pollock. She saw him set out across the road, saw a car racing towards him. He wasn't looking. It was sure to ... But he was safely across. Miss Pollock had never before felt such anxiety for someone else. There was anguish in it, but yet there was a kind of pleasure, too.

Mr Charrington was a long time inside the café. Miss Pollock looked away, her eye caught by a little steamer apparently motionless on the horizon, and was taken by surprise when he returned. He carried quite a large tray, and was panting a little as he put it down on the seat. He had brought a pot of tea, milk and sugar, a plate of bread and butter, some jam, two slices of fruit cake and two chocolate biscuits wrapped in silver paper.

'Oh, good gracious me!' exclaimed Miss Pollock. 'I shall never eat all that!'

'I shall,' said Mr Charrington. 'I missed me dinner! Come on. You be mother!'

'Oh!' said Miss Pollock, and clicked her tongue again. But she couldn't help smiling.

They sat one on each side of the tray, and Miss Pollock poured out. In the end, she ate nearly as much as he did, though she only had two cups of tea. He had three, and four teaspoons of sugar in each of them. There wasn't enough in the sugar basin, so Miss Pollock dug into her shopping bag and fetched out her bag of sugar.

'Well, I never!' exclaimed Mr Charrington, looking at her admiringly. 'Well, I never!'

It was a wonderful tea. The fresh air, the beautiful view of the sea, and the novelty of eating it alone together in the shelter, like two children with a doll's tea set in a summer house, all gave a feeling of adventure and escape. Miss Pollock felt that she wanted the tea to go on for ever. While the tea tray lay between them, and Mr Charrington dipped his bread and butter in his tea and pushed the plate towards her with a kindly, rough, 'Go on! Go on!' she was safe.

But it couldn't last for ever. Finally it was over. They looked at each other across the empty cups, empty plates and two little screws of silver paper.

'Well,' said Mr Charrington, 'I suppose I'd better take the tray back.'

He stood up. Again, Miss Pollock felt a sharp stab of terror. He would take the tray away and he wouldn't come back. He would say goodbye, and leave her here all alone on the windy promenade with night coming on. She felt her breath come short at the thought, and looked up at him, painfully still and silent.

'Time's getting on,' said Mr Charrington. 'Hadn't you better be getting home, then?'

An obstinate look came into Miss Pollock's face.

'No,' she said. She hesitated. The brown eyes weren't twinkling now. They were profoundly troubled. For the first time since her mother died, she knew that someone really cared what happened to her, and for the first time since Mr Simmonds came to throw her little world into terror and confusion, her own eyes filled with tears.

'I haven't anywhere to go,' she said.

'You what?'

'They're pulling down my house,' said Miss Pollock, stubbornly. 'I haven't got anywhere to go.'

He suddenly gave a great laugh and sat down again.

'Well, I never!' said Mr Charrington. 'That makes two of us!'

Eighteen

When Mr Charrington went to live with his son, it all began quite well. He had the two hundred pounds from the house, quite apart from his bit of savings, and he was able to give the children a few treats and buy Gwen a new carpet for the sitting room. He even bought a television set. Ken offered to treat the money for the TV as a loan, but Mr Charrington said, 'Go on! It's a present. If I'm living here, I want you all to have a good time. You want a TV, well, come on, here it is!' But, what with the carpet and the television and tickets for the summer show for them all, with bus fare to Brightlesea and back, somehow the money went very quickly. Christmas was expensive, too. He asked Gwen what the kids would like, and that turned out to be new bicycles. Then he bought Ken a watch and Gwen an electric mixer, and suddenly there he was, with nothing to live on but his pension. By the time he'd paid Gwen for his room and his keep, there wasn't even much left of that.

Mr Charrington wondered at first if he was imagining things when he wasn't quite as comfortable as he had been. He supposed you got a bit too much used to a place, and people started to get on your nerves. Only, where it had once been, 'Johnny, don't bother your Granddad!' now it seemed to be, 'Oh, Dad, leave the kids alone! It's *their* home, after all!' What was more annoying than anything else was that it was the television which *he* had bought which caused most of the trouble. Mr Charrington liked a bit of a chat in the evening. He'd been alone most of the day, sitting in his room, or in the public library reading the papers, or sitting on a park bench. When the kids got back from school, he wanted to know what they'd learnt, and whether they'd played any games. And when Gwen and Ken got back from their jobs, he wanted to hear a bit of gossip from them. Instead, as soon as the kids got inside the house, before they even took off their caps or blazers, on went the telly, and down they sat gawping at it, and it never went off again until eleven o'clock or what-ever time it stopped. A load of rubbish it

85

was, too. The only programmes Mr Charrington really liked were the travel stories, but whenever they came on, Gwen would say, 'Oh, we don't want that! Turn it over, Johnny! Go on, turn it over!' and there was some young fool trying to sell hair cream, or some girl in a bath, or some idiot with a guitar shouting out a lot of nonsense and knocking his knees together.

Mr Charrington grumbled a good deal, but then he always had. He used to grumble at his wife, and she used to grumble at him. Neither of them took much notice, and he didn't expect anyone else to. So when the shocking thing happened, it wasn't only shocking, it was also a shock, a blinding, staggering shock, like a hand-grenade landing in the living room.

Mr Charrington always found Sunday an awkward day at Ken's. In the old days at Brightlesea he'd looked forward to Sundays, but here, with the children home all day, there wasn't a bit of peace. This particular Sunday was worse than usual, because it started with Johnny bashing his bicycle into the wall.

'You ought to be more careful!' said Mr Charrington, sharply, thinking of all the tobacco he could have bought with the money he'd spent on that dented, mistreated object. 'Why don't you ride it properly?'

'Oh, for goodness' sake!' said Gwen. 'It's

his bike, isn't it?'

'Well, I didn't give it to him for him to knock it about,' said Mr Charrington. 'Look at the way he's bent that mudguard. You won't be able to mend that, you know.'

'Well, then he'll have to have a new one, won't he?' said Gwen. 'I know it won't be *you* buying it!'

The words swept through Mr Charrington like a cold wind. As Gwen banged back into the kitchen, he stared after her, astonished and horrified. He looked away and saw Johnny deliberately putting out his tongue at him before jumping on his bicycle and clattering away down the path.

Mr Charrington had always looked forward to Sunday dinner, too. During the week, he got his own midday meals, usually a bit of cold meat and pickle, or some bread and cheese. Sunday was the one day he had a cooked dinner. But he was usually disappointed in it. His wife always used to do something special on Sundays. Emily had had her faults, but, to do her justice, she was a lovely cook. Gwen was different. She got up late on Sundays and slopped about the house in a dressing gown, drinking cups of tea and reading the papers. Half the time, it was after twelve o'clock before she got the joint in the oven, and sometimes they didn't sit down to eat until three o'clock. On this particular Sunday, the meat was beef, which was Mr Charrington's favourite, but the potatoes were boiled instead of roast, there was no gravy, and the peas were those frozen packet ones which Mr Charrington thought had no flavour at all.

'Don't we get any Yorkshire pudding, then?' he asked as they sat down.

'Listen,' said Gwen, 'if you want Yorkshire pudding, you can make it yourself!'

And Johnny looked sideways at Timmy and they both laughed.

'What are you grinning at?' said Mr Charrington.

'I suppose they can laugh if they want to,' said Gwen. 'It's a free country.'

Mr Charrington glanced at Ken, but he was carving the meat and didn't seem to have noticed anything.

It was an irritating afternoon. Mr Charrington liked a nap after dinner, but there the boys were, as usual, shouting and banging about and quarrelling, and Ken and Gwen swore at them, but never really did anything to stop them, as Mr Charrington would have if it had been *his* house. If it had been *his* house ... It came to him with a sickening discomfort that it was not his house and never would be. Never again would he have a house. Never again would he have things to suit himself, as he used to in Brightlesea. He was just an old man, a lodger in someone else's house. For a moment he felt frighteningly helpless. Then he gathered himself together. This wouldn't do. He must assert himself. He wasn't going to be pushed around.

There was a programme on the television that evening about going up the Amazon which Mr Charrington very much fancied. (People were always going up the Amazon in the boys' papers he used to read, and he wanted to see what it looked like.) But just as it was about to come on, Johnny jumped up and said, 'Cor! We're on the wrong programme!'

'No, we're not,' said Mr Charrington. 'We're on the right programme.' And, as Johnny still reached for the knob, he added menacingly, 'You leave that alone.'

'But Billy Fury's on the other,' said Johnny.

'Who's he when he's at home?' enquired Mr Charrington, sarcastically.

'He's a singer.'

'A singer!' said Mr Charrington, disgustedly. 'What does he do? Shake his hips or knock his knees together? You leave that alone!'

'Dad, if he wants it, let him have it!' said Ken. 'What's the matter with you?'

'I want the other,' said Mr Charrington. 'It's *my* television.'

'Oh no, it isn't!' said Ken. 'You gave that to me. It's *my* television, and it's *my* house, and I'm not having anyone else telling my kids what to do. Johnny, you want the other programme, you turn it over!'

'You touch that knob,' said Mr Charrington, suddenly trembling with rage, 'and I'll walk out of this house.'

'I don't see anyone stopping you,' said Ken.

There was a brief, breathless pause. Even Johnny, standing by the television set, felt the enormity of the moment and didn't move. Mr Charrington stared at Ken unbelievingly.

'I'm fed up with you always shouting the odds,' said Ken, 'grumbling at everything and trying to boss the show. If you don't like it here, you know what you can do.'

'You ... you *asked* me to come here!' gasped Mr Charrington.

'Yeah, well, now I'm telling you the other thing,' said Ken. 'Shut up or get out. I've had enough. So's Gwen. If you don't like it here, you can get out.'

'I shall, don't worry,' said Mr Charrington. 'I know when I'm not wanted.'

He got up and went stiffly out of the room. He paused at the foot of the stairs, holding on to the banister, and heard from the sitting room the sudden moronic moan of guitar and voice, indistinguishably twanging away together. It was as though the whole family put their tongues out at him. He knew that, whatever happened, he couldn't stay.

90

Next morning, Mr Charrington stayed in his room until they had all left. Then he came downstairs, made himself a pot of tea and two slices of toast, meticulously washed up his own cup and plate, leaving the rest of the breakfast things – which he usually washed up – dirty in the sink, put his razor, pyjamas and dressing gown in an old brown holdall with a change of underwear, put on his overcoat and hat, put his pension book in his pocket, and walked out of the house.

It was a quarter of an hour's walk to the bus, and half an hour's journey into Brightlesea. He tried ten different bed and breakfast places and five different boarding houses. Either they didn't take lodgers, or it was too late in the season, or they charged more than he could afford.

By the time he walked up on to the promenade, he was tired out. His legs were trembling, his feet hurt, and he could hardly breathe. He sat down in the shelter, trying to fight off the panic which rolled irresistibly in upon him like waves from the sea. Then he saw a little old lady struggling along the promenade. She was carrying a huge, unwieldy suitcase and a shopping bag. Her hat was crooked, and her eyes were very blue.

Nineteen

'Well, this is a fine kettle of fish!' said Mr Charrington.

'I don't know what to do,' said Miss Pollock, with a quaver in her voice.

'We shall have to do something, shan't we?' said Mr Charrington. 'We can't sleep here all night!'

There was magic in that 'we'. The mere use of that one word put loneliness to flight.

'I don't know,' said Mr Charrington, looking round the shelter. 'It wouldn't be bad, would it?'

'What, *here*?' cried Miss Pollock, but she was smiling, not scandalised. It passed through her mind that this was, after all, a bit of a lark.

'We could cuddle up close together,' said Mr Charrington – and then Miss Pollock *was* scandalised!

'Here!' exclaimed Mr Charrington, suddenly. 'You ever been down under the promenade?'

'You can't get under there,' said Miss Pollock.

92

'You *can*,' said Mr Charrington. 'We used to go down there when we was kids. They got ... like ... shelters there. Keep boats in them, and that. If we could get in one of those, we'd be quite cosy. We might sleep in a boat.'

He chuckled. Miss Pollock felt quite dazed. He was so very ... He seemed so much more ... It came to her suddenly that he was a *man*. That was what made the difference. For the first time in her life she had a man looking after her – just her. There was something daring in the thought, and yet at the same time it made her feel safe.

'How do we get there?' she enquired, eyeing Mr Charrington severely, as her mother used to look at her father when he was 'having her on'.

'Down that slope,' said Mr Charrington, delightedly. 'I'll just take the tray back and then we'll explore, eh?'

Miss Pollock felt she had never in her life enjoyed anything quite so much as going down that slope. Mr Charrington went first, carrying the suitcase and the holdall, and then he came back and held out his hand to her. It was a brown, freckled hand, square but not podgy, and his eyes twinkled as she came down the slope, nervous as a kitten, step by step in her tiny, dusty shoes. When she stepped on to the shingle at the bottom – and that was an adventure, too, because her mother never had let her walk on the shingle for fear of spoiling her shoes – she saw that Mr Charrington was quite right: the cavelike space under the promenade was divided off by wooden partitions.

'Why,' cried Miss Pollock, charmed, 'they're like a lot of little houses!'

The first little house was inhospitably boarded up, with a makeshift door and a padlock at one side. The second little house looked, as Miss Pollock said, 'nasty', with broken bottles, orange peel and dirty paper. But the third little house looked, somehow, inviting, in spite of the fact that a boat took up half the room in it. There were nets, too, draped over the boat.

'We could go fishing,' said Mr Charrington, and they both giggled like a pair of children.

'Ooh!' cried Miss Pollock, suddenly alarmed. 'What happens when the tide comes in?'

'It don't come up here,' Mr Charrington replied. He kicked the shingle over with the toe of his shoe. 'Look, quite dry,' he said.

Miss Pollock watched him admiringly. She would never have thought of that. The shingle was quite dry. They were safe.

'The first thing we gotta decide,' said Mr Charrington, 'is where we're going to sleep. I wouldn't mind getting into the boat. How about you?'

'What, up there?' cried Miss Pollock. 'Never!'

For the boat towered above them, rearing unexpectedly up from its rigid keel.

'There's a little ladder – look,' insinuated Mr Charrington. He chuckled suddenly. 'You ever been to Arundel Castle?'

'Where?' said Miss Pollock, dazed again.

One never knew what he would say next. After living alone for so long, it was hard to follow him. It was disconcerting, but ... it was an adventure. Just listening to him was an adventure!

'Arundel Castle,' said Mr Charrington. 'I went there once on a choir outing. They got a bedroom there what Queen Victoria once slep' in.'

'They what?' said Miss Pollock, faintly.

'That's right,' Mr Charrington insisted, delightedly. 'A great big bed what Queen Victoria and Prince Albert slept in. On'y, her legs being rather short to climb up, they had a little ladder for her – little wooden steps. Well, there you are. There's your little steps, just like you was Queen Victoria.'

Miss Pollock eyed him severely, but she could not quite keep the amusement out of the corner of her mouth, no matter how firmly she pressed her lips together.

'I'm not climbing up there,' she said, 'not even for Queen Victoria!'

He laughed heartily and, try as she would, she had to smile, too. She remembered how her father used to tease her mother, and how

95

her mother used to pretend to be annoyed but was really pleased. She had never understood it until this moment.

Mr Charrington went up the rough wooden steps which stood against the side of the boat, and Miss Pollock put down the shopping bag and came to stand below him, with some indistinct idea of catching him if he should fall. She thought how wonderfully strong and brave he was. *She* would never dare to climb up there.

'Here!' said Mr Charrington. 'We'll be all right for something to sleep on. There's a bundle of old nets here and some canvas.' He looked down at her. 'Shall I chuck that canvas down for you?'

She nodded, and as he leaned over the edge of the boat, she ventured to take hold of the skirts of his coat, just so as to have something to hang on to if he should slip off the steps. The canvas was heavier than he had thought, and in the end she crept up on to the first step so that she could help him, trying to grasp the stiff, unyielding creases with her fawn woollen fingertips.

'Look out!' exclaimed Mr Charrington, breathlessly. 'If it comes down on top of you, it'll knock you flat. You stand back and I'll shove it over.'

After a determined struggle, he dragged the canvas over the edge while Miss Pollock watched anxiously. When it thumped down on to the sandy shingle, she started forward again.

'Leave it!' Mr Charrington commanded, descending. 'It's too heavy for you.'

It was nearly too heavy for Mr Charrington, but he did somehow manage to drag it along to the smooth, rock-walled corner at the back.

'How's that?' he said, panting but triumphant.

It looked like a crumpled grey nest. Miss Pollock was delighted. She sniffed.

'It's all right,' she said, with a little nod.

Mr Charrington fetched her suitcase and shopping bag and set them down near the canvas, and then went off to pick up his brown holdall and climbed step by step, gasping a little, into the boat. It was suddenly important to Miss Pollock to unpack her suitcase at once, as though she needed, after all, something safe and normal in the midst of all this strangeness.

She opened the suitcase and, because she had to take her dressing gown out first, anyway, she laid it on the canvas as though it were a bedcover. She folded the crocheted throw, too, and put it on the end like an eiderdown. By a bit of luck, there was a little ledge on the rock at the back, and there Miss Pollock put the donkey-and-basket and Uncle Alfie's jug. Her father's photograph she stood up beside the bed. She decided that she wouldn't undress to go to bed – it wouldn't be nice with Mr Charrington there – so she took out her nightdress and folded it up to make a pillow.

'Well, I never!' said Mr Charrington, leaning over the edge of the boat. 'It looks quite like home!'

Miss Pollock was pleased. That was just how *she* felt about it.

'Here,' said Mr Charrington, 'do you want to see mine?'

He went back to the middle of the boat and leaned over to take Miss Pollock's hand as she came nervously up the steps and peered over. It was beginning to get dark in there now, but she could just see a bundle of nets with Mr Charrington's thick dressing gown laid over them.

'You want to roll your pyjamas up as a pillow,' she said.

'A pillow!' said Mr Charrington, admiringly. 'I never thought of that. You've got it up there, haven't you?'

He fished about in his bag and fetched out a clumsy-looking pair of striped pyjamas while Miss Pollock watched him. It was quite a new feeling for her to be advising someone else, and to be thought clever. No one had ever thought she was clever before. She'd never done well at school. She didn't mind geography, but with all the other subjects – especially English and history and arithmetic – she hadn't known most of the time what the teachers were on about, so she had kept very quiet and hoped they wouldn't notice her, and mostly they didn't.

'There!' said Mr Charrington. 'Now, how about a bit of supper?'

'Supper?' exclaimed Miss Pollock. 'We've only just had our tea!'

'Never mind,' said Mr Charrington. 'We could do with an early bed. I'm tired, aren't you?'

Miss Pollock *was* but she wasn't going to say so. She went down the steps again and waited while he climbed over the edge of the boat and came down after her.

'I wish I could fill my hot-water bottle,' she said.

'Why not?' said Mr Charrington. 'Ask at the café. They wouldn't mind.'

'Ooh, I couldn't!' cried Miss Pollock.

'All right, then,' said Mr Charrington. 'You bring it over and *I'll* ask them.'

She looked at him doubtfully.

'Go on!' he said, grinning at her.

Still hesitating, she went to the suitcase and got out the hot-water bottle in its purple knitted cover.

'Coo, that's a smart one!' exclaimed Mr Charrington. 'Come on, then, let's see what they got for supper.'

Miss Pollock became very quiet as they trudged out of the little house and up the slope. Something was worrying her – something she couldn't possibly mention to Mr Charrington. She clutched her handbag and the hot-water bottle, thinking that what a little while ago had been a jolly adventure was suddenly dreadful and hopeless and shameful. She stepped up on to the promenade and paused, and Mr Charrington paused, too.

'I wouldn't mind going to the toilet, would you?' he said.

For a second, Miss Pollock was too shocked even to think. You didn't talk about things like that. Even when you were going to the 'outside', you pretended that you weren't. But, of course, if there *was* a nice toilet somewhere near, well, she *had* been wondering about it. Relief began to take the place of her embarrassment – tentative and nervous, but still relief.

'They got a nice new public lavatory along there,' said Mr Charrington.

'A public lavatory!' repeated Miss Pollock, dismayed.

'There it is,' said Mr Charrington. 'Ladies one side and gents the other. Lovely flowers they got outside, ain't they?'

Miss Pollock didn't answer. She walked along at his side, her face set in a mutinous frown of embarrassment and fear. She had only been to a public lavatory once in her life, when she was a little girl and out for the day with her parents. She still remembered her mother's shocked and indignant whispers when she confessed that she had forgotten to go before she came out, and how her mother had taken her off like a prisoner under escort while her father pretended not to notice. She remembered, too, the dark, evil-smelling place down a flight of stone steps, and the horrible iron turnstile. Supposing she couldn't work the turnstile?

'Here we are,' said Mr Charrington. 'I'm round the other side. If I'm out first, I'll wait for you there, by the flower bed.'

Miss Pollock nodded. The flowers *were* nice, and the place itself looked different from the one she remembered. She tiptoed inside, her footsteps echoing disconcertingly. But there wasn't any turnstile, and it wasn't dark at all. It was brightly lit and very clean, and the tiles were pink and blue. In fact, it was nicer – she really had to admit it – than her own 'outside'. And there were washbasins, too, and a place where you could put threepence in and get a towel out. Miss Pollock suddenly realised that she could come here any time she liked, and have a wash and all. She felt wonderful. She came out as happy as a sandboy. She didn't mind in the least that Mr Charrington wasn't yet waiting by the flower bed and that she had to stand there all alone outside the public lavatory. She just stood and looked at the flowers and watched the cars go by and waited for him. She didn't worry about whether the few people walking past were staring at her or not. She didn't even notice the policeman.

PC Whitehead noticed Miss Pollock, however. As he walked slowly along the promenade, he saw her from quite a long way off. She looked exactly like his mother-in-law.

Twenty

What drove Arthur Whitehead mad was the thought that *he* had been the one who said they must have her to live with them. Joyce said that her mother would only try to rule the roost, just as she'd always done at home, but he'd said the poor old lady had nowhere else to go, and that they must take her in. 'Poor old lady!' Much he'd known about it!

It started as soon as she got inside the house. He'd decorated the spare room specially for her – cream paint and a nice flowered wallpaper. He carried her case upstairs and opened the bedroom door. He expected her to say, 'Well, that does look bright and clean!' or perhaps, 'Oh, Arthur, you've done it up!' But what she said was, 'I hope you don't expect me to sleep in there, with that smell of paint!'

'There, Arthur!' exclaimed his wife. 'I *told* you! I told you you should've got on to it sooner!'

The old woman *wouldn't* sleep in there, either. The girl had to move into Tony's room, and young Tony had to sleep on the settee downstairs. That was the start of it, and it had gone on like that ever since.

PC Whitehead felt it most when he came in from duty. In the old days, it made no difference what time he came in – Joyce always seemed glad to see him. In the daytime, it was always, 'Tea's ready, love,' or, 'Going to have your supper in the other room, Arthur?' Even in the middle of the night, he used to make her a cup of tea, and she'd sit up in bed and drink it while he got undressed. But now, the first voice he heard was always his mother-in-law's. 'You're late, then, aren't you?' or, 'I suppose you want something to eat now!' And at night Joyce wouldn't let him make tea because the water made a noise in the pipes in the spare room, so he had to creep upstairs and get into bed without even washing, 'and even then the old woman usually had something to say at breakfast about what a row he'd made, and how she'd never got off to sleep again until five o'clock in the morning.

And the worst of it was that Joyce was different, too. She'd never got on with her mother, and yet now ... He'd only got to say one wrong word about her, and Joyce was down on him like a ton of bricks. And the kids, too. With the old woman sitting there in the lounge, grumbling and mumbling on and on about how untidy they were and what a lot of rubbish they watched on television, they soon got out from under. Instead of him and Joyce and the two kids sitting together in the lounge on his evenings off, watching television, and Joyce wheeling supper in on the trolley, and them all cosy and jolly together, now it was just him and Joyce and that old ... devil. She was. She was an old devil, with a tongue like poison. And somehow the fact that she was so small made it worse. There he was, six foot two in his stockinged feet, and his whole life was being ruined by a little woman only four foot ten. It was like being dominated over by a malevolent dwarf. Even when she was ill in bed, there was no peace, with Joyce up and down to her, and saying 'Shush!' every time he spoke. And if *he* took a tray up, it was always, 'Mind you don't spill it!' or, 'What've you got there? I don't want *that*!' before he was even inside the door.

And there was no end to it. That was the worst of it. She hadn't got anywhere else to go. Joyce was her only daughter, and her two sons had gone abroad, one to Canada and one to New Zealand – getting away from her domineering ways, most like. And she was only seventy-three. She might live to ninety. She might live to a hundred. He found himself thinking, Oh, God, don't let her live to ninety! and then he was horrified at himself. But to go on, day after day, knowing that there was no escape, and that wherever he was, he must take her with him ... It was like being put in prison for a crime he hadn't committed.

PC Whitehead came nearly level with the old lady standing by the flowers outside the public lavatory. She seemed to be holding a purple woollen shield in front of her, and she was also clutching a shabby handbag. It was an odd time of day for an old lady to be standing there alone. If she had been a child, now, he would have stopped and spoken to her. Or if she had been a young girl, or, well, or even a middle-aged woman. Just to make sure she was all right, and not stranded by a belated coach outing or something like that. PC Whitehead saw the fawn hat skewered on with a hatpin, and the lips pressed together, just as his mother-in-law pressed hers when there was something she didn't approve of – and that was all the time.

He walked on. No need to worry about old ladies out alone in the evening, he thought. Old ladies were tough. He ought to know that, if anyone did.

Twenty-One

Miss Pollock couldn't remember the last time she'd eaten a meal out. Her mother and father were never much for going out to meals. The few times they went for day trips, they mostly took sandwiches. And now here she was, sitting in a restaurant with a stranger – for Mr Charrington was a stranger, really – trying to read the menu. It made her feel queer. She could hardly believe that it was true.

As a matter of fact, 'menu' was the only word Miss Pollock could read, because that was printed in great big letters. The rest was written in ink, and Miss Pollock had forgotten to bring her spectacles.

'What'll you have?' said Mr Charrington.

Miss Pollock gave up trying to read that blue blur and put the card down.

'I don't mind,' she said.

Mr Charrington picked up the card. He had to hold it rather a long way away from him, but he seemed to be able to read it without glasses.

'Poached egg on toast,' he said. 'Baked

beans on toast. Poached egg on toast and baked beans. Plaice and chips. Cod and chips. Mixed grill.'

He looked up at her.

'What d'you fancy?'

Miss Pollock pressed her lips together and frowned. She wondered what 'mixed grill' meant. Mr Charrington's brown eyes twinkled at her.

'How about poached egg on toast and baked beans?'

'I don't mind,' said Miss Pollock.

Poached egg on toast and baked beans was just what she fancied.

'And a pot of tea, eh?' suggested Mr Charrington.

She nodded. He put the card down and smiled at her.

'Here!' she said. 'How much does it cost?'

'Oh, that's all right,' said Mr Charrington, easily. 'I'll do this one.'

'You did the tea,' said Miss Pollock.

He chuckled.

'Oh well,' he said, 'when I run out, I'll touch you for it!'

The man who came to see what they wanted to eat was fat and didn't look very clean. He wore a dirty shirt and no tie and his pullover had a hole in the sleeve.

' 'Ullo,' he said.

' 'Evening,' said Mr Charrington. 'We'll 'ave poached eggs and baked beans and a pot o' tea.'

'Right,' said the fat man, and went away behind the counter.

Miss Pollock let her breath go and relaxed. She could never have said it like that – never! She sat back and looked about her. It wasn't a very big restaurant. There were about six tables, covered with green and white checked plastic cloths, and each one had a cruet and a bottle of Worcester sauce and a vase with plastic roses in it. And there were white lace curtains over the lower part of the windows, so that people outside couldn't look in and watch you. It was nice, thought Miss Pollock, really nice. She looked across at Mr Charrington and found him looking at her and looked quickly away and felt that she was blushing. She still couldn't quite believe that she was sitting here with a man in a restaurant on Brightlesea Front at seven o'clock in the evening.

There was a sudden, frightening blare of noise from behind her and she jumped.

'Whatever's that?' she cried.

'It's a jukebox,' said Mr Charrington.

'A what?'

'Ain't you never seen one? It's a kind of gramophone – plays any kind of music you want.'

'Huh!' said Miss Pollock. 'Call that music?'

She looked over her shoulder and saw the brightly coloured box roaring out this

108

strange noise, and then she saw something else which made her forget it again. She turned back to Mr Charrington and spoke under her breath.

'There's a black feller!' she said.

'Oh yes?' said Mr Charrington.

Miss Pollock stole another fascinated glance over her shoulder.

'I don't know as I've ever seen one before,' she said.

'Go on!' said Mr Charrington. 'Oh, there's a lot of them round here. They work on the buses mostly.'

'What, as conductors?'

'That's right.'

Miss Pollock was shocked.

'Ooh, I wouldn't like them on the buses.'

'Oh?' said Mr Charrington. 'Why? What've you got against them?'

'I ain't got nothing against them,' said Miss Pollock, indignantly. 'I just don't fancy them on the buses. I mean, they're different from us, aren't they, black fellers?'

'Oh, they're all right,' said Mr Charrington, easily.

Miss Pollock took another peep at the black feller, who sat by the jukebox, stirring a cup of tea or coffee very slowly, and looking into it as though he was going to tell someone's fortune. She felt exactly as she had when she was a little girl frightened of a big dog, and her father had patted the dog and showed her that it was gentle.

'They're like us, really,' said Mr Charrington. 'Not much different.'

'Fancy,' said Miss Pollock, turning back.

She really meant, fancy sitting in a restaurant with a black feller and taking it all as a matter of course! When the fat man came with their poached eggs and beans and a pot of tea, she just sat quite calmly while he put them down, and when he asked if they wanted bread and butter, too, she actually said, 'No, thank you,' before Mr Charrington did.

When the noisy music finished, the black feller got up and went out, and it was very quiet. Miss Pollock and Mr Charrington didn't say much. They were both tired, and they didn't mind just eating their supper, there in the warm, with the fat man reading his paper behind the counter. When they'd finished, Mr Charrington got up.

'Give us yer hot-water bottle,' he said.

'Ooh, you can't!' whispered Miss Pollock.

'*Can't* I?' he said. 'Come on.'

She fished it up from its hiding place on her lap and gave it to him. She didn't watch him as he went over to the counter, but just sat very still, clutching her handbag and pretending not to know anything about it. She was quite taken by surprise when he came back.

'Ready, then?' he said.

She looked up. His eyes twinkled at her, and he'd got the hot-water bottle under his arm.

'Come on, then,' he said.

'What about paying?' she asked.

'I done that up at the counter,' he said.

He put threepence down on the table under his saucer.

'What's that for?' she asked.

'Well,' he said, 'I thought I'd leave a tip as we had a big meal. I don't bother for a cup of tea.'

'Oh,' said Miss Pollock.

She felt again how much he knew compared to her, and how safe she was while she was with him. He took her by the elbow as they went out of the door, and when they were outside he gave her the hot-water bottle.

'Ooh!' cried Miss Pollock, feeling the warmth right through her coat. 'He filled it!'

' 'Course he filled it,' said Mr Charrington. 'I just said we was having a new stove in at our house, and we hadn't got no hot water.'

'Ooh, what a fib!' cried Miss Pollock.

But she wasn't shocked. She was giggling, and Mr Charrington chuckled, too.

They both glanced back inside, through the uncurtained glass door, and saw the fat man leaning on the counter reading his paper.

'Did he believe you?' asked Miss Pollock,

breathless with that unaccustomed feeling of shared mischief.

' 'Course he did!' said Mr Charrington. 'Come on. Let's go to the crossing.'

Twenty-Two

Ed didn't really believe Mr Charrington. But then, he wasn't really interested. He never took much notice of customers as long as they paid. A woman he'd had living there for a while used to ask him why he didn't try to get a better class of customer. But he used to say, 'Why? They got a different kind of money, then?' She didn't want him to serve blacks, either. But he didn't mind blacks. He'd fought enough of them in the old days. Only thing he said about blacks was, they'd got harder heads than white people. His manager used to say he imagined it, but he knew better. Time and again, when he'd got back to his corner, he'd look across the ring and say, 'Cor! Head like a cocoanut, that one!' He never bore malice, though. Some people said that was why he never got far in the fight game. 'You gotta be a bit nasty,' they used to say to him.

Ed wondered sometimes what it would

have been like if he *had* got to the top. Light-heavyweight champion of Europe – the world, maybe. Still, fighters all ended up the same. Big success – they bought a nightclub or one of them restaurants where Lord Muck-a-Muck came from the sporting club. There wasn't much, in the end, between that and a caff in Brightlesea. He did good business in the summer. And in the winter, he'd got somewhere to live, hadn't he? And if he got fed up with it being too quiet, he could always shut the place up and go and have a game of snooker with the boys.

Ed finished the sports page of the evening paper. He only read the sports page, but he read it very slowly, so it took him the best part of the evening, what with serving customers and all. He'd finished it earlier than usual this time, though, with everything being so quiet. Most likely some of the kids would come in later, when the cinemas ended. They liked a cup of coffee and a bit of music before they got on their bikes or caught the last bus home. Ed hoped they'd come. They didn't always. They were like a flock of birds or something – always went about together, now one place, now another. It wasn't half quiet of an evening in the winter when they didn't come.

Ed heard the door open behind him. It was the woman who cooked. She always went home at eight. Wasn't nothing but coffee after that, anyway.

'I'm off,' she said.

'OK,' said Ed.

She went out. Ed wondered what she'd got in her shopping bag. The plaice, most like. Frozen plaice – it'd do for tomorrow, but that'd be what she'd take home. Not the cod that he'd probably have to give to the cat. It was the woman who was then living with him who put him wise to what was going on.

'She's robbing you blind,' she said. 'You want someone to look after you.'

Ed guessed she meant she'd like to stay and marry him, but he wasn't having any of that, and he soon got rid of her.

Not that there weren't times when he thought he wouldn't mind being married. Not to her, mind, but there were times when he was alone of an evening and things were quiet when he thought it'd be nice to have someone who'd sit and have a cup of tea with him, or maybe be waiting for him in the bedroom of the flat upstairs – not a whore, but *someone*.

He'd always gone around with whores when he was in the fight game. They were no trouble as long as you gave them money, and they didn't expect nothing. They didn't expect to get married, neither, and that was what did for boxers. Get married, and first thing you knew, you'd gone soft. Funnily enough, he'd only ever met one girl he'd

114

fancied to marry. Doris, her name was. She wasn't a whore.

'I don't do it for money,' she used to say. 'I do it for love.'

Then she'd laugh that big laugh of hers. She'd got a way with her, Doris had. She was ... company. Real company.

Funny thing, it was Doris who saw the advert for this café.

'Brightlesea,' she said. 'I love Brightlesea. Go on, why don't you buy it? Somewhere for your old age!'

And then that laugh of hers, as though life was a big joke, even growing old. Even growing old was a big joke to Doris. They came down to Brightlesea together and saw the place. They had a meal, sitting in the corner by the window, and when they came back, Ed told his manager where they'd been. His manager gave him a funny look.

'You know what she wants, don't you?' he said. 'She means to marry you, boy.'

That was enough for Ed. He dropped her. Just never called her again. Funny thing was, soon after that, his manager gave him the chuck. Said he wasn't never going to get there, and he might as well quit. Ed had a couple more fights, but they weren't much good. He'd bought the caff so he thought he might as well run it for a bit. He could always go back into training later. He never did, though. He'd been here ever since.

Ed came to clear the table. He tossed Mr Charrington's threepenny bit and caught it. Mean old devil! Might have made it a tanner. 'New stove', indeed! Did they take him for a green one? There wasn't no houses anywhere along the front, only hotels and boarding houses. Not that it was his business. The fight game had been his business once. Now nothing was.

Twenty-Three

'We'd better go to the toilet before we go to bed,' said Mr Charrington.

'It'll be too dark in there,' said Miss Pollock.

'No, it won't. They keep the lights on all night. Come on, I'll see you inside.'

Miss Pollock would have expected to feel shy at the idea of a gentleman taking her into a lavatory, but Mr Charrington was so kind and matter-of-fact that she never even thought of it. He was quite right – it was light inside.

'There you are,' he said. 'When you come out, you stay here in the doorway. I'll come round and fetch you.'

It *was* very dark, though, going down the slope from the promenade. Even with Mr

Charrington's hand in hers, Miss Pollock felt rather frightened. They stumbled together along the shingle, with the waves hissing and roaring not far away, and paused before the pitch-black hole which in the daylight had looked like a dear little house.

'I can't go in there!' cried Miss Pollock, panic-stricken. 'Supposing there's something in there!'

'Wait a minute,' said Mr Charrington.

He took his hand out of hers and moved away. She stood and trembled. Then she heard a little scrape, and a light sprang up, a small, flickering flame.

'There you are,' said Mr Charrington, shielding the match with his hand. 'It's all right. There's your little bed. Come on.'

She came forward. The match went out, but he struck another one, and by its light she saw the familiar things – her dressing gown and nightdress, the crocheted throw, her father's picture. She let her breath go. It wasn't a frightening dark hole any more. It was a little house by the sea – hers and Mr Charrington's.

'I'm going upstairs, then,' said Mr Charrington. 'I'll leave you the matches, shall I?'

'No, you keep them,' said Miss Pollock, boldly. 'You need them, going up into that boat.'

'Like Queen Victoria,' said Mr Charrington, and they both giggled. 'We'll get some candles tomorrow,' he added.

He went off up the steps. Miss Pollock took off her hat and coat and shoes, and laid the coat on top of the dressing gown, and then, clutching the hot-water bottle, she got into bed. The canvas felt hard and bumpy, but the hot-water bottle brought a comforting warmth. She heard Mr Charrington thumping about in the boat, grunting a little as he took off his coat and shoes.

'Eh!' he said.

She looked up. She could just see his head over the top of the boat.

'Night, night,' he said. 'Sleep well.'

It was what her father used to say.

'Sleep well,' said Miss Pollock.

As she lay looking out of the little house, she could see the stars in the sky, and hear the sea, very loud, coming and going, coming and going. It was all very strange, as though she had travelled far away to a distant country. But she wasn't alone. She could hear Mr Charrington's breathing up in the boat, rather creaky but companionable. She didn't think she'd ever fall asleep, but while she was thinking that, she did.

Twenty-Four

Ann Waterlow went along to Hampton Row on the way to her office on Tuesday morning. She knew that she should have gone the day before, and she was angry that she hadn't done so. She was angry with Mr Harper and ashamed of herself. Not going just to spite him – it was behaving like a loony old spinster.

She was so early that the milkman had only just left the milk. He slammed an empty half-pint bottle into the basket as she reached the gate, but he didn't look at her, just climbed up on to the cart and drove away.

Ann Waterlow walked up the little garden path. The new half-pint of milk stood on the step. The door was shabby, with peeling paint, and had no knocker or letter box. Only the ancient lace curtain at the window and the unbroken glass distinguished the house from the empty shells on each side of it. Miss Waterlow felt a new surge of anger against Mr Harper. While a poor, defenceless old woman was living miserably in this cheerless slum, he was swilling whiskey in some bar or other. (She had never accepted his invitation to a drink, so she didn't know about the pink gins.)

Miss Waterlow knocked on the door with her knuckles. It hurt her knuckles and made no sound, which annoyed her still more. If *she* were housing manager, she'd have knockers put on all the doors. She hesitated, glanced round, and then, feeling like a criminal, she picked up a stone from the bare little garden and banged on the door with it. Experience taught her to watch the lace curtain and she did so, but it remained motionless.

She stepped up to the window. The lace curtain was heavily darned, but it was thick enough to prevent her from seeing more than dim outlines in the room. She knew that it would be the usual uneconomically designed house with a tiny, dark hall leading up the staircase and a kitchen/living room with a door opening into a scullery. Miss Waterlow, peering through the thick yellow-white cloud of lace, fancied that she would have been able to see a fire if it had been alight. Perhaps the old lady wasn't up yet. Old people, she thought, sometimes got up very late.

She stepped back to the door and banged again with her stone. The little house was like a fortress. The houses on each side prevented access to the back door, and there wasn't even a letter box to call through.

There were no neighbours to ask, either. Ann Waterlow, glancing around, felt a sick chill in her heart at the awful loneliness and stillness. *Miss* Pollock – she was a spinster, then. She was old and alone and friendless. In a sudden panic, Miss Waterlow banged on the door again, rattled the door handle and even called out to the closed bedroom window.

'Miss Pollock! Are you there? Miss Pollock!'

But there was no reply. The house was as still as death.

Miss Waterlow saw the grocery shop on the corner and with a feeling of relief walked quickly back towards it. Just as she reached it, she saw a policeman on the other side of the road. She hesitated, wondering if it would be a good idea to speak to him first. She probably would have done so if he had glanced at her. But he was walking heavily along, looking at the ground and frowning.

It had been a bad morning for Arthur Whitehead. His mother-in-law had told his wife that she was a fool to cook him bacon and eggs for breakfast, and that cereal and bread and butter was quite enough for anyone. Arthur had told her to mind her own damn business, and his wife had burst into tears and run out of the room. She came back and finished cooking his breakfast and he forced it down somehow, but he felt

121

sick now at the thought of it. He'd always enjoyed breakfast, with the kitchen warm and noisy from the radio, and Joyce calling the kids down while he read the paper and relished the smell of cooking bacon. Now, he thought, he'd never eat it with pleasure again. That filthy-tempered old woman had poisoned it for him – along with everything else.

PC Whitehead didn't see Miss Waterlow as she hesitated, her hand on Bickstead's door. He saw his wife choking down her tears as she cooked his bacon, and saw the children frowning and embarrassed, and saw that homeless old woman who repaid his hospitality by destroying his home.

It had been a bad morning for Mrs Bickstead, too. She'd always prided herself on her courage. 'It takes a lot to frighten me!' she used to say when the flying bombs fell, or when a young thug with a gun tried to hold her up in the shop. But there was one thing she was afraid of, really afraid. She didn't want Donald to be like his father. Except for the roving eye, she knew what her husband was when she married him. He was weak and he'd do what suited him for the moment, no matter who suffered for it, and she knew that he had lost his last job for pilfering. She didn't mind that. She knew it when she married him, and if he hadn't made a fool of her by seeing that other woman, he could have done what he liked. But Donald was different. He was hers. Every time he did something that showed him to be like his father, her whole life shook under her feet.

She'd been saving some money to spend on Christmas presents – not much, just the odd sixpence or threepenny bit in a big jar. It was just a fancy of hers to have some loose cash that she could really splash about on clothes for Donald and perhaps a new raincoat for herself. But she knew exactly the level of the jar, and after breakfast that day she noticed that it had dropped by about an inch. It had to be Donald. She knew that. No one else came into their back room. There was only the two of them. That's what her husband used to say to her. 'Come on, love. There's only the two of us. Don't let's quarrel.'

It was when she found that it wasn't just the two of them, that he was seeing that other woman, that she took Donald and walked out. Since then, it had been her and Donald, just the two of them. But if Donald ... If he could steal from her, then that meant ... What if it wasn't just the two of them, but just her, her alone? She wouldn't think of it, she thought.

But when Miss Waterlow came in, she was putting the new goods on the shelves and thinking of nothing else. She turned towards the woman, her automatic smile less bright than usual.

'Yes?' she said.

'Excuse me,' said Miss Waterlow.

Oh, damn, thought Mrs Bickstead. Not even a customer. Just wants to ask the way or something.

'I'm from the Welfare Department.'

Oh, my Gawd! thought Mrs Bickstead. *He's been stealing from someone else, too!*

'I'm trying to get in touch with a Miss Pollock.'

Relief made Mrs Bickstead brusque, relief and an illogical feeling that she still needed to defend Donald from attack.

'She lives down the road. Hampton Row.'

'Yes, I know.'

Well, if you know, why do you want to ask me, you silly bitch? The words were unspoken, but some echo of them escaped to Miss Waterlow. She felt that she wanted to cut short the conversation and leave as soon as possible.

'But I couldn't get any reply at her house. Does she ever come in here?'

'Oh yes,' said Mrs Bickstead, 'she usually comes in on Saturday mornings.'

'Do you happen to remember if she came in last Saturday?'

'Let's see,' said Mrs Bickstead.

She thought back, and remembered the crowded shop, and Miss Pollock's hesitant entry, and Donald moving forward. Donald. What did he want the money for? Was it for

124

clothes? Or records? He knew he could have anything he wanted. He only had to ask.

'Yes, she came in as usual. My son served her. They don't buy much, these old ladies.'

'I don't expect they can afford to,' said Miss Waterlow, sharply.

She had meant to explain the circumstances and ask for Mrs Bickstead's help, but what was the point? She was obviously a disagreeable and heartless woman.

Mrs Bickstead was going to add that Miss Pollock usually walked along on Tuesday mornings to the newsagent's to buy the weekly paper, and was going to offer to speak to her, but at Miss Waterlow's tone she changed her mind. Welfare, indeed! She probably only wanted to harry the poor old thing. If she was so clever, let her find her!

'Well, thank you very much,' said Miss Waterlow. 'If you should see her, perhaps you'd say that I want to get in touch with her.'

Mrs Bickstead nodded, her face expressionless, and Miss Waterlow turned and went out.

When she returned to her office, a stern conscience drove her to telephone Mr Harper to report her ill success, but to her relief he was out – swilling whiskey, of course! – and so she spoke to Mr Simmonds.

'I called on Miss Pollock this morning,' she said.

There was a pause before he repeated feebly, 'Miss Pollock?'

Ann's voice sharpened. What a hopeless little man he was!

'The tenant in Hampton Row.'

'Oh yes.'

'She was out.'

'But she never goes out!' cried Mr Simmonds.

Alone in her office, Ann still made a pantomime of throwing her eyes up and heaving a sigh. However much one might dislike Mr Harper, at least he had some go and intelligence. This Simmonds man was just a chair-polisher, sending out forms all week and growing roses in his beastly garden on Sundays.

'Presumably,' said Ann, very slowly and distinctly, 'she goes out shopping occasionally.'

'Oh ... yes,' replied Mr Simmonds, 'but not often. She ... I went to see her,' he added, inconsequentially.

'You did?' said Ann, surprised.

'Tried to explain it to her.'

Oh well, thought Ann, no wonder! He'd probably frightened the poor old thing out of her wits with his bureaucratic jargon. If it had been Mr Harper, at least he ... Mr Simmonds was mumbling on, but she cut him short, looking at her diary.

'I have committee meetings all this morning, and I have to go out to Barrowfield Estate this afternoon...'

'Oh,' said Mr Simmonds. 'Would you like me to—'

'Please tell Mr Harper that I will go and see her again tomorrow.'

She put the telephone down. Dreary, unfeeling little man! What did he care?

Twenty-Five

When Miss Pollock awoke that morning, the sun was shining quite brilliantly. She lay with a strange feeling of peace and contentment, listening to the sea and looking at the semicircular piece of blue sky outside their little cave. She knew it must be early because it was so cold. In fact, she had been woken by the cold as much as by the brightness. But when she put her coat on and tucked down again under the dressing gown and the crocheted throw, she felt quite cosy. And somewhere in the peace and contentment was an odd feeling of excitement, too. She'd never felt anything quite like it before, but she knew that it had something to do with Mr Charrington, and that, just waiting for him to wake up and speak to her, she was

127

happier than she had ever been in her whole life.

She must have dozed off again after all, for the next thing she knew, Mr Charrington was coming backwards down the ladder. She lay and watched him until he reached the shingle and turned to look at her.

'There!' he said. 'Did I go and wake you up, then?'

'No, I was awake,' she said. 'What time is it?'

He fetched a big silver watch out of his pocket.

'Eight o'clock.'

'Never!' cried Miss Pollock, scandalised.

'Oh well,' said Mr Charrington, easily, 'it don't matter. We're on holiday.'

'I've never slept so late in my whole life!' cried Miss Pollock.

But even that was part of the fun of it.

'You stay there and enjoy it,' said Mr Charrington. 'I'll go up and have a wash.'

Miss Pollock *did* stay there. It wasn't only that she felt tired after the worry and exhaustion of the past few days. Somehow, lying there in the little nest which he had made for her was a way of pleasing Mr Charrington, of ... She couldn't express it in her mind, but somewhere, far hidden and unacknowledged, was the thought that it was a *feminine* thing to do. And when some time later she heard Mr Charrington's crunching footsteps returning, he came with a cup and saucer precariously balanced in his hand.

'There you are,' he said. 'Cuppa tea in bed.'

Miss Pollock sat up on her elbow and drank it and felt like a queen. It was the best cup of tea she had ever had, even if it was slopped in the saucer and a bit cold. When she had got up and made her 'bed', she went along to the public lavatory and walked in as bold as brass. She even bought a towel from the machine and had a wash. It wasn't a bad towel for threepence, even if it did have something stamped on the corner to show where it had come from. (Miss Pollock didn't notice the bin marked 'Used Towels', and certainly wouldn't have put the towel in there if she had. It was *her* towel, after all. She'd bought it fair and square and she wasn't going to throw it away.)

'Well, what are we going to do today?' said Mr Charrington, when they were sitting in the restaurant having their breakfast.

'You said we ought to buy some candles,' suggested Miss Pollock.

'Well, I never!' he exclaimed, looking at her admiringly. 'So I did. You don't forget, do you?'

Miss Pollock looked severe, just to show that flattery had no effect on her, although of course it did. It delighted her.

'Candles,' said Mr Charrington. 'Better go

to Woolworth's.'

Going to Woolworth's had always been a treat to Miss Pollock. She and her mother used to go there to buy their Christmas cards and Easter eggs and sometimes, if they were in town on a Saturday morning, they would join the jostling crowd who struggled round the long counters, just for the pleasure of staring at the artificial pearls, the toys and ties and drawing pins. 'Whatever will they have next?' Miss Pollock's mother would exclaim.

It was something of a disappointment to Miss Pollock to discover that the goods were no longer all threepence or sixpence as they used to be, but Mr Charrington said that had changed a long time ago. They bought four candles, and this time Miss Pollock insisted on paying half.

'Here!' said Mr Charrington, suddenly. 'How about buying a spirit stove?'

'A what?'

'Wouldn't you like to be able to make a cup of tea when you fancied it?'

'What, in our little house?' said Miss Pollock, charmed. 'Then we could have our dinner there, too. I got some ham and a bit of bread and some milk.'

'You got some sugar, too,' said Mr Charrington, teasingly.

Miss Pollock eyed him quellingly.

'And some tea,' she said.

'Come on, then,' said Mr Charrington. 'We'll get a stove and a little kettle and some cups and a teapot, and then we're all set up.'

They shared the cost between them. Miss Pollock was alarmed at the price of it all, but Mr Charrington was consoling.

'Cheaper in the long run,' he said. 'That chap charges fi'pence for a cup of tea.'

'He never!' cried Miss Pollock, aghast.

They realised they also needed to buy a spoon.

'There!' said Miss Pollock. 'I coulda brought a spoon from home. I *was* a silly-billy.'

Mr Charrington didn't answer, and when she looked up at him he was smiling down at her with a look in his face which made her suddenly turn away, and she could feel her breath coming quickly and her heart beating, as though, as though ... She didn't know why.

Miss Pollock made her way out into the street. She was rather surprised to find that Mr Charrington wasn't with her, but he had insisted on carrying all the parcels, so she supposed it had taken him longer to get out. He joined her at last, clutching brown paper parcels and smiling with a pleased look.

'Ten o'clock,' he said. 'Now we'll buy a bottle of meth and take these things back, and then we're on the loose.'

'On the loose?' said Miss Pollock.

'On the loose!' said Mr Charrington, and he winked at her.

Miss Pollock clicked her teeth.

'Well, I don't know!' she said.

It was a glorious day. The sea was blue and sparkling. As they came up the slope from their little house, they could feel the wind in their faces, fresh but mild.

'Here!' said Mr Charrington, suddenly. 'Let's go to the fun fair!'

'The what?' said Miss Pollock.

Mr Charrington tucked her gloved hand under his elbow.

'Come on,' he said.

It wasn't Miss Pollock's idea of a fun fair. There weren't any roundabouts or hoopla stalls. Instead it seemed to be a row of funny-looking shops along the seafront, with lights inside the doors, and music coming out of them.

'Let's try this one,' said Mr Charrington. There was a great big board over it which said 'Lots o' Fun' and had coloured lights round it. A man in a white coat with a leather bag over his shoulder stood at the entrance.

'You never gave him nothing,' said Miss Pollock, as they walked inside.

'Oh, you don't have to pay to go in,' replied Mr Charrington, carelessly. 'He's just there to give you change.'

The long room was full of brightly colour-ed machines, and there was some noisy music coming from somewhere. A few young men in leather jackets were standing around looking at the machines.

'What do we do?' asked Miss Pollock, nervously.

'I'll show you,' said Mr Charrington.

There was a machine standing against the wall with a picture of a heap of gold coins and the words 'Strike It Rich' on it. Mr Charrington put a penny in and a little silver ball popped out. He flicked a silver handle at the side, and the ball shot up and whizzed about and disappeared again.

'Missed it!' said Mr Charrington. 'You got to get it in that hole marked "Pay-off".'

'Pay-off,' repeated Miss Pollock, blankly.

She fumbled for a penny and got one out.

'I'll put it in for you,' said Mr Charrington. 'Go on, then. Buzz the ball round and try and get it in that hole there.'

Miss Pollock banged the handle. Her gloved fingers slipped. The silver ball shot wildly up, jolted about a few times and then disappeared. A shower of coins fell down into the scoop.

'You got it!' shouted Mr Charrington. 'The pay-off! You got it!'

'I never!' cried Miss Pollock, and she laughed so much that she had to lean against the next machine.

'One, two, three, four, five,' said Mr Charrington, counting the pennies. 'There you are. Your own penny back, and four more. You going to have another go, then?'

'Not me!' said Miss Pollock. 'I might lose it this time.'

And then Mr Charrington laughed, too.

'Want a game of football?' he said.

'What, in here?' said Miss Pollock, but she was ready for anything now.

There was a sort of glass box in the middle of the room, with little men in football jerseys. Mr Charrington showed her how to wiggle a little handle to and fro, so that the footballers kicked with one foot.

'Well, I never!' said Miss Pollock. 'Whatever will they think of next?'

Mr Charrington put some money in, and a ball popped up out of the green board.

'There you are,' he said. 'That's your team, the ones in the yeller jerseys. You go up that end, and try to stop the ball going through your goal.'

'My what?'

'Them white posts there. Now, watch it!'

He made his little men kick their legs and the ball shot towards Miss Pollock's end.

'Ooh, no!' she squeaked. 'No!'

She seized her handle. The ball escaped the first man, and the second, but the third kicked it squarely back towards Mr Charrington.

'Well played!' he cried. 'Whoops! Nearly got me. Go on, you lot! Kick it! Kick it!'

It was a grand game. Miss Pollock had never really played a game with anyone before, except for snap and ludo and beggar-my-neighbour with her mother and father. Mr Charrington roared and shouted and laughed, but Miss Pollock, after her first squeak, didn't make a sound. She was too excited.

In the end, Mr Charrington kicked the ball through Miss Pollock's goal, and she was rather pleased. It was all right for her to win the pay-off, but when it came to football, she felt that the gentleman *ought* to win the game rather than the lady.

'What's that?' she asked, as they turned away and she saw another big glass case.

There was a big silver claw-like thing, and a lot of things that looked like coloured beads, with packets of cigarettes and a fountain pen sitting amongst them. Miss Pollock spelt out the letters above the case.

' "Treasure Chest",' she said.

'That's right,' said Mr Charrington. 'You put tuppence in and work that crane thing. Here, I'll show you.'

He put the money in and twiddled the knob.

'I'll try for them cigarettes,' he said.

But all he got was a lot of coloured beads.

'Do you want a go?' he said. 'I'll put the tuppence in.'

'No, I will!' cried Miss Pollock, made reckless by her success in Strike It Rich.

It had suddenly occurred to her that if she could get hold of the fountain pen, she could give it to Mr Charrington as a present. She took her glove off, so that the knob shouldn't slip in her hand, and Mr Charrington put the tuppence in for her, while she tried with all her might to turn the crane towards the fountain pen. It moved forward and down. The claws closed over the fountain pen. The crane began to rise and move back. But at the last minute, the fountain pen slipped between the claws and fell back. Tears rushed into Miss Pollock's eyes.

'Oh, it fell out!' she cried.

'Never mind,' said Mr Charrington, consolingly. 'You got the sweets.'

'Is them sweets?'

'Try one,' he said, and popped one of his own into her mouth.

'I thought they was beads,' she said, and they both laughed again, and walked out of Lots o' Fun, happily eating their liquorice sweets.

'Want a go of bingo?' enquired Mr Charrington.

'Bingo? What's that?'

'Ain't you never played bingo?' said Mr Charrington. 'Housey-housey, they used to call it in the old days. Come on. Here's a bingo place. Let's have a go.'

There was a big circular table, with a man

sitting on a stool in the middle. Some other people were sitting on stools round the outside.

'Come along, come along,' called the man in a loud, booming voice. 'Wonderful prizes. Something for nothing, ladies, something for nothing. I know that's what you like. Something for nothing!'

Miss Pollock hung back. 'Something for nothing' was not what she liked at all. 'Something for nothing' was almost like ... well, stealing. Mr Charrington looked down at her, feeling the slight drag on his arm.

'Come along, sir,' called the man. 'Come along, madam. Still a few places left!'

There were quite a lot of places left, as a matter of fact, and Mr Charrington helped Miss Pollock up on to a stool and climbed up beside her.

'How many cards?' asked the man.

'Two,' replied Mr Charrington. 'One each.'

'Here, you're going it a bit!' said the man, and the other people there laughed. 'Two bob.'

Miss Pollock was so horrified that she didn't even offer to pay her share. Tuppence was bad enough, but a shilling each! For the first time, she began to wonder if she had not been rather rash to hitch her fortunes to Mr Charrington's. He did seem to throw his money about rather, and he *had* said that when his money was all gone, he would 'touch her for it'. A mulish look crept on to her face, and when Mr Charrington put the card in front of her, she just frowned at it.

'Here you are,' said Mr Charrington. 'When the chap starts calling out the numbers, you keep your eye on your card, and if he shouts one you've got, you shove one of them bits of cardboard over it. If your card's the first one to be full, then you've won.'

Miss Pollock still frowned. She remembered that her father used to say gambling was a bad thing and only led to trouble. Was this gambling? And, anyway, a shilling! Two shillings! They'd never get that back!

Mr Charrington seemed to have no idea how she felt. He sat on his stool and looked cheerfully around him, whistling between his teeth in time to the music. Then the man in the middle got down and stooped under the table and went to the open space leading on to the street. Mr Charrington jerked his head towards him.

' 'E won't start till 'e's got a few more in,' he said. 'Fine day like this, he might get a few bus trips.'

'Come along, come along!' the man was shouting. 'Come along, ladies! Game of bingo just about to start. Come on, ladies! Great, big, wonderful prizes! In you come! In you come!'

'There you are,' said Mr Charrington. 'What did I tell you?'

A whole crowd of women came jostling in and sat up at the table. The man went back into the middle, talking and laughing with them, and some of them bought as many as five cards. Miss Pollock felt quite alarmed, and shrank against Mr Charrington's arm. Then the man was calling out numbers one after another in a loud voice. Miss Pollock stared desperately at her card, rigid with nervousness and the strain of concentration. It didn't help that the man called the numbers in such a funny way. 'Legs eleven. Doctor's orders – number nine.' Whatever did he mean?

'Unlucky thirteen, that's one of yours,' said Mr Charrington, and Miss Pollock fumbled a cardboard disc on to her card with awkward woollen fingers. She wished Mr Charrington had never thought of bingo. Two shillings!

But after a while she found that the numbers on her card came up so slowly that she had plenty of time to cover them when they did come. She was even able to glance at Mr Charrington's card now and then, and once she spotted a number on his card before he did.

'All the twos – twenty-two,' said the man.

'Bingo!' roared Mr Charrington. 'Bingo! Twenty-two! That's your last one. You got it! Bingo!'

'What happened?' said Miss Pollock, dazed

by the suddenness of it all, just when she was enjoying the peaceful game.

'You won,' said Mr Charrington. 'What prize you going to have?'

All the women from the coach trip were chattering and exclaiming. The man checked Miss Pollock's card and then waved his hand towards the things piled up on shelves at the back of the room.

'Fruit bowl?' he suggested. 'Nice rubbish bin? Set of glasses?'

'Here,' said Mr Charrington. 'How about that thermos flask? That'd come in handy.'

Miss Pollock nodded. She couldn't speak, and scowled at the man ferociously. He didn't look too pleased, and went with a touch of reluctance to fetch the shiny red and chromium flask.

'There you are, then,' he said, sourly. 'Worth a fiver, that is. Now then, ladies! Who's having another go?'

'How about you?' enquired Mr Charrington, but Miss Pollock had already got down from her stool and was halfway to the street, clutching the thermos flask in slippery woollen fingers.

'Not me!' she said, as Mr Charrington caught up with her. 'He might take it away again!'

Mr Charrington laughed until he coughed and wheezed and had to lean against the wall.

'You're a one!' he gasped. 'You really are a one!'

And Miss Pollock looked up at him, clutching the thermos, and smiling her slow, reluctant, unaccustomed smile.

As they walked away down the street, Mr Charrington took her arm, holding her hand and pressing his elbow against hers. It was very strange to her to be so close to someone. It had never happened to her before. Even when she had walked along between her parents, they had only held her small, gloved hands in theirs at arm's length. To feel the bone of Mr Charrington's elbow digging into her side and to find her hand cramped in his gave her an odd, breathless feeling. Suddenly he stopped short.

'Wanta go to the pitchers?' he said.

Miss Pollock felt dazed again. He pointed to a brightly coloured poster.

'They say that ain't bad. It's a musical. Shall we go and see that this afternoon?'

'How much does it cost?' asked Miss Pollock, suspiciously.

'Not much. You got your pension book?'

Miss Pollock was aghast. He was going to take all her money out and spend it on going to the pictures! She drew her hand away from his, clutching her handbag and the thermos, and glared at him. He grinned at her.

'You got your pension book,' he said, 'you

can get in for ninepence.'

'In the *pictures*?'

'Tha's right.'

He took her arm again.

'Eh!' he said. 'Let's 'ave some fish'n chips first.'

She pulled away from him a little, still suffering from the remnants of her recent suspicion, but when he nudged her and she glanced up at him and met his twinkling brown eyes, she couldn't help smiling back at him. She allowed him to take her hand again, and, before she knew what she was doing, she actually pressed his elbow with hers.

'We shan't be able to afford this every day,' said Mr Charrington, as they went to sit down with their fish and chips and bread and butter and cups of tea.

Miss Pollock had never eaten in a fish and chip shop before. Her mother said they were vulgar places, and that it was all right to buy fish and chips and carry them home, but not to eat there. Still, it wasn't too bad. The table was clean, and had a nice bottle of vinegar on it, and a cruet and a bottle of tomato sauce as well. And it was good to eat the fish and chips while it was hot, as it never was when you had to carry it home. (Of course, her mother would never have thought of sitting on the seafront and eating it out of a bit of newspaper with their fingers.)

'It's a good batter that makes the difference,' said Miss Pollock, after the first few mouthfuls.

It was what her mother used to say, but she saw no reason to mention that, especially when Mr Charrington looked at her admiringly and said, 'You're right! Quite right!'

'I suppose we shouldn't be long,' said Miss Pollock.

'Plenty of time,' said Mr Charrington. 'You enjoy your meal.'

She did, too, and the banana fritter which he insisted on getting for afters, although she still felt a bit uneasy about the cost of it all – and supposing he was wrong about the cost of the tickets for the pictures!

Mr Charrington was quite right, however, although Miss Pollock could hardly believe it when she saw the picture house. It was a great big place, like a palace, not a bit like the old Ritz where she and her mother used to go before the War. In fact, it looked so grand that she would never have dared to go in there, but Mr Charrington walked in as bold as brass, right across the carpet to the golden cage in the middle of the floor and asked the smart lady inside for two pensioner's tickets. They had to show their books, but once they did that they only had to pay ninepence, and the lady inside with the torch said they could sit anywhere they liked.

When they came out into the street more than three hours later, Miss Pollock couldn't speak.

'Did you like it?' asked Mr Charrington. 'It wasn't bad, was it? Did you like it?'

She could only smile at him and shake her head wonderingly, and he took the thermos from her so that she could walk along clinging to his arm with both hands. The music and singing, the beautiful story and the scenery had all left her stunned and breathless. And it was all in colour. She had had no idea that they made pictures in colour now.

'Cor, there's a nip in the air, ain't there?' said Mr Charrington. 'You all right?'

Miss Pollock was shivering as she walked along. She met his kind, anxious brown eyes and made a tremendous effort, holding his arm tighter than ever.

'I never seen nothing like it!' she said.

Mr Charrington beamed delightedly.

'It warn't bad, was it?' he said. 'I like a good pitcher meself. Come on, let's get home and have a nice tea.'

It was Mr Charrington who filled the kettle from the tap up on the promenade and got the stove going. Miss Pollock was still in a sort of dream. She cut and buttered some bread and cut some rather ragged pieces of ham off, and then sat and watched Mr Charrington while he made the tea and poured it out.

'Here!' he said. 'Let's have a bit o' light on the scene!'

He lit two candles and stuck them in the sand, wedged in with stones.

'How's that?' he said. 'A candlelit supper, eh?'

He reached across and patted her hand, and then helped himself to sugar out of her little paper bag.

'I could peck a bit now,' he said. 'What you got there? Ham, eh?'

He picked up a slice of bread and butter and ham, folding it over with his freckled hand and stubby fingers.

'That knife ain't very sharp,' said Miss Pollock, 'for cutting it up.'

Mr Charrington took a big bite and spoke with his mouth full.

'Tastes all right,' he said.

Miss Pollock held her own piece of bread and butter and ham and watched him. He was eating the food she'd got ready for him, and he was drinking the tea and milk and sugar she'd brought out with her. She was glad he'd spoken with his mouth full, and she liked to hear him slurp his tea. She didn't know why, but somehow the candlelit cave and the picture they had just seen and Mr Charrington eating and drinking and wiping his moustache with his handkerchief was all part of the same thing. Was it that it seemed to make him belong to her, as her father had seemed to belong to her mother?

'Aren't you going to 'ave some, then?' asked Mr Charrington.

Miss Pollock took a bite. The bread was dry and the ham was dry and the butter was a bit 'off' from being wrapped up in the shopping bag. She looked up and found Mr Charrington watching her.

'Fancy you bringing all that away with you!' he said. 'You're a wonder, that's what you are.'

'Get along with you!' said Miss Pollock, in just the tone her mother would have used, and she took another bite and thought the butter wasn't really off after all. 'Would you like a bit of boiled pertater?' she said. 'It looks a bit dry. I'll spread some butter on it for you.'

When Mr Charrington took it from her, he hummed the tune from the film they'd just seen, and kept his eyes on hers as he put the potato in his mouth, and she felt herself blushing.

'We won't fill the thermos tonight,' said Mr Charrington. 'We'll need some more milk tomorrow, so I may's well get our morning tea from the caff.'

'How will we do the washing-up?' enquired Miss Pollock.

'I'll fill the kettle again an' put it on the stove.'

'I'll do that,' said Miss Pollock hastily, getting up. 'It's my turn.'

'Wait a minute,' said Mr Charrington.

He got to his feet. The effort made him short of breath, and he wheezed for a moment, feeling in his inside pocket.

'I got something for you.'

He brought out a little package and held it out to her.

'What is it?' asked Miss Pollock.

'Have a look.'

She opened the package and found something gold with brightly coloured jewels in the middle. She said dazedly, 'It's a brooch.'

'That's right,' said Mr Charrington. 'I got it in Woolworth's. Didn't you think I was a long while coming out?'

Miss Pollock still looked from him to the brooch, frowning a little, unable to realise that he had actually bought it for *her*.

'I noticed you liked the jewellery,' said Mr Charrington, smiling, 'and I seen how disappointed you was when you never got that pen with the crane.'

'But I wanted it for you!' cried Miss Pollock. 'I was going to give it to *you*.'

He took hold of her hand, with the brooch in it. Tears came into her eyes, and she saw tears in his eyes, too. He bent forward and kissed her. She felt his moustache soft and bristly on her cheek, and she knew that she loved him.

A sharp gust of wind blew in from the sea, and the flame in their little stove flared up and then went out. Miss Pollock shivered.

'Wassermatter?' said Mr Charrington, smiling. 'Ghost walked over your grave?' He put his arm round her. 'Want me to pin that on?'

He took the brooch and began to pin it on her coat. The wind blew again but more steadily, and this time it was Mr Charrington who gave a little shiver and then coughed and wheezed.

'Cor, we'll have to wrap up warm tonight,' he said. 'The weather's on the turn.'

It crossed Miss Pollock's mind that winter was coming on, and she wondered how they would manage if it got really cold. For a second the chill in the wind was matched by a chill in her heart. Then he finished pinning the brooch on, and she put her hand to it, and he put his hand on hers and they smiled at each other.

Twenty-Six

That Ann Waterlow approached Hampton Row on Wednesday morning even before John Weatherfield was a sign of her uneasiness. Something about the narrow little house standing desolately amidst the ruins of its neighbours had touched her heart and conscience, and fear of a desolate old age for herself made her superstitiously afraid of neglecting this one old lady whose doom seemed to foreshadow her own.

'My goodness, you're an early bird this morning!' her mother had said, wandering about the kitchen in her Marks & Spencer's quilted nylon gown. 'I haven't got your breakfast ready yet.'

'I only want coffee,' said Ann. 'I've got a call to make.'

'You work too hard,' said her mother. 'You want to get out more. Oh, by the way, don't be late home. There's a lovely old film on television – Ronald Colman. I love Ronald Colman, don't you?'

Oh, God! thought Ann, as she pulled the front door shut behind her. *Now she wants me to marry Ronald Colman!*

She was shaken by a wave of hatred for her mother, but she fought it off. She didn't hate her mother. She loved her. She was good to her, and patient. She loved all old people, especially lonely old people. She took care of them, and she would take care of Miss Pollock.

Miss Waterlow walked up the path and saw the half-pint bottle of milk still outside the front door. She paused, and frowned. But perhaps it was a new half-pint, left by the milkman that morning. Yes, that was it. She felt an illogical sense of relief, and at that moment she heard a rattle and hum in the otherwise silent street behind her. She turned and saw the milkman's cart approaching.

So it was the foreman from the garage. John Weatherfield had known it as soon as he saw them together in the pub. Now he'd got to decide what to do. She hadn't got in until midnight, and then he'd pretended to be asleep. He'd got the boy in bed with him, so she got into bed with the girl. He knew from her breathing that she was asleep almost at once. He didn't go to sleep. He lay and wondered what to do. He must do something now. But what? When he got up and dressed and made a cup of tea, with the wife and the boy and the girl still asleep, he was still wondering what to do. And when he went down the stairs and out into the cold morning air, and at the depot and driving the cart down Hampton Row, he was still wondering. What was he going to do? What was he going to do? The half-pint of milk was in his hand and he was walking up the path before he saw Miss Waterlow.

He saw the half-pint of milk on the doorstep, too, but his mind was working very slowly, still clogged with misery and shame. When Miss Waterlow said, 'Did you leave this milk yesterday?' he looked at her blankly.

'Hasn't she taken it in, then?' he said at last.

She shook her head.

'I knocked at the door yesterday,' she said, 'but I didn't get any answer.'

'Oh,' he said. He could take the children to his mother, and then ... How did you get a divorce, anyway? But a divorce would mean he'd never see her again. Was that what he wanted?

'When did you last see her?'

'The old girl?'

'Miss Pollock.'

Catching the note of reproof in her voice, John Weatherfield looked at Miss Waterlow properly for the first time, seeing the smart navy-blue suit and the close-fitting hat and the briefcase. He knew her sort – sat in an office all day telling someone like him that he and his family were lucky to have a roof over their heads and then went home to a posh house and garden.

Ann Waterlow tried again.

'Did you usually see Miss Pollock when you left her milk?'

'No, just every Saturday when she paid her bill.'

'And did you see her last Saturday?'

'Yes, that's right,' replied John Weatherfield, with a touch of irritation. 'She came to the door, paid her bill, same as usual.'

Miss Waterlow looked back at the silent little house with its motionless lace curtains, and John Weatherfield followed her gaze. Just as someone in pain is only half aware of what is going on around him, so his perceptions were still dimmed, but he seemed to see the small figure of Miss Pollock standing in the open doorway, purse in hand. And she had said ... Yes, that was it.

'She said she'd got to move.'

Ann Waterlow looked relieved.

'She told you she was moving out?'

John Weatherfield wasn't listening.

'Said that they were going to pull these houses down. I told her, about time, too! One old woman living in a place that would house a whole family!'

'You told her *that?*'

It was as though he came to himself.

'Well, no ... not ... I just said ... I can't remember exactly. She paid the bill, and—'

'She didn't say anything about not leaving any more milk?'

'No. And she put the empty bottle out, same as usual, so...'

They both looked at the half-pint of milk on the doorstep. A chill crept over Miss Waterlow's heart. An elderly woman so set in her ways – shopping at the same shop every Saturday morning, always paying her milk bill on the same day, always putting out an empty half-pint bottle – surely she wouldn't do something so out of character as leaving without cancelling the milk.

'She might have been taken ill,' said Miss Waterlow. 'Or...'

Suddenly she was avoiding his eye, and, glancing towards Bickstead's, saw the policeman entering the shop.

When Mrs Bickstead turned away from the back of the shop at the tinkle of the bell over the door and saw the policeman, she thought for a moment that her heart had stopped. It was Donald, she was sure. He'd been shoplifting, or thieved some money at school. His father's bad blood was coming out in him, just as she had always feared.

Somehow she managed to put on her bright shopkeeper's smile.

'Can I help you?'

'A packet of biscuits, please. Digestive.'

She felt relieved as she went to fetch them, but still anxious. Perhaps it was just a blind.

Out of the corner of her eye she saw him glancing round the shop. What had he really come for?

Arthur Whitehead went in to buy a packet of digestive biscuits because he hadn't had any breakfast. He'd told his wife that he was on early turn, but that was a lie. He just didn't want the bother of deciding whether or not to accept a cooked breakfast and risk more snide remarks from that damned old woman. And then, after all, would Joyce offer it to him and, if she did, would she give that sideways glance at her mother which meant she was afraid of another row? Oh God! Would there soon be a single moment of his home life which hadn't been turned into a battlefield?

He'd spotted the look of fear on the face of the woman behind the counter as she turned and saw him in the shop. He recognised it at once, and also the smile which was just a bit too bright. She'd been up to something, and he wondered what it was, but he couldn't be bothered to find out. Time was when he loved his work, and especially that bit of detection in it. Being a cop on the beat suited him fine, and it gave him a chance to spot trouble before it happened, to prevent crime, but also to give a hand when it was needed, even sometimes to save life. He wouldn't call himself a goody-goody, but that's what he really joined the Force for –

not just to uphold law and order but to help other people. But that was in the days when, much as he enjoyed his work, he always looked forward to going home, to the warmth of the welcome from his kids and from Joyce, and then sitting with her and telling her all about his day. It was as though once he'd lost that, his work had gone sour as well. If people were in trouble, so what? He was in trouble himself. He'd do his duty, but that was it.

'Is there anything else?' asked Mrs Bickstead, brightly.

The bell over the door tinkled and a voice said, 'Officer!'

Arthur Whitehead recognised that voice, and when he turned and saw Miss Waterlow it was no surprise. She was quite pretty, but she represented petty officialdom, and if you were a copper you did well to go along with petty officials because if you didn't they could give you a lot of bother – even female ones.

'My name's Miss Waterlow,' she said. 'I am in charge of Old People's Welfare.'

Oh, are you? thought Arthur Whitehead. *Perhaps you'd like to take charge of my mother-in-law!*

'I am concerned about an old lady who lives in Hampton Row, just down there,' said Miss Waterlow, pointing.

'Miss Pollock?' said Mrs Bickstead.

'Yes. I can't get any answer, and she hasn't taken in her milk.'

Arthur Whitehead looked at his watch.

'It's early yet. Old people don't get up that soon.'

They lie in bed, waiting for breakfast to be brought up, and then say, 'You've burned the toast!'

'Miss Pollock does,' said Mrs Bickstead. 'On Saturdays, she's my first customer.'

'And, anyway,' said Miss Waterlow, 'it was the milk that the milkman left yesterday. She hasn't taken it in.'

'That's not like her!' exclaimed Mrs Bickstead.

Miss Waterlow looked PC Whitehead firmly in the eye.

'I really am concerned about her,' she said.

Arthur Whitehead would have found it hard to explain the reluctance with which he approached the old lady's house. It was the sort of problem which once would have been right up his street. 'Here comes Dixon of Dock Green!' the fellows at the station used to say when he turned up with some old biddy who'd lost her purse or her dog or who couldn't remember where her daughter lived. But that was before...

'You haven't got a key?' he enquired.

'No. She's a Council tenant...'

'Well, then, they've probably got one.'

'I don't think we should wait. She may

have been taken ill, or had a fall...'

I hope not, thought Arthur, remembering the time his mother-in-law had fallen down in her bedroom and couldn't get up again. Joyce had called him in a panic, and by the time he got there the old woman hardly seemed to know where she was. He lifted her up rather awkwardly – she was heavier than she looked – and as he put her down in the armchair she seemed to come to herself. 'What are you doing?' she demanded. 'Get away from me!'

'Or even...'

Peering in at the window, he became aware of a strange note in Miss Waterlow's voice and looked back at her.

'She was very ... I understand she was upset at the thought of moving.'

'You think she might have done herself in?'

And fleeting across his mind was the unacknowledged thought, *I* should be so lucky!

Miss Waterlow looked shocked at the unfeeling bluntness of his words.

'No, no, I'm sure not! But I think we should make sure as soon as possible that she is all right.'

The milkman was still there.

'Did you want me to wait?' he asked, uneasily.

'Just till we see she's all right,' said PC Whitehead.

It wasn't difficult to break a pane of glass, slip the catch, raise the window and climb in. He could see at once that the kitchen was empty, and ... At least she hasn't gassed herself, he thought, looking at the cold grate. No gas stove. Looking round, he saw a key on a hook with an ancient label attached to it and the words 'Front Door' in faded ink. He unlocked the door and stood back to let Miss Waterlow enter.

'Doesn't look as though she's here,' he said.

'You haven't been upstairs yet?'

He shook his head and took his helmet off and put it down on the kitchen table. Seeing that she was afraid of what she might find, he led the way up the stairs. The milkman lingered in the doorway.

There was no stair carpet, only linoleum, and the stairs creaked loudly in the desolate, silent house.

'Miss Pollock!' called Ann Waterlow. 'Are you there?'

But it only took a few moments to glance into the bedroom and the tiny room behind it which might once have been a child's bedroom but now seemed to be used as a storeroom, the tiny bed piled up with old newspapers and battered cardboard boxes. He smiled at Miss Waterlow and stood aside again. She went nervously into the bedroom and he followed her.

158

'Left neat and tidy,' he said. He turned the faded cover back. 'Clean sheets, so...'

'So?'

'So she's still living here.'

'Then where is she?'

He opened the wardrobe door.

'Not many clothes here. Looks as though ... Ah.'

He had seen the rectangular indentation on the end of the bed.

'Looks as though she packed a suitcase.'

Ann Waterlow drew a breath of relief.

'Oh, so she ... But I wonder where she's gone.'

'Well, that's not our business, is it?' said Arthur Whitehead.

Now that she knew that there was no horrifying corpse to be found, no shocking memorial to her heartless negligence, Ann Waterlow was herself again.

'It may not be *your* business,' she said, 'but it certainly is *mine*. Still, as long as she's all right...'

Oh, she's all right! said Arthur Whitehead to himself, adding, Gone to dump herself on some poor bastard who's unlucky enough to be related to her – or whose wife is!

John Weatherfield was in the kitchen when they came downstairs.

'Is she there?' he called.

'No, she seems to have moved out,' replied Miss Waterlow.

159

Arthur Whitehead saw the milkman glancing round.

'Not much of a place, is it?' he said.

'Better than one room!' said the milkman, and then, suddenly, to Miss Waterlow, 'Did you say you were from the Council?'

'Well ... yes ... but only Old People's Welfare.'

'I might have known!' said John Weatherfield. 'Unmarried Mothers, Old People, bloody Blacks! I've got a wife and two children – or *did* have! Funny I never seem to be in the right category for a decent home!'

He turned on his heel and went out and slammed the half-pint of milk into a basket and started up the cart and drove off. So the old girl had moved out, but too late. If they'd knocked those slums down and built new houses, maybe he could have got hold of one. Maybe he could have saved his marriage. He had never hated anyone as much as he hated Miss Pollock at that moment.

'You'd better get the Council to fit a new pane of glass,' said Arthur Whitehead. 'Don't want someone breaking in. Not that there's much to take.' His eyes rested on the coronation mug and the *Little Sweetheart* picture.

As Arthur Whitehead moved towards the door, Ann Waterlow remained where she was, trying to make sense of it all. The clean sheets on the bed, the washing-up done, everything so neat and tidy – just what, well,

160

what any spinster would do if she was going to kill herself and wanted to do it decently. But Miss Pollock hadn't killed herself, at least not here – and she had forgotten to stop the milk. Something was wrong, but what was it?

'Are you going to keep the spare key?' enquired the policeman.

She hesitated.

'I don't think I should. She's been given notice to quit, but legally she's still the tenant of the property.'

Somehow, Arthur Whitehead didn't want the old woman to win. He glanced at the window.

'I suppose the Council will need to gain access to secure the premises?'

'Yes. Yes, that's true.'

They went outside and he locked the door and gave her the key. Even as she took it, Ann Waterlow felt a sense of betrayal to the old spinster who had so heroically defended her territory and now was ... where?

Twenty-Seven

Miss Pollock didn't sleep as well that night. The noise of the sea was so loud that she was afraid it might come into their little house, but, even through the rush and surge of the waves, she could hear Mr Charrington's breath wheezing and creaking. Now and then she would hear him snoring a few times, and she would think with relief, Oh, good, he's fallen asleep. But then, almost at once, there would be a snort and a gasp, and the laboured breathing would start again. It should have been strange to her to lie there so much aware of this man she hardly knew, but somehow it didn't seem strange. It seemed perfectly natural – and natural, too, that she should lie all night listening and worrying about him.

She didn't know when she fell asleep at last, but she was awoken by a harsh voice in her ear and started up in a fright to see Mr Charrington, a clattering cup and saucer in his hand.

'I'm a bit late this morning,' he said, smiling at her, but gasping a bit, too.

And the fact that he had struggled across

the road and back to bring her a cup of tea which was cold and most of it slopped in the saucer gave her the strangest feeling of – what was it? – an almost painful caring for him, as though she needed to protect him as a mother did her child.

'Ooh,' she said, quickly, 'a cup of tea. Just what I fancy!'

'Weather ain't up to much,' said Mr Charrington. 'I think we'd better have our breakfast at the café.'

It started to rain as they crossed the road.

'There, now!' exclaimed Miss Pollock. 'I never thought to bring the umbrella.'

'No more didn't I,' said Mr Charrington. 'We *are* a pair, aren't we?'

And as he smiled down at her, Miss Pollock smiled back, and held his arm more tightly, because, of course, they were a pair, and that was all that mattered.

Oh, no, thought Ed, not them again – Darby and Joan! What were they up to? Couldn't be staying at a bed and breakfast, unless it was one that didn't serve breakfast. In fact, for a moment, he wondered if they weren't sleeping rough. But as he came to take their order, he could see that she was clean and tidy and the old man had shaved. Besides, they weren't the type.

'I don't think I fancy very much this morning,' said Mr Charrington. 'A pot of tea and a bit of toast will do me. But you have your poached egg – or do you fancy egg and bacon?'

'No, tea and toast's enough for me,' said Miss Pollock. 'That's all I have at home.'

'How about a boiled egg? You need building up.'

'Oh ... no...'

But she did fancy a boiled egg.

Mr Charrington looked up at Ed. He had to wait a moment to get his breath, before he said authoritatively, 'Pot of tea for two, buttered toast for two and a boiled egg.'

She clicked her teeth, but smiled at him. He always seemed to know what she wanted. A gust of wind came in as the door opened.

'There's that blackie again,' whispered Miss Pollock.

'Oh yes?' Mr Charrington turned round in his seat. 'Morning,' he called.

'Good morning,' said the black man, and went to sit down in the corner.

He had a deep voice and an accent which sounded quite posh, thought Miss Pollock, surprised – although, since she had never met a black man, she didn't know quite what she expected.

Twenty-Eight

Norman Taylor noticed the little old lady stealing cautious glances at him while the man went to fetch their order. He didn't mind, but he felt surprised. It was as though she had never seen a black man before. People used to look at him with that kind of astonished curiosity during the first years after he landed, but that was nearly ten years ago. When people stared at him now, they weren't thinking, Cor, there's a black man! but rather, You're black! You've no business to be here! Go back where you belong!

But where did he belong? Sitting with his bare feet in the dust in front of his Granny's one-room shack? Or in London, where he'd tramped looking for somewhere to live, and had to stand in front of notices which read 'No dogs, no Irish, no Blacks'?

The old gentleman had a coughing fit, and Norman's eyes rested on him for a moment. Nice old fellow. He reminded Norman of his father.

'Get your education, boy,' he'd said. 'Get an education, it'll carry you all over the world.'

165

That was just before he left them. They never knew where he went. But Norman took his advice, stayed on at school and worked hard, and his teacher said he had high hopes for him. And this was it, thought Norman. This was the end of the high hopes – working on the railway and living in one room in a seaside town, trying to save enough money to bring his family over, and not sure if they'd do better to stay in the sunshine, sitting with their bare feet in the dust, rather than standing looking at a notice which read 'No dogs, no Irish, no Blacks'.

The café owner took the breakfast to the old couple by the window and paused on his way back.

'Same as usual?' he said.

Norman nodded. He was accustomed now to the fact that people here didn't talk as they did back home, where they all knew each other and never missed a chance to exchange family news and local gossip. He'd been eating breakfast here ever since he came to Brightlesea, and yet he didn't even know the café owner's name.

This was his only hot meal of the day. His landlady had told him that she didn't do any meals. There was an old electric kettle, and...

'I've no objection to you making yourself a cup of tea,' she said, 'but no cooking in the room.'

'No, Madam,' he had replied.

He knew he was lucky to find someone who would rent him a room, even if it did cost him two pounds a week. Coming downstairs the next day, treading softly so as not to disturb his new landlady, he had heard a voice coming from the sitting room.

'I don't know how you can have a black man in your house!'

'Oh, he's quite pleasant,' his landlady had replied. 'You'd never know he was black if you didn't know it.'

Time was that Norman would have laughed at that, but he wasn't laughing now when he thought of it. A gust of wind threw a heavy splatter of rain against the window. Winter was coming, with cold and rain – maybe even snow like last year. He felt such a longing for warmth and sun that he could hardly bear it.

Miss Pollock had just tapped the top of her egg when she was startled by the sudden gust of wind and rain against the window.

'Ooh, that made me jump!' she exclaimed.

She smiled at Mr Charrington and returned to the engrossing task of picking off small pieces of eggshell when she became aware that he was watching her. His smile made her blush.

'You know what I do?' he said. 'I just tap the side and take the top off.'

'That's what my father used to do,' said Miss Pollock, 'but half the time the yolk ran

167

down the side. My mother used to say, "You're wasting half that egg!" '

'Ah,' said Mr Charrington, 'but you want to cook it a bit more firm, then it's all right.'

'I like mine runny,' said Miss Pollock.

She felt very daring as she said it, as though she was, well, setting herself up against him, but it wasn't really that so much as that, well, that he was a gentleman and she was a lady, and tapping the eggshell was more, well, ladylike. But Mr Charrington didn't give in. Well, he wouldn't, would he, being a gentleman?

'You can still do it, even if it's runny,' said Mr Charrington. 'I'll show you one day.'

And because the words 'one day' seemed to say that they would be together for quite some time, she felt brave enough to say, 'What are we going to do today?'

'Well,' replied Mr Charrington, cheerfully, as the rain streamed down the window, 'I don't reckon we'll be going for a five-mile run along the Front, do you?'

It was as though he didn't realise that behind her words was the unspoken question, What are we going to do if it goes on raining, and gets colder and colder? How are we going to manage? And somewhere in the back of her mind was the thought that perhaps he *did* know what she meant but that he didn't know what they were going to do and didn't want to think about it. She took a spoonful of white from the top of her egg, and then found she had a tiny piece of shell in her mouth and had to fish it out.

'There you are!' cried Mr Charrington, triumphantly. 'You got a bit of eggshell. You should've done it my way!'

She couldn't help smiling, and he laughed and coughed and laughed again. But they still hadn't decided what they were going to do.

Twenty-Nine

'Ah, Hampton Row,' said Mr Harper. 'I think Miss Waterlow may have some news about that?'

He directed that smile at her across the table which he thought held a hint of an intimate understanding between them, and which she thought was a disgusting leer. The Housing Committee was preparing for the report which would be given to the Council the following week and Mr Harper was in the chair. He always felt that he was at his best on these occasions, bluff, efficient and in command.

You can't help admiring him, thought Mr Simmonds.

Pompous ass, thought Miss Waterlow.

She usually tried to put him down, but today she felt a slight uneasiness. She shuffled her papers to avoid meeting his eye.

'Er ... yes. I visited Miss Pollock again, or rather, endeavoured to...'

'Pollock!' repeated Mr Harper, with jovial enthusiasm. 'That's right! That's our obstinate old lady, isn't it? I hope you talked some sense into her.'

'I hoped to speak to her,' said Ann Waterlow, coldly, 'but she wasn't there.'

'Not there?' exclaimed Mr Simmonds. 'But she never goes out. That is, only to buy her groceries, or—'

'Yes, thank you, Bill,' said Mr Harper, crushingly. 'If you wouldn't mind addressing your remarks through the chair. Perhaps we should allow Miss Waterlow to continue.'

'Oh ... yes ... sorry. Sorry, Miss Waterlow.'

He really was a silly little man, thought Ann. Although, of course, he was right.

'She seems to have gone away,' she said.

'Excellent!' cried Mr Harper. 'If the tenant has left the premises we can proceed with demolition. Well done!'

'No, I'm afraid we can't. Not yet. Her possessions are still in the house.'

'Well, tenants do tend to leave a few things behind, but—'

'Even her clothes are there.'

Mr Harper looked puzzled.

'Where?'

'In her wardrobe.'

'I thought you said she wasn't there.'

Ann Waterlow could avoid it no longer.

'No, I ... I had to gain entry.'

'Gain entry?'

This time, Mr Harper's tone was more appropriate to that he would use to a recalcitrant aircraftman than to a damned attractive WAAF, and Ann Waterlow, in spite of herself, found that she was replying defensively.

'I was concerned for her safety.'

Glances went round the table, and she responded to them.

'I was afraid she might have had a fall.'

'Or killed herself,' said Mr Simmonds, rashly.

This time there was a slight catch of breath around the table, and Mr Simmonds glanced nervously at Mr Harper, but found that he was looking at Miss Waterlow.

'That was hardly likely,' she said, briskly, and if there was a touch of defiance in her voice, only she was aware of it. 'But there happened to be a policeman nearby, so I thought it was just as well to make sure that everything was all right.'

'A policeman?' Mr Harper began to feel that he was losing control of the situation. If there was an unexpected development, he liked to receive it typed out, preferably in duplicate, so that he could read it and study it before the meeting. Truth to tell, he never had been very quick-witted, which was why the RAF had suited him so well, with its carefully laid-down rules and its insistence on precise paperwork. And, of course, in the RAF, if things went wrong, there was always someone else to blame.

'You didn't tell me that the Police had become involved.'

'They haven't,' replied Miss Waterlow, and hoped she was right. Would the policeman have to report himself, and her, for breaking and entering? 'The constable helped me to ... to gain entrance, just to ensure that everything was in order. And I've arranged for the Council Building Department to repair the broken pane of glass.'

'That's a bit of a waste,' said one of the other committee members, 'if we're going to demolish the building.'

'Not at all,' said Miss Waterlow. 'As I said, Miss Pollock has left some of her property there, and the house had to be secured until—'

'Mr Simmonds,' interrupted Mr Harper, deciding to take charge, 'did you send the Final Notice?'

'Yes, yes I did, but ... but we can't evict her until October the sixteenth.'

'If she's left, we can't evict her at all,' remarked the same committee member as before, and there was a general laugh.

172

'Yes, yes, thank you,' said Mr Harper, repressively. 'Mr Simmonds has followed the correct procedure, and when the Final Notice expires, we can arrange for the tenant's goods to be collected and stored, and then we can officially take possession. Problem solved. Jolly good show.'

He nodded to Mr Simmonds and then gave a warm, approving smile to Miss Waterlow, indicating that, between them, with their special relationship, they had sorted the whole thing out. He then shuffled together the papers relating to 'Pollock, Ellen Mary', placed them in the file marked 'Hampton Row', closed it and put it aside. Mr Simmonds opened his mouth and shut it again. So did Miss Waterlow.

Mr Simmonds was struggling with the impulse to say, *But where has she gone?* as he thought of the old lady defending her little den like a defiant dormouse. Would she really have ventured out into the great world, and, if so, how would she survive? But he knew that Mr Harper would simply have replied that it was none of their business, and, of course, he was right. Mr Simmonds remembered his wife saying that he was too soft, and, of course, she was right, too. The premises were vacated. That was what mattered. Everything else was, well, sentimentality.

Miss Waterlow was thinking of the rectangular impression on the bed where, according to the policeman, Miss Pollock had packed a suitcase. But where had she gone? Was it Ann's responsibility to ensure that she had relatives and had, perhaps, travelled to stay with them? Should she check at the railway station? But, no, that would be absurd. In her work for Old People's Welfare, Ann was all too familiar with the heroic, frail old men and women who had lived through dire poverty, the Depression, bombing and near starvation and bereavement, and who still declared that they didn't want charity and that they could manage, thank you very much. Like the old woman in Dickens' *Old Curiosity Shop*, Betty Whatsit, they fled the welfare state just as they had defied Hitler, clinging to the tattered flag of their absurd, enfeebled independence.

The old lady had made a decision to pack a suitcase and leave, and that was her own affair. If Ann should ever be left old and alone, she, too, would fight for her independence.

'Next business,' said Mr Harper.

Thirty

The rain had been unremitting all morning.

'We can't stay here all day,' whispered Miss Pollock when they had finished their breakfast.

'Eh?' said Mr Charrington, putting his hand up to his ear.

Miss Pollock glanced at the café owner, who was leaning on the counter reading his paper. Everyone else had left, and it was very quiet except for the sound of the rain. She leaned across the table.

'I think he wants us to leave,' she said.

'He's had our money,' replied Mr Charrington, loudly. 'And I tipped him again!'

'Sh-sh!'

She glanced at the man again, but he was folding his paper over and didn't seem to have heard.

Ed had heard every word, of course. The old man was deaf, and his aggressive tone reminded Ed of his father. It was because of his father that he'd gone into boxing. He was fed up with being knocked about, and the happiest day of his life was when he'd come home from the gym and caught the old devil unawares with a lovely straight left. Laid him out cold on the linoleum at the foot of the stairs. He always remembered the look of astonishment in his father's face just before Ed's fist landed on his jaw. As he turned to leave, Ed caught sight of his mother shrinking back with the familiar look of helpless fear. He knew there was nothing she could have done, but he still blamed her. He never saw his father again, and only saw his mother once, when she was in hospital just before she died. She gave him the same helpless look of misery, and he felt bad about it, but neither of them said anything, and after a bit he got up and left. He paid for her funeral, but he never saw her again. He felt bad about that, too, but there was one good thing. Having a family like his – a father who beat him up, a mother who did nothing about it, and two brothers and a sister who got out as soon as they could and never came back – at least it taught him to look after number one, and not to get involved with other people.

He wondered now what this old couple were up to, and why they didn't seem to have anywhere to go, but it was none of his business. He turned to the horse racing page, reached for the stub of pencil on the cash register and began to mark possible winners.

They decided to spend the morning in the

public library.

'No one cares how long you stay in there' Mr Charrington had said. 'Just keep reading the papers, or get a book out of the shelves.'

Miss Pollock thought how clever he was, and how much he knew. She had never been in a public library. 'We're not much for books in our family,' her father used to say, and her mother had once told her that Grandfather Pollock couldn't read or write and had to 'make his cross' instead of signing his name. She lowered her voice as she said it, and Miss Pollock had nodded solemnly. It was true that, since leaving school, she hardly ever had to write anything, but how embarrassing it would be not to be able to sign your name!

'We'll have to find a nice grocer's soon,' said Miss Pollock, as they left the café. 'We need to get our rations.'

'Rations?' repeated Mr Charrington. 'That's going back a bit.'

'Oh, you know what I mean!' she said.

She sounded cross, but she wasn't really. It was as though it was a game and she knew the rules, even though she had never played it before. Although that wasn't quite true. When she was at school, a boy had waited for her outside the 'Junior Boys' entrance and had offered to carry her satchel home.

'I can carry it myself, thank you!' she had said, with a little toss of her head, and as she

off, she became aware, with a quite unaccustomed sense of triumph, that he was
following her, and she glanced over her
shoulder, and didn't quite smile at him.
When she reached her house, she paused,
and he opened the gate for her, and then she
looked at him and did give a sort of smile,
and he gave a great, beaming smile back, and
she went through the gate and he closed it,
and she cast a quick, final glance over her
shoulder and saw him running and leaping
away up the road. It was the last day of term,
and she never saw him again, probably
because he had gone up to the senior school,
but she had never quite forgotten him, and
sometimes wondered what had happened to
him.

Mr Charrington chuckled.

'I know what you mean,' he said. 'We've
got our little house, and now we've got to fill
our little store cupboard.'

'Oh, *you!*' she said, but she couldn't help
laughing.

He tucked her hand more closely in his
arm as they turned into the road which led
into town. It was still raining, but at least the
sharp north-east wind which had gusted
along the seafront was now behind them.

'You all right?' said Mr Charrington.

She wasn't the one who was panting and
gasping for breath, but she said, 'Better out
of the wind.'

'That's what *I* thought,' he said, and she felt a sense of relief at having somehow said the right thing.

The public library was very big and very quiet, a bit like a church, thought Miss Pollock, but it didn't seem to worry Mr Charrington. He was rather out of breath after climbing the big flight of steps outside, but he only paused for a moment before setting off for the rack of newspapers.

'Here we are,' he said, rather loudly.

There was a tall, thin man in spectacles standing behind the counter. Miss Pollock saw him frown, and felt that she should apologise, as though Mr Charrington belonged to her, but she just trotted after him to the place where the newspapers were spread out on a kind of wooden rack.

'Which one do you want?' he enquired.

Miss Pollock had never read a daily newspaper. Her father used to read the *Daily Mirror*, but her mother said it was a nasty common paper and she didn't know how could, and when he had finished with i used it to light the fire, or to put down kitchen floor after it was washed. had always bought the local pa week, and after her father died on with that. So Miss Pollock see the *Brightlesea Gazette*, came out on Tuesdays, an chance to read it that week.

'I'll have that one,' she said.

He got it down for her and spread it out on the table, and then came and sat beside her. She saw that he had the *Daily Mirror*. She was surprised to find that she didn't mind, even though it had a picture on the front of a girl in a bathing dress, or rather, she thought, daringly, more *out* of it. She didn't even mind when Mr Charrington nudged her and said, '*She's* going to get a bit chilly, en't she, if this weather holds up!'

'Quiet, please!' called the librarian.

'Sh-sh!' said Miss Pollock, and nudged him back, and they both giggled.

Miss Pollock read the *Brightlesea Gazette* just as she always did, very slowly from the front page to the back page. She even read the sports pages, and now and then recognised a name, like Reg Tully, captain of the Brightlesea football team, and knew that the Brightlesea team was called The Greens, although she didn't know why. But her favourite part of the paper was called 'Julian's ...er'. There was a picture of Julian Brown ... the title, and he looked, she thought, ...ry nice young man. And then, the ... told seemed to be about real ...ouple who had just celebrated ...vedding, or a young girl who ...up for swimming, or a man ...'d watch on the beach. She thought he must have a very exciting life, meeting all those interesting people.

Mr Charrington had finished the *Daily Mirror* and got up to return it to the rack.

'You want another one?' he enquired.

'I haven't finished this one yet.'

He peered over her shoulder.

'Brightlesea lost again. You interested in football?'

She didn't quite like to say that she'd only read about it all these years because she had nothing better to do, so she enquired, 'Why do they call them The Greens?'

'Because of their green jerseys. En't you never seen 'em?'

She shook her head.

'We'll go together on Saturday,' he said.

The woman at the next table clicked her teeth in annoyance, and the librarian said 'Quiet, please!' but Miss Pollock didn't mind. Fancy going to a real football game! Whatever next?

It was still raining when they left the Library.

'This en't no weather for one of our picnics,' said Mr Charrington. 'Look, there's a milk bar over there. Let's try that.'

Miss Pollock had heard of milk bars, but she had never been in one, and, truth to tell, if they were all like this one, she didn't think much of them. There were no proper tables, and if you wanted to sit down, you had to sit on a stool at the counter or at shelves round the room. There were young men and girls who looked as if they'd just got off their motorcycles, and when she asked for a cup of tea, the man behind the counter said they didn't do tea. What kind of café was it, she thought, which 'didn't do tea'?

'You can have coffee,' said the man.

Miss Pollock had only tried coffee once. It was called 'Camp Coffee' and it came out of a bottle like Worcester sauce, except that it had a picture of a soldier on it, and when you poured it out, it looked like gravy browning. Her father had said that they used to drink it sometimes in France during the Great War and he fancied trying it again, so her mother had bought it from old Mr Dewsbury.

'Makes a change from tea, I daresay,' he had suggested as he wrapped it.

'Huh! A change for the worse!' her mother had remarked, as they all sat round the kitchen table and tried it, and her father said he reckoned it had tasted better in the trenches.

'Fancy a cup of coffee?' Mr Charrington enquired now.

Miss Pollock didn't answer, but just looked mulish. Too many strange things were happening at once, and he shouldn't have brought her to this place where you couldn't even get a nice cup of tea. Mr Charrington looked up at the menu, which was painted in

white on the wall behind the counter.

'You could have a milk shake,' he said. 'How about a strawberry milk shake?'

It seemed a funny thing to have for dinner, but at least it was better than coffee, so Miss Pollock nodded. It wasn't too bad. It was like melted ice cream, and when she had struggled up on to a stool by the window, she drank it while eating a ham sandwich which had mustard in it, and she'd never liked mustard. Mr Charrington had a cup of coffee which had a lot of froth on top, as if it was beer.

'Aren't you going to eat something?' she asked, anxiously.

'I'll have something later,' he said, but she gave him half of her ham sandwich, and it turned out that he liked mustard, so that made her feel better, even if he did leave most of it in his saucer.

They found a grocer's shop on a corner not far away from the front. It wasn't a real grocer's shop like Mrs Bickstead's.

'It's a "Help Yourself",' said Mr Charrington.

'What, don't you have to pay nothing?' demanded Miss Pollock.

That made him laugh so much that it brought on a fit of coughing, so she was sorry she'd said it, because, of course, she did really know that they had to pay.

'It's what they call "Self Service",' he said.

'Huh!' she said, just like her mother. 'I s'pose that means we have to run about looking for what we want, and they just sit by the door and take our money!'

But in fact, it was rather enjoyable to wander about the shop together deciding what to buy, like, well, like an old married couple. They even argued about it, and Miss Pollock was secretly astonished to find herself standing up against him when he wanted to buy something too expensive. 'Men have no idea of money,' her mother used to say, and she was right, but they did agree on soup and baked beans and half a dozen eggs and biscuits and a bit of cheese, and tea and sugar and a pint of milk.

They had agreed to share the cost, and Miss Pollock was a bit startled to find how little money she had left in her purse. Unobtrusively glancing at Mr Charrington as he put his wallet away and fished in his trouser pockets, she knew that he felt the same, but he didn't say anything until they were out of the shop.

'We'll take this lot home,' he said, 'and then I'd better go along and collect my pension.' He stopped short. 'Oh, bother!'

'What is it?' she asked, alarmed.

'I'll have to go back to the sub-post office where it's registered.'

'Oh yes? Where's that?'

'Near where I used to live,' he said. He paused, as though he was sort of getting himself together. 'It's not far,' he said. 'I can get the bus from the pier and then ... then it's not far to the post office.'

He smiled at her and began to walk on, but she could see his breath coming shorter than ever, and suddenly she knew that the journey would be too much for him, and that he knew it, too. He had bronchitis, same as her father used to get in the winter. She was so unused to taking decisions, even for herself, and much more so for someone else, that he was some feet away and she almost had to run to catch hold of his sleeve and say, 'No.'

'Hm?'

He looked down at her.

'Mine's much nearer,' she said.

'Eh?'

'Where I get my pension. It's just down the road from the front. If you take our...'

'Rations?'

She saw his eyes twinkling at her, and she was so relieved that he felt well enough to make a joke of it that she pretended to speak severely, even though she couldn't help smiling.

'Never mind that,' she said. 'You take them home and put the kettle on, and I'll get my pension and then we'll have a nice cup of tea.'

They walked together as far as the café,

and then paused and looked at each other.

'You sure you're all right to go there on your own? Don't want me to come with you?'

' 'Course not,' she said. 'It's just down there.'

But they still lingered, as though reluctant to part.

'Got your pension book?'

She looked in her handbag.

'I got it.'

'Well,' he said, 'cheery- bye.'

He turned to cross the road.

'Mind how you go,' she called, and he turned and smiled at her.

She walked to the corner and paused and looked back to make sure he was safely across the road. He turned – as she knew he would – and waved, and she waved back.

She knew that she had done the right thing, but as he disappeared down the beach she had a terrible empty feeling, as though she would never see him again. But that was silly, she thought. He would light the little stove and put the kettle on, and the sooner she got her pension and joined him, the sooner they could have their tea.

As she walked towards the Pavilion Hotel, Miss Pollock saw a young man coming down the steps. He turned and gave a cheery wave to the fair-haired woman standing outside the open door. Miss Pollock knew that was the hotel owner and turned her face away, half afraid that if anyone spotted her, even someone who didn't really know who she was, she would be reported to the Council and dragged off to be put in a home. As she passed the young man, she thought that she had seen his face somewhere, but she couldn't remember where, and she put her head down and hurried on.

Betty Sparkes had recognised Miss Pollock – or rather she had recognised the hat. She started forward instinctively, inclined to call after her, saying, Are you all right? Did you find somewhere to stay? But no, she thought, that was the kind of silly, sentimental thing which her father had told her she must *not* do. The poor old lady must have found a bed and breakfast somewhere. She *must* have. It was much more important that Julian Brown had come to see her and that he was going to do a piece in his column about the Pavilion Hotel.

Thirty-One

Julian Brown had seen the old lady walking by with her head bent down. In fact, he had nearly bumped into her, but, even so, he didn't exactly notice her. There was no reason why he should. There were dozens of old ladies bumbling about the streets of Brightlesea, and he sometimes thought that during the last year he had interviewed them all.

His name wasn't really Julian, it was John. His father was William Brown, a gas-fitter in Nottingham, and his grandfather had been a farm labourer. Julian – because now he always thought of himself as Julian, even if they did still insist on calling him John at home – was the first in the family to have a job where he could keep his hands clean. He had managed to get into grammar school, and he would have liked to have gone on to university, but of course they couldn't have afforded that, and the truth was that he wasn't quite good enough, anyway. So he took a job as office boy with the local paper, and when he saw the advertisement for a junior reporter with the *Brightlesea Gazette*, he applied for it under his new name of Julian Brown. He had been practising speaking without his Nottingham accent, and he had saved up his wages and bought a matching shirt and tie from Marks & Spencer. He didn't lie at the interview. He said that he wanted to be a journalist, which was true, and that he took the job of office boy in order to learn the business from the bottom, which was not entirely true, since he had no choice. The editor of the *Brightlesea Gazette* was a mild, sandy-haired man, and he sat and looked at Julian in silence for a moment, and then remarked with a slight sigh, 'Well, if you really want to be a journalist, you might as well start here.'

Accustomed to the rather larger resources of the Nottingham paper, Julian was surprised to find that, in addition to being junior reporter, he was also sole reporter, the editor himself filling most of the other functions, with the exception of the column entitled 'Brightlesea People', which was written by the proprietor's maiden aunt. A lady of advanced years and quiet gentility, she lived in a private hotel on the front, and tapped out her copy on an ancient Underwood typewriter. When she died as quietly as she had lived, the editor suggested that Julian should take the column on. He surprised them both by saying that he would like to think about it, and then returned next day to say that he would be happy to oblige, but that he wanted his own by-line and that he wanted to change the name of the column to 'Julian's Corner'. The editor was perfectly agreeable to the request for a by-line, but absolutely refused to consider the change of name, certain that the proprietor, a pompous local businessman, would consider this to be an insult to the exertions of his late departed relative.

'In that case,' said Julian, 'I think you will have to get someone else.'

'Mm,' said the editor.

Next day, he casually remarked that Julian could have his column. It was some months later that, during a somewhat inebriated late evening in the pub, he revealed that the proprietor didn't give a damn what went into the paper as long as it didn't offend the advertisers. Presumably his maiden aunt, now six feet down in the local churchyard, didn't carry the same weight.

Julian was at first elated. He knew that several famous theatrical people lived in Brightlesea. It had begun with retired music-hall performers building bungalows on the greensward along the coast. Then a musical-comedy star built a rather grander mock-Tudor house and gave weekend parties there for theatrical friends, and since then, several distinguished actors and actresses had bought elegant Georgian houses on South

Crescent. Julian looked forward to intimate and exclusive interviews and even, perhaps, since several of them were also film stars, visits to the studios at Ealing and Pinewood. Suddenly the *Brightlesea Gazette* would become a sort of theatrical weekly, with 'Julian's Corner' valued for its knowledge-able gossip and inside information. 'Dear Julian,' they would say as they drank tea with him in their first-floor drawing rooms overlooking the sea, 'it isn't generally known that I am going to play the lead in Terence Rattigan's new play, but I'm sure he won't mind if it is mentioned first in your column.'

But he soon discovered that the distin-guished actors and actresses came to Bright-lesea to escape from press interviews. They took no part in the social life of the town, but, like the musical-comedy star, preferred to mingle with their own friends, leaving their formal theatrical and cinematic lives behind them in the dining car of the South-ern Railway train which so conveniently carried them down after their evening per-formance and took them back in time for lunch at the Ivy. If Julian wrote to any of them requesting an interview, he would receive a brief refusal typed by a secretary from a London address. He did once venture to accost an actress while she was walking her little white poodle along the front. She was famous for those film performances in which she bravely and graciously sent her officer husbands off to war in a doomed submarine, or undertaking a gallant bombing raid, or leading heroic missions behind enemy lines, but when Julian introduced himself as the theatre correspondent of the *Brightlesea Gazette*, she gave him a glare which would have chilled the zeal of Trevor Howard, John Mills or even Noel Coward, picked up the dog and walked away.

There were, it was true, occasional touring companies playing at the Theatre on the Green, and the actors and actresses were happy to be interviewed, especially since they were not usually of the first rank, but it emerged, disappointingly, that the editor had reserved for himself the duty of dramatic critic, together with the free seats. So 'Julian's Corner' differed from 'Brightlesea People' only in its name, consisting, as before, of heart-warming but all too familiar stories of golden weddings and talented young violinists, interspersed with reports of even more familiar local amateur operettas and pantomimes – familiar not just for the events themselves but also for the sturdy, not to say stout performers who, with supreme confidence if slightly off the note, undertook the leading parts year after year.

And here he was now, thought Julian, turning to wave at Mrs Sparkes, plugging a tarted-up bed and breakfast because the owner's father had done business with the proprietor of the paper. What happened to journalistic integrity? He had thought of refusing, but when he began to demur, the editor had pointed one long finger and said, wearily, 'Julian, just do it,' and he knew that the editor's fifty-year-old aspirations and his own twenty-six-year-old ambitions were held in the same grim clamp of financial reality.

What did it mean to be a journalist? he thought. *Why did he want to be a journalist? Was it just to get his name in the paper?* Descending the last step and turning, he nearly knocked into an old lady, and stepped aside to avoid her. Subconsciously he noticed that she glanced quickly at him and then turned her face away as though not wanting to be recognised, but his conscious mind was thinking that this was another old girl who could get her name in the paper. She looked about right for a golden wedding. 'Me and my Jack, we first met at school, and we've been sweethearts ever since.' Then the familiar stories of wartime partings and reunions, and the photograph with them and their grown-up sons and daughters all having moved up in the world and the grandchildren sitting cross-legged on the floor. As the photographer adjusted his lens, Julian would see the old, gnarled hands clutching each other on the draylon sofa, and remember his own grandparents back in Nottingham and wonder what more interesting moments of sexual passion, disappointment or fulfilment, rage, despair, grief and reconciliation lay behind the smooth and well-worn story.

Oh well, he thought now, no place for any of that in 'Julian's Corner'. Back to the office to hack out a crawling piece about the Pavilion Hotel, and how important it was for Brightlesea to have a small hotel – not a bed and breakfast, and not grand like the Royal Hotel, but elegant and informal – and what a charming hostess Mrs Sparkes was, and how she looked upon her guests as more like friends, or even family. 'I like to think of my guests as my family,' she had said, 'and I do all I can to make them happy.' Ugh! Yuck! What a hypocrite! She took in 'guests' because they paid. She did it for the money, just as her father's friend expected his newspaper to make money and not offend the advertisers who brought in the money. That's what journalists were, in the end – the means by which people were persuaded to buy the paper and thus enable the proprietor to make money. Had he really ever thought that a journalist could do something worthwhile?

He reached the front, and turned to look back at the newly painted sign – 'Pavilion Hotel' – and saw in the distance the old lady turning the corner out of sight.

Thirty-Two

The sub-post office where Miss Pollock got her pension was also a newsagent's and a sweetshop. The postmaster wasn't at all friendly. Her mother used to say he had a face like a wet weekend. In the last year that her mother was ill, he never asked whether Mrs Pollock was poorly, or why Miss Pollock was collecting her pension. He just stamped the book and pushed the money towards her, and sometimes Miss Pollock thought he didn't even see her. It used to upset her a little bit, especially after her mother died, but now she was glad of it. She needn't worry about him recognising her and handing her over to the Council. She would just collect her money and leave and go back to Mr Charrington, and then she would be safe.

But as she walked towards it, she saw that there was a crowd of people outside the shop. Then she saw that they were schoolchildren, yelling and screaming and pushing each other. She had trouble getting through them into the shop. 'Excuse me,' she said, 'excuse me,' but they didn't take any notice.

They didn't even seem to see her. It was worse inside, with boys and girls jostling each other and picking up bars of chocolate or packets of sweets and shouting, 'How much?' at the woman who was trying to serve them. *Where was their teacher?* thought Miss Pollock. She remembered the day she had gone into a sweetshop on the way home from school because she had been given a shiny new penny by Uncle Alfie. There was another girl with her who had said something cheeky to Miss Stacy, who owned the shop. The young Ellen had giggled and then felt a sudden sharp pain as someone jerked her pigtail. 'Ow!' she said, and turned to see their teacher.

'Don't you "ow" me, Ellen Pollock,' the teacher had said. 'I heard you being rude to that lady. Apologise at once. And you, Mabel Booth.'

Mabel Booth had been indignant afterwards, saying, 'It wasn't none of her business,' but Miss Pollock remembered that she had felt ashamed, because it wasn't nice to be cheeky to older people, and she knew she shouldn't have giggled. It alarmed her now to find that these schoolchildren didn't seem to care that the woman trying to serve them was old enough to be their mother, or that Miss Pollock herself, still saying, 'Excuse me,' as she tried to reach the post office counter, could have been, well, their grand-

196

mother. She realised that until now she had
collected her pension in the morning when
the children were in school. Were they always
like this? she wondered. Were all children
now rude and noisy? Times change, her
mother used to say, but Miss Pollock didn't
want them to change if this was the way they
were going. Suddenly she longed to be back
in her own house in Hampton Row where
nothing changed and where she felt safe.

She managed to reach the post office
counter and put her book down.

'You haven't signed it.'

'Oh!'

She was horrified. The last thing she
wanted to do was to draw attention to herself. But she realised that the postmaster
wasn't looking at her. He just pushed the
book back and she signed it. He stamped it,
returned it and counted out the money, and
she gathered it up with fumbling fingers and
quickly turned away, almost glad of the
jostling crowd of children who instantly hid
her from the view of the postmaster. Supposing the Council had warned him to look
out for her? Supposing they cancelled her
pension unless she agreed to go into a home?

Outside, she paused to put the money
away in her handbag. It had begun to rain
again. If only she had her umbrella! But her
umbrella was in her house in Hampton Row.
She still had the key. She saw it in her purse.

And there was another thing: she and Mr Charrington had bought a kettle, but not a saucepan, and you needed a saucepan to heat soup or baked beans or to make scrambled eggs. She had left just the right saucepan behind in her kitchen, but did she really dare to go back there? As she hesitated, the rain came down harder than ever.

I shall go to my house, she thought, as though speaking defiantly to someone. *I shall go to my house and fetch my umbrella.*

And she set off in the direction of Hampton Row.

Thirty-Three

It felt very strange to approach her own house as though she was a burglar. The gate squeaked as it always did, and she felt like saying, 'Sh-sh!' She was about to unlock the door when she saw the broken window pane and gasped. They had talked about pulling her house down. Surely they hadn't started already? She looked round nervously, but the little street was, as usual, deserted, and the rain, which had let up a little, began to come down more heavily. She quickly unlocked the door and went inside, and, on an impulse, locked it behind her, finding her

198

hands trembling, and then stood quite still, her back to the door.

Everything was just as she had left it, as though she had died and come back to earth like a ghost. She stood there in the silence, almost afraid to move, as though she had no business being there. Looking round, she saw the umbrella in its usual place and moved to pick it up, although she felt almost guilty doing so. Still, it was good to have it in her hands. The bit of elastic which was supposed to hook round a button to keep it neat and tidy when it was closed was rather worn, and the loop of plaited silk which went round your wrist was distinctly ragged. But her father had given it to her mother as a birthday present not long before he died, and many was the time she and her mother had walked along under its shelter, and always with the words, 'Lucky we brought the umbrella!' Now she and Mr Charrington could shelter beneath it. She put it on the table and went to fetch the small saucepan, which, like everything else, was in its usual place. In fact, she could have gone straight to it if she had been blind, and, again, she felt great satisfaction in holding its familiar form – no longer quite circular after long use and with its bottom slightly blackened. But it was the soup saucepan, and that evening she and Mr Charrington would open a tin of soup and ... Open a tin of soup? But they hadn't bought a tin-opener!

'Oh!' she exclaimed aloud, and put a hand to her mouth, thinking how dreadful it would have been if they had settled down in their little house and Mr Charrington had fancied a bowl of soup, and they didn't have a tin-opener.

She opened the dresser drawer very quietly, still feeling like a thief, but she couldn't help smiling as she took out the battered tin-opener, and heard in her head Mr Charrington saying, Fancy you thinking of that! Next to the tin-opener was the big kitchen spoon they used to stir the soup, so she took that as well, and then she saw the spare sardine-tin key, and a daring thought came to her.

It was a pity, Miss Pollock thought, that she hadn't got her shopping bag with her, but she knew that there was a carrier bag hanging behind the door. As she opened the door of the store cupboard, it came to her that it was all a bit of a lark, stealing from her own house, especially since she was doing it for Mr Charrington. Truth to tell, she never kept much in the way of stores because she really couldn't afford to. The packages of cornflower, custard and blancmange powder were a bit musty, and most of the tins had been there since before her mother died and were rather rusty and bent, but she found a tin of sardines and a tin of corned beef, and a tin of salmon which her mother had bought for when Uncle Alfie came, but he had died first, so they had kept it for a special occasion.

Well, if this isn't a special occasion I don't know what is! thought Miss Pollock, and put her hand to the brooch pinned to her coat.

She was still smiling as she turned towards the door to fetch the carrier bag, but at that moment she heard the squeak of the garden gate and the sound of men's voices. She stood for a moment motionless, terrified. They must have come from the Council. The footsteps approached. They mustn't see her! They mustn't know that she was there. She could feel her heart beating as she waited for them to knock at the door. But instead she heard the sound of a key in the lock. They had a key! They were coming inside! They were coming into her house!

She looked round helplessly, and then she stumbled towards the stairs and, clutching the banister, tried to hurry up. The sound of her footsteps on the worn linoleum sounded very loud in the silent house, and the stairs which she had run up and down ever since her childhood now had to be taken one at a time as she gasped for breath. For the first time she realised that she was old. She really was an old person. They were coming to get her, and she couldn't run up the stairs. That was what it meant to be old. She could still hear the rattle of the key in the lock.

'Probably they gave you the wrong key,' said a young man's voice, and, relieved, she found the strength to climb the last few stairs.

'No, it's all right, I got it,' said a louder, older voice, and suddenly she realised that the door was open and that they were inside the house.

She managed to tiptoe into the bedroom and flattened herself against the wall.

Fred finally managed to open the door with the key which that woman in the Old People's Welfare had given him. She reminded him of that ATS officer who'd been after the captain, and seemed to think that ordering Fred about would bring her closer to him. 'Do this, please,' and 'Would you do that?' Fred had soon put her right. He knew the captain would back him up – and if he didn't, Mrs Onslow would. The great thing about the Army was that everyone had their place. Of course you tried to beat the system, but that was different from taking liberties. In bloody Civvy Street nobody knew their place and everyone took liberties – usually with Fred.

'You'd better stay outside, Terry,' he said. 'Lady Muck said we'd got to be careful because the tenant's property is still here and we mustn't damage it.'

He looked round him.

'Don't think we need to worry about that too much,' he said, his eyes resting on the coronation mug and the *Little Sweetheart* picture and the scrubbed wooden table with the pile of junk on it. 'Terry,' he called, 'come in and sweep up this glass. And wipe your feet ... Oh, too late. Never mind. It won't hurt the Persian carpet.'

Terry, a great lumping boy of eighteen, looked at the big, wet, muddy footprints he had left on the linoleum and then looked blankly at Fred. Thick as two planks of wood.

'Go on, find a dustpan and brush. They must have one somewhere.'

Fred hated these fiddling little Council repair jobs, but at least with this one the house was empty. Hadn't got some bloody tenant looking over his shoulder and saying, 'Oh, while you're about it, you might as well put this shelf up.' The women were the worst. Living rent-free, most of them, but you'd think it would kill them to knock a nail in. They put him in mind of those officers' wives in Germany. Husbands risen from the ranks, never had a servant in their lives, but their idea of showing they were officer class was to work their German maids and nannies half to death while they lay in bed, and to treat a batman like a skivvy. Not like Mrs Onslow. When he first joined up, he had been Captain Onslow's batman. He didn't think he'd like it, but he found that he did. A Barnados boy, he'd never had a family of his own, and he got on a treat with Mrs Onslow and the children.

'Oh, Fred,' Mrs Onslow would say, 'I know I shouldn't ask you, but I've got to take Rosie to her riding lesson. 'Could you bear to...?'

And of course he'd be glad to do whatever job it was, like putting up a pelmet or nailing down that bit of carpet, and he enjoyed doing it because the Captain would always say, 'Sally, you are the limit! That's not Fred's job.' And then Fred and Mrs Onslow would exchange a look, and he'd give her a wink. Captain Onslow was a regular, so Mrs Onslow had always been an Army wife, living in quarters and bringing a few bits and pieces with her, like a couple of Persian rugs, a small antique bureau, or curtains which had to be lengthened or shortened according to the size of the windows, and always managing to make every place a home. When the regiment was posted to the desert, she hugged Fred and said, 'Take care of him,' and he did – although taking care usually consisted of brewing up in petrol tins. The Captain came back an MC and a Lieutenant Colonel, and somehow it was fiddled so that they all went together to Germany with the army of occupation.

But then the War was finally over, and the

Onslows went to Kenya. ('No chance of promotion in the Army now.') Fred was demobbed and went back to the wife he'd never really liked, and found that the only job he could get was in the Council Repairs Department.

Upstairs, Miss Pollock listened, horrified, to the sound of cupboard doors being opened and banged shut. What were they doing? Were they stealing her things? Perhaps they weren't from the Council at all. Perhaps they were criminals. She must stop them. She crept round the door and heard the rattle of glass being swept up.

'What shall I do with it?'

'Chuck it in the dustbin and then give me a hand mending this window.'

Leaning back out of sight, she could just see a man with a tool bag by the window. So they weren't criminals. They were from the Council. At first she was relieved, but then she remembered the umbrella and the other things which she had left on the table. If they saw them, they would know that she was there. They would come upstairs and look for her.

When she was sure that they were busy mending the window, she very cautiously edged her way back into the room and hid behind the door. She had always hated the game of hide-and-seek, and now ... She stood motionless, hardly daring to breathe.

205

If they realised that she was there, they would come and find her and drag her away to a home and she would never see Mr Charrington again.

Fred had finished replacing the window pane – not quite as neatly as if it had been for Mrs Onslow, but well enough – and prepared to leave, glancing round the room. What had that Old People's Welfare woman said? 'The tenant has left the property, but we need to secure it.' His eyes rested on the table. Funny to go away and leave those bits and pieces there. Were they to be thrown away? The rusty tins, maybe, and the battered old saucepan, but ... the umbrella? When a woman left the house she usually took her umbrella with her.

'Come on, darling!'

'Just getting my umbrella!'

He remembered Mrs Onslow's favourite umbrella – slim and wine-coloured with a delicately rounded leather handle. Dear, oh me! the number of times he'd chased that blooming thing up, and always when he brought it back, 'Oh, Fred, you angel! Where did you find it? What would I do without you?' He looked again at the direfully shabby umbrella on the table. It looked more like his wife's, except that it was brown instead of navy blue. 'Why don't you get a new one?' he had demanded once, but his wife had replied irritably, 'What for? It's only something to keep the rain off.'

Terry had finished cleaning up, and there was a clatter as he threw the dustpan and brush back in the cupboard and slammed the door shut.

'Can we go now?' he said.

'Mm?'

It was a pretty shabby umbrella. Probably the tenant had put it with the other things to be chucked out, but was too idle to put them in the dustbin. None of his business, anyway.

Miss Pollock heard the front door being slammed and locked, but it was several minutes before she ventured to come out of the bedroom and creep step by step down the stairs, looking nervously round in case one of them had stayed behind. She knew that she must be quick. Mr Charrington didn't know that she was going to come to the house and he would be worried. She fetched the brown paper carrier bag which had the words 'Dewsbury, Family Grocer' on it, and put the saucepan and tins and other things in it. Then it occurred to her that if they were having soup they would really need soup bowls, so she got two bowls and wrapped them in an old copy of the *Brightlesea Gazette* and put those in as well. She longed to take the two willow-pattern plates on which they always had their dinner, but she wasn't sure how much she could carry, or how strong old Mr Dewsbury's carrier bag was.

As she picked up her umbrella and prepared to leave, she thought it might be a good idea to take the spare key, but, glancing at the hook beside the door, she was shocked to see that it wasn't there. That was how the men had got into her house. They had broken into her house and stolen her key, and they could come back any time they liked. She knew then that she must never come to the house again, because next time they might catch her.

Standing by the kitchen table, holding her umbrella and handbag and the string handles of old Mr Dewsbury's carrier bag, it was as though she was aware of every single object in the house, from her father's long combinations laid to rest in the chest of drawers to her mother's beaded jacket hung in the wardrobe, from the burnt frying pan which they had never managed to get clean but couldn't bring themselves to throw away to the best glass bowl which they used for banana custard when they had visitors. The last time she had left, she had it in the back of her mind that in a little while the Council would forget all about her and she could come back again and go on as before. But now ... To walk out and leave the house and everything in it, knowing that it was for ever, was like walking out on her whole life, including her mother and father and her own childhood, just as people who had lost their memory had to start with nothing – not even the knowledge of those they loved.

For a moment she felt that she couldn't bear it. Then she thought of Mr Charrington. At least *he* would be waiting for her. She took a deep breath and prepared to leave. But at the very last minute she took down the coronation mug and put it in old Mr Dewsbury's carrier bag.

Thirty-Four

Mrs Bickstead was just shutting up. It was nearly dark outside, and she had turned the sign from 'Open' to 'Closed' and was just pulling the blind down when she saw the little figure hurrying along under an umbrella.

'Miss Pollock!' she called, and tried to open the door, forgetting that she had already locked it.

The blind flew up, and she hastily unlocked the door and looked out. In the growing dusk, the small figure had almost disappeared down the ill-lit street. She gazed after it anxiously, feeling the rain on her face.

Donald's voice spoke behind her.

'Shall I cash up?'

'No,' she answered, hastily withdrawing. 'No, I'll do it.'

She locked the door and pulled the blind down and Miss Pollock was forgotten in that instant.

In spite of everything, Miss Pollock felt her spirits rising as she hurried along towards the front. The worst thing about living alone was that there was no one to tell about anything, even if it was only about Mrs Bickstead's son being rather offhand or how she tripped over that rough bit of pavement and only just saved herself. But now she had had a real adventure, and she could tell Mr Charrington all about it. 'Well, I never!' he would say. 'Lucky you got upstairs in time!' And they would sit down and have a cup of tea, and everything which had been so frightening when she was alone would be interesting and exciting when she could share it.

She had no trouble crossing the road, but the slope down to the beach seemed much steeper without Mr Charrington's arm to hold on to. She had thought that she would be able to see a little light from the stove, and perhaps also a candle, and that he would be looking out for her and would call out and come to meet her, but he didn't. Her feet slithered under her when she stepped down on to the shingle. The rain had almost stopped, but it was too difficult to put the umbrella down with her handbag over her wrist and the carrier bag in the other hand, and she was afraid of falling as she slipped unsteadily on the shifting stones past the other boathouses, her footsteps sounding very loud in the silence. And when she arrived at their little house it was all dark and silent.

No stove, no kettle, no lighted candle. Mr Charrington wasn't there.

It was like the shock of a sudden bereavement. She was there alone. She had lost him and she didn't know where he was. She might have been standing there amidst the rubble in the aftermath of a bomb. After a moment, without conscious thought, she put the carrier bag down on the shingle. The bowls and coronation mug clanked together slightly, but it didn't matter. In the face of this great calamity nothing else mattered. In the same sleepwalking state she lowered and closed the umbrella, opening and shutting it a few times to shake off the rain and, as she did so, she heard a rustling noise from inside the house. There was someone there! She took a nervous step backwards and, in the gloom, saw Mr Charrington's head appearing over the side of the boat.

'Hullo,' he said. 'I must've dropped off.'

He began to struggle over the edge of the boat and on to the ladder.

'Oh, deary me!' he gasped. 'I only meant to have forty winks.'

He reached the bottom of the ladder and his feet crunched on the stones.

'Well, I am a one!' he said. 'I was going to have the kettle on before you got back. Almost dark, in'it? What time is it?'

She couldn't move or speak.

'You all right?' he said.

He put his hands on her shoulders, and she made a strange, high-pitched sound, like a small cry of despair.

'Here!' he said. 'What's this?'

'I thought you'd ... gone.'

'Gone? Gone where?'

He put his arms round her and held her close, damp umbrella and all.

'Come on,' he said. 'You know I'd never go anywhere without you.'

He could feel her trembling.

'Come on,' he said. 'Come on. We'll put the kettle on and have a nice cup of tea.'

Mr Charrington said that he reckoned that sleep had done him a power of good. He admired all the things she'd brought, and they both had a good laugh about the tin-opener.

'Pair of dumbos we'd've looked,' he said. ' "I just fancy a bowl of soup." "Oh, yes, going to open it with yer teeth?" '

'Lucky I thought of it, then,' she answered, and gave him a little, triumphant nod in the candlelight as they drank their tea.

'You know,' he said, when she told him about the Council men, 'I don't reckon they could put you in a home if you didn't want to go.'

'They'd put me somewhere.'

'Not while I'm here, they won't!'

And she knew it was true. As long as he was with her, she was safe.

It was an evening of pure pleasure. Mr Charrington had put the stores away, but, of course, all in the wrong places, and he sat watching her as she clicked her teeth and moved them about.

'There,' she said, 'that's better.'

'Oh, yes,' he said, 'much better!'

She looked at him and saw the twinkle in his eyes.

'Oh, you!' she said, and gave a little slap on his brown, freckled hand.

They both fancied tomato soup for supper. He opened the tin, and she warmed the soup in the familiar saucepan. As they drank it, sitting close together and smiling at each other now and then, she watched him wiping the bowl round with the slice of bread which she had buttered for him and she knew that she was perfectly happy.

Thirty-Five

Next morning, Miss Waterlow had finished dealing with her correspondence and was just preparing to go and visit Pinelea Old People's Home when the Council repairs man arrived.

'Key from Hampton Row,' he said.

'Oh ... yes,' said Miss Waterlow, taking the key. 'Was everything in order?'

The man shrugged.

'Seemed all right.' He half turned to go, but paused. 'There was a pile of junk on the table.'

'Oh yes,' replied Miss Waterlow.

Because she had been so young when she was put in charge of Old People's Welfare – a department which did not carry high priority in the publicity-conscious minds of Council Members and Officials – she had taken care to seem to be fully aware of everything which was going on, whether she was or not, and, finding that this seemed to strengthen her position, had continued with it ever since. But the moment she had said, 'Oh yes,' she was thinking, *But there was nothing on the table – nothing at all.*

214

'Old tins,' said the man, 'and ... an umbrella.'

'An umbrella?'

'Put there to be thrown out, I s'pose,' said the man. 'I just left it there.'

'Yes, of course,' said Miss Waterlow. 'But you mended the window?'

'That's right,' said Fred. He hesitated. 'Did you say the tenant had left?'

'I believe so,' replied Miss Waterlow, briskly, 'but we had to secure the premises, anyway.'

'Right,' said Fred, and turned and went out.

He'd done his job. That was all he did do these days, and whether the umbrella on the table was a shabby brown one or slim and wine-coloured with an elegant leather handle was none of his business.

Miss Waterlow's secretary had been hovering, notebook in hand, preparing to retire to her own small office and type the letters.

'Shall I hang the key on the board?' she enquired.

'Er ... no,' said Miss Waterlow. Her hand closed round the old-fashioned key with its faded label. 'I ... I think I'll just check on the property – make sure it's been properly secured.'

She was immediately conscious of Mrs Price's disapproval. Her secretary was many years older than she was, and her attitude was that of an elderly governess, protective but subtly authoritarian.

'You shouldn't have to do that,' she said. 'That's the business of the Council Repairs Department.'

'It's no trouble,' said Ann Waterlow. 'I have to go near Hampton Row, anyway.'

She walked out quickly, aware of having lied, and even more aware that Mrs Price probably knew that she had lied. And, all the way to Hampton Row, she thought, What pile of junk? What umbrella?

Because she had no real reason to be there, Miss Waterlow, too, felt like a burglar as she unlocked the door and went inside. Her eyes went at once to the kitchen table. It was completely bare, just as she had seen it last, standing there with the policeman at the door.

She tried to count back. She had gone to the house on Tuesday morning, and got no reply, and returned early on Wednesday, when they had broken in. She had made a great point of insisting that the house should be instantly secured, and that had been done that same afternoon. So who had put the things on the table, and when? And who had removed them, and when? It could only be Miss Pollock, but if so, where was she? Surely she must be hidden somewhere in the house!

In sudden panic, Ann ran upstairs. The bedroom looked just as she had left it, the rectangular shape still on the bedcover. She looked underneath the bed. Nothing there but a flowered chamber pot. She opened the wardrobe, and saw the same few garments on hangers carefully covered with ribbons or cretonne and several worn pairs of shoes. There was no space for anyone to hide in the smaller room, but she did look under the bed (another chamber pot) and, absurdly, in the small, white-painted chest of drawers which contained a child's clothes carefully wrapped in newspaper and mothballs. With increasing alarm, she wondered if there was a loft, but there was no sign of a trapdoor above the landing.

For a moment she stayed perfectly still, listening, and even held her breath, half believing that she could hear someone else breathing nearby. But no, there was nothing. She knew there was nothing. She went downstairs and unbolted the back door and looked out into the little yard. She could see the tin bath hanging on the wall and ... Of course, there was the outside toilet! The perfect hiding place.

She had to get her courage together to open the door, expecting to be confronted by the unknown Miss Pollock, but there was no one there, just the wooden-seated lavatory and the chain with its wooden handle, and the roll of Bronco toilet paper. It all looked very clean, but a faint smell lingered. How disgraceful, thought Miss Waterlow, that an old woman should have to live in such conditions!

She went back inside and closed and bolted the back door. *It's my fault*, she thought. *I should have come on Monday. I might have been able to talk to her, persuade her to let me help her.* She shivered. The wind had gone round to the north, and with no fire or any kind of heating the little house was very cold. If the old woman had been hiding there, she would have been suffering from hypothermia. But where *was* she? Miss Waterlow went to the front door and paused, looking round the room, as she had the day before. She saw the *Little Sweetheart* picture, but ... Something was missing. Of course. The coronation mug wasn't there.

Unexpectedly, she found her eyes filling with tears. *How ridiculous of me!* she thought. So the old lady, now alone in the world, had nothing left to value but her possessions, and had come back to collect them, paltry as they were. So what? Ann Waterlow blinked back the tears and stiffened her shoulders. The situation of the old lady in Pinelea was much more pathetic. She had been evicted from Mrs Sparkes' hotel and was now incontinent, so that the home could no longer keep her, and she had nowhere else to go. But Ann Waterlow, who was neither incontinent nor pathetic, would deal with it sensibly, which was much better than indulging in soggy sentimentality.

She went firmly out of the front door without a backward glance and locked it. She would return the key to the board and never come near this horrid little house again. Miss Pollock had left. She had made it very clear that she wanted no help from the Welfare Department, and where she was and what she was doing was entirely her own business. Moreover, thought Ann Waterlow, if her disappearance inconvenienced Mr Harper, so much the better!

She shut the little, creaking gate with a determined clack.

Thirty-Six

Miss Pollock had woken late that morning. The day before had been so busy – the public library, the milk bar, the post office and going to her house – that by the time she and Mr Charrington called out, 'Night, night, sleep well,' she was really tired and fell asleep at once. She woke with a start, and was immediately aware that it was quite light, and also that she felt very cold. She sat up and pulled the crocheted throw about her shoulders and looked up at the boat. There was no sign of Mr Charrington, but, through the noise of the sea, she thought that she could hear his creaky breathing. She got up and put her shoes on and tidied her bed and then, hesitating, went to the foot of the ladder.

'Mr Charrington!' she called. 'George!'

There was no reply. She began to climb the ladder, uneasily, because it was, well, like going into a gentleman's bedroom. She saw him lying on his back, his breath coming in a strange, gasping way.

'Mr Charrington,' she said.

She reached out and touched him, and he started up with a sort of groan.

'Uh? Uh?'

'Are you all right?'

'Yes,' he gasped. 'Yes.'

But she could see that he wasn't all right at all.

'I'll ... I'll make a cup of tea,' she said.

He seemed to struggle to come to himself, and she even saw the familiar look of amusement.

'You know how to light the stove?' he asked and, as she hesitated, he quickly said, 'Don't worry, I'll come.'

She was so relieved that she didn't protest, but only said, 'It's very cold.'

'We'll have to make ourselves a little fire,'

he said, and she smiled and retreated down the ladder, glad that he was in charge again.

But when they went to the toilet, she found that she almost had to hold him up as he struggled along the shingle and on to the slope. He stood still at the top, trying to get his breath, although in a few minutes he smiled at her and nodded, and they set off again.

She came out before he did and had to wait a long time in the cold wind. He had washed and shaved, but he didn't have his usual ruddy look, and his eyes were dim.

'Would you rather go to the café?' she asked, uncertainly.

'Why, do you fancy a cooked breakfast?'

'Oh no, just a cup of tea.'

'Same here,' he said.

'You'd better learn me how to light the stove,' she said, and he smiled at her and tucked her hand under his arm.

She made him sit down on her bed and folded her dressing gown and put it behind him before she went to fill the kettle. When she returned, he was leaning back with his eyes closed, but he managed to sit up, and told her how to light the stove and, breathless as he was, even teased her when she got it wrong.

'I've put an extra spoonful of sugar in,' she said, as she passed him his cup of tea. 'You need building up.'

'Just the ticket,' he said.

But, anxiously watching him, she saw that he only drank half of it.

'I think I'll have a little lie-down,' he said, beginning to struggle to his feet.

'Why don't you tuck down there?' she suggested, feeling obscurely that it was rather bold to invite him to sleep in her bed.

'No, I'll be better in me own bed. You might want to have your afternoon nap there.'

'I don't never have an afternoon—!' And then she saw that he was teasing her, and said, 'Oh, you!' and helped him to his feet.

It wasn't easy to get Mr Charrington up the ladder and into the boat, and when she took his hand, Miss Pollock could feel that it was burning hot, and yet he was shivering. She fetched the crocheted throw and tucked it round him.

'No, no,' he protested, 'you'll need that.'

'No, I won't. I've got my coat and my dressing gown. And I don't have afternoon naps!'

He tried to smile, but even that was too much for him, and he lay back on his rolled-up pyjamas with a strange, creaking noise as though his lungs were a pair of worn-out leather bellows. Miss Pollock began to descend, but he gasped, 'Here!'

'Yes?'

'It's too cold out there. Go to the caff. Get

a bite to eat.'

'Oh, I...' she started to protest, and then saw his anxious look, and continued, 'Yes, all right.'

She felt guilty, because she didn't really intend to go there, but then she thought about it and decided that it was a good idea. It was dreadfully cold, and she wanted to go to the chemist just up the road. Besides, she did fancy something to eat, and she couldn't face getting breakfast just for herself in their own little house without him.

Norman Taylor had nearly finished his breakfast when the old lady came in, but he was spinning it out because he had a week's holiday. He would much rather have been at work, because he had nothing to do and nowhere to go, but the other men said that it was bad enough him coming over here to take their jobs without him trying to make them look bad.

He saw that when the old lady sat down by herself at the table even the café owner, who never seemed to notice anything, looked surprised, and glanced out of the window as he came to take her order.

'Your husband not coming this morning?' Ed enquired.

The old lady gave him a startled look. She was holding the menu card very tightly in gloved hands, and, without answering his question, recited as though she had learned it off by heart, 'A poached egg on toast, please, and a pot of tea.'

'Pot of tea for one?'

She threw him another startled look and then nodded, and put the menu down and sat very still, clutching her gloved hands in her lap.

The café owner paused by Norman's table.

'Not going to work today?'

'I've got a week off.'

'Want another cup of tea?' enquired Ed, and added, 'On the house.'

Norman looked up at him and smiled. It felt as though it was the first time he had smiled since he arrived in the country.

'Thank you,' he said, and they both glanced towards the old lady in the window, as though their shared interest in her had given them something in common.

It had taken all Miss Pollock's courage to enter the café on her own. She had never done such a thing in her life. She hadn't tried to read the menu. She remembered what was on it, and had already decided what to have, but she hadn't expected the man to ask her about Mr Charrington, and it gave her a funny feeling to realise that he thought they were married. It was almost shocking. The words 'living in sin' came into her mind, although, of course, it wasn't quite like that, but ... It was lucky she had her gloves on, she thought, or he would have seen that she wasn't wearing a wedding ring, and when he brought her breakfast she waited until he had gone before she took them off.

But still, as she sipped her tea and ate her poached egg, she felt that unaccustomed little lift of her spirits, thinking that if only Mr Charrington could get well again, she might tell him what the man had said, and they would both have a bit of a laugh about it. When she had finished eating, she quickly put the glove on her left hand. The man came to take the plate and told her how much it was. She took the exact money out of her purse and then hesitated. Mr Charrington had said you ought to give him a tip. She had a threepenny bit, but that had been for both of them. Carefully she took two pennies out and put them down on the table, looking up at him.

'That's the tip,' she said, nervously.

Ed gave her a grin, rather uneven from all the times his teeth had fetched up on the floor in the ring, but wide and joyous all the same.

'Thanks, lady,' he said, and picked up the two pence.

Funny old girl, he thought. That tuppence was a fortune to her, but she thought she ought to give it, so she did. On his way back to the counter, he gave Norman a wink.

By the time Miss Pollock had set off across the road, Norman had finished his extra cup of tea, returned the cup to the counter and gone to the door. He looked out, puzzled, seeing the little figure descending the slope to the beach, and turned to say something to the café owner. But Ed – he supposed his name was Ed because of the name 'Ed's Café' – had gone back to his usual occupation of sitting behind the counter reading his paper, and, despite his first sign of friendliness, Norman had learned enough in the last few years not to risk a rebuff.

He opened the door and went out, buttoning his jacket about him against the cold wind.

Thirty-Seven

Miss Pollock had hoped to find Mr Charrington asleep, but as soon as she reached their house she could hear his restless movements sounding in time to his labouring breath.

'I'm back!' she called, and was dismayed to get only a groan in reply.

But at least she knew what to do. Her father used to get bronchitis. It was true that it was her mother who had nursed him, but the young Ellen had watched and listened. She went up the ladder with some difficulty, because she was carrying a cup of water.

'Mr Charrington,' she said. 'George.'

'Uh?'

'Sit up,' she said. 'Come on, sit up.'

He struggled up.

'What? Wassermatter?'

'I got some aspirins here. They'll bring your temperature down.'

'I ain't got a—'

'Yes, you have. My father used to have bronchitis. Take this water.'

She gave him the cup. It shook in his hand, and she hastily opened the aspirin bottle and took out two tablets.

'You take them two aspirins,' she said. 'They'll bring your temperature down.'

He grinned at her through the haze of a high temperature.

'Bossy little thing, ain't yer?' he gasped.

'Never mind that,' she said. 'You just take them aspirins.'

He obeyed, and she quickly took the cup as he lay back, out of breath. She hesitated. She had bought something else, but was afraid to tire him out. 'He'll sleep himself right,' her mother used to say.

She felt very lonely when she came down the ladder again, as though Mr Charrington, being ill, had gone far away and she was on her own, but feeling all the weight and worry of his illness, too. Then it occurred to her that it was important to keep him warm, and she remembered that he had said they had better light a fire. He might have been teasing her, but she still thought it was a good idea, and, after all, she had been used to lighting the fire every morning at home.

Miss Pollock wondered what her mother and father would have said if they had seen her walking along the beach collecting driftwood. (Scuffing her shoes, too!) There was plenty of it, but when she brought it back she realised that it was so light that it would only do to kindle the fire, and would soon burn out. If only she had the coal from the coal bunker out back! Then she had a sudden inspiration. The *Brightlesea Gazette* which she had read in the public library had mentioned a woodyard by the harbour. Maybe if she went there, she could buy some wood.

Tiptoeing up the ladder, she was relieved to see that Mr Charrington was sleeping. Perhaps the aspirins would cure him. She felt a little spring of hope as she set off.

It was quite an adventure to be walking to the harbour, and Miss Pollock thought what fun it would have been if Mr Charrington had been with her. She remembered as a little girl being taken to see the fishing boats coming in from the sea, and she saw a man on the quayside selling fish, but she had no idea what a woodyard would look like. But, following the narrow street which led inland, she saw a big sign which read, 'Birkett & Son, Wood Merchants.' There was the sound of machinery and, as she paused just inside the wide wooden gates, the smell of fresh sawdust. But there didn't seem to be any logs, just lots and lots of planks. A man in a dark suit was making notes in a book.

'Can I help you?' he said.

Miss Pollock took a deep breath.

'I wanted to buy some wood.'

'Oh yes? Two-by-four?'

She didn't understand what he meant, but, looking round, she saw a lot of small pieces of wood in a heap near the gate.

'How much are those?' she asked.

'You can have those for nothing,' said the man.

Miss Pollock scowled at him suspiciously, and he suddenly laughed.

'Take what you like,' he said. 'Shall I give you a hand?'

She had brought her shopping bag, but he filled a big brown paper bag with the pieces of wood and gave it to her.

'I think that's all you can carry, don't you?'

She clutched the bulky bag to her and nodded. She wanted to say thank you, but couldn't quite manage it, so nodded again instead. She turned to go, but then paused.

'I...'

He looked up from his book.

'Was there something else?'

She said, bravely, 'I might come back for some more.'

He laughed again.

'You're welcome any time,' he said, and then, with mock severity, 'but don't forget, we're closed over the weekend.'

'Oh ... yes.'

Smiling, he watched her walk back towards the harbour. Just like his Gran. She never could resist a bargain.

On the quayside, Mrs Harrison was buying tomorrow's fish. They always had fish on Friday. They weren't Catholics, but then neither were Madam or the Master, and fish was always served for lunch on Friday in *their* house.

'I don't like fish, Nanny,' John used to say, up in the nursery.

'Never mind that,' Mrs Harrison would reply. 'We always have fish on Friday.'

'Why?'

'Because it's the right thing to do.'

Truth to tell, Mrs Harrison greatly enjoyed her weekly trip to the harbour, and people who only knew the rather grim-faced bed and breakfast landlady would have been surprised to find how lively was the repartee as she bargained with the fishermen, just as the brisk nanny in her neat uniform and starched veil used to exchange cheerful insults with the tradesmen. (That was how she had met Mr Harrison.) There were broad grins all round as she took the damp, newspaper wrapped package, having managed to knock sixpence off the price. Turning away, still smiling, she saw the small figure of Miss Pollock walking past her towards the front. She recognised the hat, and then remembered where she had seen her before.

Mrs Harrison could have walked back through the town, which was probably a shorter route, but she always walked along the front, and so she naturally followed Miss Pollock. In fact, she could easily have overtaken her – the old lady, clutching a large paper parcel, was walking very slowly – but without quite knowing why, Mrs Harrison slowed down instead. She found herself wondering whether the old lady had found somewhere to lodge in the town and even, perhaps, hoping to see where it was. But when she reached the crossing, she saw with surprise that the old lady was making her way down the slope which led to the beach.

She felt an absurd impulse to call out, 'And where do you think *you're* going?' as though the little person in the shabby coat and terrible hat was one of her charges. But, of course, she was no such thing, and there was no reason why Mrs Harrison should have lingered at the crossing, glancing back on the other side to see that the little figure had disappeared and, all the way to Crestview, have felt a burden of uneasiness, as though there was something she should have done.

Thirty-Eight

When he heard Miss Pollock approaching, Mr Charrington called out.

'Is that you? Where've you been? I kept calling out, but you wasn't there.'

He sounded quite irritable, but she didn't mind, because she remembered that her father used to speak like that to her mother when he had bronchitis.

'I went to get some wood for our fire.'

'Our what?'

'I'm going to light a fire to keep us warm. Do you want me to make you a cup of tea first?'

Instead of saying, yes, please, he gave a sort of cross grunt, but Miss Pollock wasn't offended. She just smiled to herself and quietly clicked her teeth. The fact that he was cross and irritable made her feel that he must be getting better.

It wasn't as easy to light the fire on the beach as it was at home, but she made a grate out of stones, and she had the *Brightle-*

232

sea Gazette paper which she had used to wrap the bowls, and the driftwood to act as kindling, and even some wood shavings from the bag, and once she got it going, the little blocks of wood from the woodyard burned a treat, although they did spit rather. She did worry a little about the smoke and flames, wondering if it was against the law to light a fire on the beach and whether a policeman might see it and come to investigate. If he did, and he found her, he might know that the Council was looking for her and take her away. But you couldn't really see the fire from the promenade, she thought, and it was nice to have a bit of warmth. She hoped that, when Mr Charrington felt better, he would come down and they would sit beside it together, but meanwhile, as she sat there alone, worrying about him, the fire felt like a bit of company.

Miss Pollock didn't have a watch. She used to wear her mother's, but then it stopped, and she didn't know how to get it mended. But just when she thought it was about lunchtime, she heard Mr Charrington struggling up, and came to help him down.

'I got to go to the toilet,' he said.

'Shall I come with you?'

He looked up towards the promenade and shook his head.

'I'll never get up there,' he said. 'You stay here.'

He went round the boat and outside, and, turning her back, she heard the patter of water. She should have felt embarrassed and shocked, but she wasn't. He was quite right. He'd never have got up to the toilet.

'Would you like a boiled egg?' she enquired, when he returned.

'No, I couldn't eat nothing,' he said. 'I think I'll just have another lie-down.'

'I'll warm you a bit of soup later,' she said, and then, as she helped him up, she astonished herself by saying, 'Wouldn't you be more comfortable in your pyjamas?'

'I don't know,' he gasped, exhausted. 'I don't know as I could manage it.'

'I'll give you a hand,' she said.

Whoever would have imagined that she would be standing on top of a ladder helping a gentleman out of his trousers? But it seemed quite natural. He didn't wear long combinations like her father (not that she had ever seen him in them!). Mr Charrington wore light-blue shorts and a vest with short sleeves and long socks. She was relieved when he said, 'I'll keep me undies on for warmth,' but when he reached for his pyjamas she said, 'Just a minute.'

'What is it?'

'I bought some Vick,' she said. 'That's what my father always had for bronchitis. I'm going to rub your chest.'

Miss Pollock hadn't realised that gentlemen had hair on their chests, and she wasn't quite sure that she liked it, but she did her best to rub the honey-coloured, strong-smelling jelly in, while he lay back and smiled at her with that teasing look which was also ... also...

'Now you got to sit up,' she said, 'so as I can rub it on your back.'

She helped him to sit up and rubbed the Vick into his back, but he was so tired and feeling so ill that he laid his head against her shoulder, and when she had finished rubbing the Vick in, she let him stay there for a while before helping him into his pyjamas.

Then she made a pillow out of his jacket, and covered him with his dressing gown and coat and tucked the crocheted throw round his neck. And, before she knew what she was doing, she kissed him on the cheek.

'You have a nice sleep,' she said, 'and then I'll bring you a drop of soup.'

He did manage two or three spoonfuls of soup, but no more, and she drank some and left the rest in the saucepan for later. She gave him two more aspirins, but when she put her hand on his forehead it was very hot, and he was terribly thirsty. There was a sort of ledge in the boat where she could put a cup of water, and she kept the teapot full of cold water so that she could keep filling it up. But she knew that he wasn't getting any better.

'I think I ought to call a doctor!' she said, as it began to get dark.

'I don't need a doctor!' he said. 'It's just ... just...'

'Just the bronchitis,' she said.

'Yes. Just the ... bronchitis.'

But it took three gasping breaths before he could get the word out.

She knew she ought to get a doctor for him, but where could she find one? Dr Harrowby, who had visited her father and then her mother, had told her that he was retiring. He said he didn't like the National Health Service. Too much interference. He said that she could register with someone else, but she'd never bothered.

And then, if she did find a doctor, he would want to know all about her, and she would have to give herself up. She had seen a film once about a murderer on the run who'd given himself up to the police because a little girl was ill. She did feel that she was on the run – even though she wasn't a murderer – and she wouldn't mind giving herself up if only it would help Mr Charrington to get better. But how could she find a doctor?

Worrying about it, she found Mr Charrington's eyes on her. In the fading light she could hardly see his face, but he reached out and took hold of her little cold hand in his big, warm one.

'I'll be all right,' he said. 'That Vick'll do the trick, you'll see.'

As she prepared to cross the road, Miss Pollock became aware of a strange noise, a rather frightening roaring noise, and saw that there were a number of motorcycles outside the café. The door was open, and some young men in black leather were sitting on the bikes and making a noise with the engines. She hesitated, but there was something she had to do for Mr Charrington.

There was a big man standing in the doorway, but he didn't seem to notice as she went past him inside. Others were gathered round the brightly coloured music box, and she saw the black man sitting at his usual table.

'Hey, Tog!' called the big man to one of the others outside. 'Have you brought your spade? Oh, it don't matter. There's one here.'

Miss Pollock hovered nervously inside the door, wondering what he meant, but as she looked for the café owner, the black man got up and walked out, and all the young men and girls laughed. The music suddenly started up so loudly that it made Miss Pollock jump. The café owner came out from behind the counter.

'Take it easy, boys,' he said.

The big man put his fists up.

'You want a fight, Ed?' he said, and

237

pretended to hit him, dodging about and nearly knocking into Miss Pollock.

'You'd know if I did,' said Ed, pretending to hit him back, and then spoke past him to Miss Pollock.

'Did you want something?' he said, and his voice sounded quite cross.

She was standing with one hand on her chest, and something purple peeped out above the top button of her coat. Looking at his unfriendly face, she couldn't have done it for herself, but she had to do it for Mr Charrington. She unbuttoned the top button and drew out the hot-water bottle in its purple knitted cover and silently held it out to him. He glared at her and she thought he wasn't going to take it, but at last he did, and pointed a thick finger at her.

'All right, but this is the last time,' he said, angrily.

As he turned away, tucking it under his arm, the big man pulled it out and held it up and there was a burst of laughter from all the young men and girls.

'What's the matter, Ed? Got nothing else to keep you warm in bed?'

He snatched it back and went towards the kitchen. Miss Pollock heard the laughs and jokes going on, but she took no notice. The little stove wouldn't light and she knew that she must keep Mr Charrington warm that night.

'You want something to eat?' asked the man when he returned.

She shook her head. She had thought of bringing the thermos for some hot tea, but didn't like the idea of asking him to fill that as well.

'Don't forget,' he said, as he gave her the hot-water bottle, 'that's the last time.'

She nodded, and tried to say thank you, but couldn't quite manage it. It was good, she thought, as she held it in her arms, that he had filled it up well, and it was really hot. The big man in black leather held the door open for her.

'All right, Grandma?' he said. 'Sleep well.'

This was very polite of him, and she didn't understand why the other young men laughed, but she was relieved to get away from the noise of the music and the loud voices, and she was anxious to get back to Mr Charrington while the bottle was still hot.

As she crossed the road, she saw that there was someone in the shelter, and, coming closer, she realised that it was the black man sitting there, gazing out to sea. Mr Charrington had said that he was all right, but Miss Pollock wasn't so sure. She stopped for a moment, and then went past and down the slope as fast as she could, hoping that he wouldn't follow her.

'George?' she called. 'Mr Charrington?'

He was lying on his back, and he had

pushed the coat and dressing gown aside. She put the hot-water bottle beside him.

'That's better, isn't it?' she said.

He tried to push it away.

'Too hot,' he gasped.

It was hard to go against him, but she knew she must.

'No, no,' she said. 'You've got to keep warm. You mustn't catch a chill.'

She covered him up and did her best to tuck him in. As he lay back, his breath sounded as though it was being sieved through gravel, and she was sure he should be sitting more upright. She couldn't reach his holdall, which was at the other end of the boat, so she fetched her two nightdresses and, finding they weren't bulky enough, subdued her uneasiness and wrapped them round her woollen vests. (Knickers, of course, would be going too far.)

'George,' she said, 'you must sit up a bit.'

He groaned, but her desperate care for him made her strong, and she managed to get her arm round him and add the makeshift pillow to the others. When he realised what she was doing, he struggled to help her.

'I'm all right,' he kept saying. 'I'm all right.'

But she knew that he wasn't all right. He wasn't all right at all.

She was almost sure that the reason the little stove wouldn't light was that it needed more

240

methylated spirit, but Mr Charrington hadn't shown her how to put it in, and, anyway, she couldn't really see how to do it by the light of the candle, whose flame kept fluttering and sometimes going out as the wind rose with the rising tide. But the fire was still alight, and she managed to heat a little water in the saucepan. Mr Charrington didn't seem to be able to take anything but water, and that worried her because there was no nourishment in water, but it occurred to her that if she put some sugar in it, that would keep him going.

As he became more restless, it was harder to persuade him to take anything, even the sweetened water from a teaspoon, and it was a relief when he sank into a gasping, open-mouthed sleep. But she knew now that he was ill, very ill, and that she must get help. Even if it meant that the Council knew where she was and dragged her away and put her in a home like old Mrs Briggs, that didn't matter. Nothing mattered in the whole world except Mr Charrington.

His breathing became faster and quieter, and she kept returning to make sure that he *was* still breathing. At last she became so exhausted that she fell asleep by the dying fire.

Next morning, it was bright and sunny, and, although the fire was out when Miss Pollock awoke, it didn't seem quite so cold. She was relieved that Mr Charrington seemed to be sleeping peacefully.

I won't disturb him, she thought. *He'll sleep himself right.*

She tidied up, and wondered if she should light the fire, but there wasn't much wood left and she thought they would need it more at night. She put on her coat and hat and picked up the thermos flask which she had won at the bingo. She had decided to go to the café and have beans on toast, and then she would ask the man to fill the thermos with tea. He could hardly refuse if she had a big meal as well.

At first she planned to leave quietly and wake Mr Charrington with a cup of tea when she returned. But she remembered him saying, 'I kept calling out and you wasn't there,' and she decided to let him know where she was going.

'Mr Charrington!' she called. 'George!'

He didn't answer. She put the thermos down and climbed up the ladder.

'George?'

She put her hand on his shoulder and shook him.

'Wake up, George.'

He didn't move. She could hear his breathing as though it came raspingly from far away and had nothing to do with the unnaturally motionless face – as though he, too, were far away. She stared at him in terror and after a moment she climbed down and stood trembling and helpless. Then she knew that she must do something to help him and that she couldn't do it herself.

She slipped and stumbled over the shingle and up the slope and, gazing desperately round, saw a policeman walking towards her along the front.

Thirty-Nine

Arthur Whitehead was exhausted. Having lied to his wife about not being on early duty the day before, he had not got home until ten o'clock at night, and then he was too tired to sleep. As he lay awake with Joyce breathing quietly beside him – was she awake, too? – he made up his mind. When he got home the next evening, he would tell her that he couldn't bear to have her mother living with them any longer, that she was poisoning their lives. He knew what his wife would say: 'You should have thought of that before you insisted on having her here. I told you not to, but you would have it. I can't turn her out now.'

'You'd rather destroy our marriage.'

He could imagine her hopeless look, and

243

then he would say, 'All right, then. I'm moving out!'

And if that old bitch was anywhere within earshot, which she usually was, she would say, 'Good riddance!'

Lying in bed last night, he had acted this scene out in his head, and now grimly did it again and again as he walked along the promenade, seeing nothing, hearing nothing else. Then out of nowhere came a little old lady who clutched him with tiny, desperate hands, saying, 'Help me! Help me!'

He felt almost dazed for a moment, and then pulled himself together.

'All right, Mother. Calm down. What's the trouble?'

'It's Mr Charrington! He's ill, and I can't ... I can't...'

'Your husband? Where is he?'

She pointed.

'What? On the beach?'

It was startling to see the makeshift shelter, but he didn't really have time to take it in. As soon as he took a couple of steps up the ladder, he could see that the old man was unconscious.

'How long has he been like this?'

She shook her head helplessly.

'I'll have to get him out of here,' he said.

He managed to raise the old chap's shoulders, but soon realised that it was impossible to lift him out of the boat without assistance. Going halfway up the slope, he saw a black man walking towards the shelter.

'Hey, Sambo!' he called. 'Give us a hand here, will you?'

The man hesitated, and then reluctantly came to join him.

'Old man down here in a bad way,' said Arthur.

He saw a look of surprise on the black man's face when he saw the old lady and an odd look on hers, and it flashed across his mind that they knew each other, but at the moment that wasn't important.

'Got to get him down from that boat,' he said.

Miss Pollock felt uneasy at the idea of the black man touching Mr Charrington, but she felt better about it now that she knew his name, and he was so big and so strong that he lifted him down almost by himself, with the policeman just steadying him on the ladder, and he was very gentle as he put Mr Charrington down on the sandy shore and kept his arm under Mr Charrington's head.

'We've got to get him somewhere warm,' said the policeman, 'and call an ambulance.'

'We could take him to the café,' said the black man.

Arthur Whitehead was always astonished at the speed with which the general public gathered round at the first sign of any kind of trouble. He sometimes thought it was an animal instinct for instantly spotting sickness or injury in another member of the herd, especially when they actually attacked the one they had identified as weak or damaged, as if they felt that he endangered the rest of the herd. But the little group which gathered even before he and the black man had carried Mr Charrington to the café was only mildly curious – although there was one rather hard-featured woman dressed like an old-fashioned nanny in a navy-blue coat and navy-blue felt hat who looked as though she would not have been out of place sitting beside the guillotine with her knitting.

Ed saw them carrying the old gentleman across the road like a boxer who'd been KO'd in the ring, and he moved a couple of tables together so that they could lay him down. He glanced instinctively beyond them and, sure enough, there was the old lady trotting along with a bundle of clothes in her arms. He exchanged a glance with the black man, and they both looked at the old man lying there on the tables in his striped pyjamas. The black man took his coat off and rolled it up and put it under the old man's head.

'I'll get a pillow,' said Ed.

'Better ring for an ambulance,' said the policeman, and went to hold the door open for the old lady.

She looked at the old man and tried to disentangle the garments clutched in her arms.

'He ought to have his dressing gown on,' she said.

'It's all right,' said the policeman. 'We'll put his coat over him.'

But she still held out the dressing gown.

'No,' she said. 'No, he...'

Norman knew what she meant. She meant that it wasn't dignified for the old man to lie there in his striped pyjamas with people peering in through the glass door. It wasn't ... respectful. He took the dressing gown from her.

'It's all right, Madam,' he said. 'We'll put it on.'

He saw from the policeman's face that he didn't understand, and as he began to lift the old man's shoulders, he said softly, 'Means a lot to her – a bit of dignity,' and the policeman gave a sort of shrug, but came to help him.

'Ambulance is on its way,' said Ed, returning with a rather grubby pillow and an old grey blanket.

As they tried to make him more comfortable, the old man partially recovered consciousness.

'What...? What...?'

'All right, old chap,' said the policeman.

'You just lay there. Ambulance'll be here in a minute.'

'No. No, I...'

He seemed to be looking round for something.

'Don't worry,' said the policeman. 'We'll have you in hospital in no time.'

He turned to the old lady and took out his notebook.

'You said the name was Charrington. First name?'

She seemed to hesitate, as though that was being rather intrusive.

'George.'

'Address?'

'I think they was camping on the beach,' said Ed.

'I know,' replied the policeman, grimly, 'but they must have been living somewhere else before that.' He returned his gaze to the old lady. 'Address?'

She folded her lips obstinately.

'Now, come along, Madam,' he said, and his 'Madam' had a note of official warning in it, very different from the gentle and respectful 'Madam' of the black man. 'What was your last address?'

'Number six, Hampton Row.'

She said it with a scowl, like a mutinous child, and he was just writing it down when the ambulance arrived outside with that wailing siren which, like the old air-raid warning, always has a momentary, heart-stopping effect.

'Ambulance is here!' called Ed from the door.

Arthur Whitehead hastily put his notebook away. The ambulance men took over with an impersonal and efficient kindness. The small group of bystanders had grown larger by the time they took Mr Charrington out, strapped in a carrying chair, accompanied by the policeman. Ed and Norman followed, and Miss Pollock lingered just outside the doorway. As the ambulance doors were opened, Mr Charrington realised what was happening.

'No!' he gasped. 'No, not without ... No, she ... I must...!'

'All right, Gran'pa,' said the ambulance man, cheerily. 'Up we go!'

They lifted the chair in, and the policeman followed. Miss Pollock took a few steps forward, trying to catch her last sight of Mr Charrington, unaware of the large lady in navy blue who now stood beside her.

Mrs Harrison always came out to buy the newspaper in the morning. Her excuse was that her husband was still slummoxing about in his slippers and cardigan, but the truth was that in the old days she had lived through the happenings and emotions of the family she had worked for, and so she still found her chief interest in the events of other people's lives, and, walking about Brightlesea, she kept a beady eye on what was going on around her. She saw the look on the old lady's face and recognised it as the look which must have been on her own face several years before when her husband was taken away with appendicitis and she had realised that, in spite of everything, she loved him and didn't want to lose him.

'Don't you want to go with your husband?' she demanded.

The old lady stared back at her speechlessly. Mrs Harrison saw that the ambulance doors were about to be closed.

'Just a minute!' she called, in that voice which had been guaranteed to stop a recalcitrant child at fifty paces.

The ambulance man paused. Mrs Harrison's firm but kindly hand propelled Miss Pollock forward.

'The gentleman's wife wants to go with him.'

Everything which had happened since she saw the policeman on the front had been so strange, as though it had nothing to do with her, that Miss Pollock, moving towards the ambulance, still felt that it was all a frightening dream. She was helped up by the ambulance man, and the policeman sat her down on a bench. Mr Charrington, strapped under a red blanket, was still breathing with that worrying grating noise and his eyes were shut. Hesitating, afraid of doing the wrong thing, she took hold of his hand. He opened his eyes and smiled at her, and she took a deep breath and smiled back. He was still there. They were still together.

Preparing to leave, Mrs Harrison paused, seeing a young man hurrying along and breaking into a run when he saw the ambulance pulling away.

'Damn!' said the young man.

Forty

Julian Brown had gone to the office of the *Brightlesea Gazette* early that morning with his article on the Pavilion Hotel. The editor liked features to be delivered well before the weekend, and it was already a day later than it should have been.

The telephone rang as the editor was glancing through his article.

'Not exactly inspired, were you?' he remarked.

Julian kept quiet. The editor always knew when he hadn't done his best with a story and, although he never tore a strip off him, he always let him know it, too. He put the typescript down and lifted the telephone.

'Yes, Bob? Where? Do you know what it is?

Right. Thanks for letting me know.'

He put the phone down.

'Bob Hastings says there's something going on along the front, near Ed's Café.'

'An accident?'

'Don't know. "Something odd," he said. Nip along and see if there's a story.'

'Right.'

But Julian lingered, his eyes on the Pavilion Hotel piece on the desk.

'Do you want me to...?'

He might tell himself that this was just a man who had lost all ambition and settled for being editor of a potty seaside newspaper, but his dispassionate recognition of slipshod work still made Julian feel uneasy.

'No, I'll do something with it. Hurry up, or you'll miss ... whatever it is. Oh,' he called after Julian, 'let me know if there's a picture in it and I'll get Pete along.'

He'd missed the ambulance, but he knew that it would be going to Brightlesea Hospital, and at least some of the bystanders were still there.

'Can anyone tell me what happened here?' he asked.

'Old gentleman taken ill.'

'Oh,' said Julian.

That was that, then. Another boring little incident of interest only to the old man concerned, and possibly his relatives. Still, he'd

252

better get the details. Through the open café door, he saw the tables pushed together and the pillow and blanket, and he recognised the café owner.

'Hullo, Ed,' he said. 'Taken ill in your café, was he? Must've been those baked beans.'

'He was not! He was taken ill on the beach.'

A large lady in a navy-blue coat and hat had been gazing after the ambulance as though she had a special interest in it, but now turned back.

'This gentleman helped the policeman to carry him over here.'

Julian identified her as one of those bystanders who always knows what's going on and doesn't hesitate to say so. Gratified, he observed that the Good Samaritan was black. At least that would give a touch of originality to the story. He took out his notebook.

'Could I have your name? *Brightlesea Gazette*.'

Norman gave it with a hint of reluctance. He had learned not to draw attention to himself.

Julian turned to the large lady.

'And your name is...?'

'Oh ... I really don't know ... I just happened to...' she started, but concluded, 'Mrs Harrison, Crestview,' and eyed his notebook as he wrote it down.

The other bystanders, realising that the action was over, were drifting away, but she stayed.

'Do you happen to know who the gentleman was?'

She shook her head.

'I'd never seen him before.'

But there was something in her tone which made Julian think she was holding something back, as though she'd been about to say something else.

'Ed? You don't know his name?'

Ed scratched his head.

'Well, I did hear it, but ... What was it? Charrington. That was it. George Charrington.' And, as Julian wrote it down, he added, 'I reckon they was sleeping rough on the beach.'

'*They*?'

'Him and his old lady.'

'Really?'

Suddenly Julian knew that there was a story here after all. A small one, perhaps, but still a story with something odd about it.

'Are you sure?' he said.

'They used to come here for breakfast. And supper. Even asked me to fill their hot-water bottle.'

'*What*?' exclaimed Julian, and laughed heartily.

Ed, remembering the purple knitted cover and the stricken but determined look on the old lady's face, managed an uneasy smile.

'You don't know where they came from? London?'

'No idea. The old lady gave an address to the copper.'

'You don't remember what it was?'

Julian was beginning to feel like a television detective.

'Nah,' said Ed.

'Hampton Row,' said Norman, unexpectedly. 'Number six, Hampton Row.'

'That's not far from my house!' exclaimed Mrs Harrison.

'Well, if they have a house there, why were they sleeping on the beach?' said Julian.

'Done a moonlight flit, most like,' observed Mrs Harrison, who had had her share of boarders creaking down the stairs with their suitcases. But then ... 'Hampton Row. Weren't those the houses they were going to pull down?'

'Oh, yes,' said Julian. 'I remember. The Council bought the property to demolish it and then couldn't decide what to do with it.'

(He couldn't know that it was another of Mr Harper's brainwaves, conceived after a couple of pink gins, which had not been entirely thought through.)

'So that was why—' began Mrs Harrison, and then stopped short.

Julian looked at her enquiringly.

'She came to my house a few days ago,'

255

said Mrs Harrison, reluctantly. 'If the Council had evicted them, that was why ... She was looking for somewhere to stay.'

'For her and her husband?'

Mrs Harrison thought back.

'She didn't say so. I thought it was just for one. I had to tell her I don't do boarders – only bed and breakfast. And, anyway, the season's over.' She spoke as though challenging Julian to contradict her, and then added hastily, 'I must go. My husband will be wondering what's happened to me.'

'You going to write about this?' enquired Ed.

Julian was still looking after Mrs Harrison as she walked quickly away, as though trying to escape.

'I might,' he said. 'Can I use your telephone?'

' 'Long as you mention the café.'

'We might even use a picture of it.'

As they prepared to go inside, Ed saw Norman moving off.

'Want to come in for a cup of tea, Norm?' he called.

Norman hesitated.

'Might throw in a bit of toast,' said Ed.

Norman suddenly realised that this was Ed's way of apologising for not standing up for him with the bikers – and it occurred to him that Ed might be short of friends, too.

Besides, instead of breakfast at the café

that morning, he had had a weak, cold cup of tea with a stale roll at the kiosk along the way, and had been overcharged. He nodded and turned back.

By the time he followed Ed inside, Julian was already heading for the telephone at the end of the counter.

'Right,' said the editor. 'I'll get Pete along at once.' And then, pensively, he added, 'Hampton Row. It might be worth having a word with the Council Housing people.'

Forty-One

When the ambulance arrived at Brightlesea General Hospital, Arthur Whitehead descended first, and watched as the ambulance men rushed Mr Charrington inside. He knew that there had been several moments during the journey when it was touch-and-go whether he would make it.

Looking back, he saw the old lady trying to get out of the ambulance. The step down was really too big for her with nothing to hold on to, but she wasn't looking around for help, just trying to work out how she could get her foot, in its lisle stocking and shabby shoe, down on to the step. She was game, he thought, which in a way you could say about his mother-in-law – always determined, never giving in, and yet ... and yet not really able to manage on her own.

'Just a minute!' he said. 'Let me give you a hand.'

She opened her mouth and then shut it again, and he thought that she wanted to say, 'I can manage on my own!' but then knew that she couldn't. He held up his hands, but she was clutching her handbag in both of her hands, and in the end he lifted her down like a child. She looked up into his face and he knew that she wanted to say thank you, but she couldn't, because she didn't want to admit that she needed help. She was still clutching her handbag, and he remembered his mother-in-law continually exclaiming, 'Where's my handbag? Who's got my handbag?' and thought that to an old lady her handbag was like a comfort blanket to a child, something to give assurance of safety and continuity, and also that with its diary, family photographs, money and pension book, it identified a person, that same person who had once been strong and independent, someone with a place in the world.

'All right?' he said.

She nodded, and then turned her face, as though drawn by a magnet, towards the entrance to the hospital through which Mr Charrington had just been carried.

Miss Pollock followed the policeman into the hospital and saw him talking to a man in a white coat who she thought must be a doctor. Then he came back to her and said, 'They're taking him straight up to Princess Alice Ward.'

She gazed up at him, uncomprehending. 'Can I...?'

'Yes, you can go up. They'll let you know when you can see him.' He hesitated. 'I'm sure he'll be all right,' he said.

Being in a hospital was like being in a foreign country – or at least how she imagined it would be in a foreign country – with meaningless signs everywhere and people whom she didn't know hurrying about. But she saw a board which had various names on it, including 'Princess Alice Ward, Second Floor'. There was a lift, but she didn't fancy that in case she didn't know how to work it, so she went up the stairs to the second floor, stopping often because she was trembling so much that it was hard to get her breath, and saw large doors with the sign 'Princess Alice Ward'.

Inside, she saw a nurse writing something in a sort of glass office who looked up and said, 'Can I help you?'

'Mr Charrington,' said Miss Pollock.

She was unable to think of anything else to say, but that seemed to be enough.

'Oh yes,' said the nurse. There was an odd

259

look on her face, and for a moment she didn't seem to be able to think what to say. 'Er ... if you would like to wait?'

Miss Pollock saw a wide passage with doors opening off it, and through two big glass doors on the other side she saw men in bed and guessed that was where Mr Charrington was. There was a chair just outside, and she went to sit down on it. The important thing was to be there if he asked for her.

After she had been there for a long time, the nurse came and said, 'Sister would like a word with you, please.'

The sister was a small, sharp-faced woman, sitting in an office with a lot of papers and files. Her navy-blue uniform fitted her as snugly as a one-piece bathing costume, with a watch firmly pinned to it and a very tight belt with a silver buckle. On her head was a white cap folded like the sails of a ship, as though it might take off at any minute. Miss Pollock had never seen anything like it. She was glad that she had her best hat on.

'Come in, Mrs Charrington. I am Sister Payne, the ward sister. We have managed to make Mr Charrington comfortable, but he is quite ill.'

She drew a sheet of paper towards her and picked up a pen.

'Now,' she said, 'if you would give me a few more details.'

Miss Pollock felt alarmed. She didn't know

anything about illness. She wasn't even sure that Mr Charrington had bronchitis, except that it seemed the same as what her father had had, until the last time when the doctor said that it had turned to pneumonia and he died, but she didn't want to think about that.

'Name, Charrington,' said the sister. 'First name, George.'

Miss Pollock nodded, relieved.

'Address, Number Six, Hampton Row.'

Miss Pollock said nothing.

The sister looked up at her.

'Is that right?'

'Yes.'

Remembering that she had given the address to the policeman, Miss Pollock decided that there was nothing else to do but to agree, even if it wasn't Mr Charrington's address, and wasn't even hers now.

'Age?'

Miss Pollock looked blank.

'How old is he?' enquired the sister, impatiently. 'Come along, surely you know your husband's age?'

'I ... I can't remember,' said Miss Pollock.

It was a bit of a fib, because she had no idea how old he was, but she was afraid that if she said he wasn't her husband, they wouldn't let her stay with him. The sister shook her head and said, 'Oh, really!' just as Miss Pollock's arithmetic teacher used to when she couldn't remember whether

261

subtraction was taking away or dividing. Sister Payne put the top back on the pen, glanced towards the ward and nodded to the nurse who stood beside her.

'Very well, Nurse,' she said, resignedly.

It felt rather peculiar and unpleasant to be in a room full of strange men all in bed, but Miss Pollock followed the nurse through the two rows of beds and saw Mr Charrington at the far end, lying propped right up with pillows, his eyes closed.

'Is he asleep?' she asked.

The nurse hesitated.

'He comes and goes,' she said.

She tucked the bedclothes in even more tightly than they were already, and moved away.

Miss Pollock sat down beside the bed. Mr Charrington looked very white and clean, and he was propped up against big, white pillows. Even his hands on the blue knitted blanket looked white and clean. It would be nice, thought Miss Pollock, if he woke up, but she didn't really mind. The important thing was that he was in a place where they knew how to look after him properly, where he would get better. Still, she was glad when the nurse came to take his pulse, and he opened his eyes.

'Where ... where is she?'

'It's all right, Mr Charrington,' said the nurse. 'Your wife's here.'

He frowned, and Miss Pollock was afraid that he was going to say, 'My wife's dead,' but luckily the nurse put a thermometer in his mouth and took hold of his wrist, and he closed his eyes again. When the nurse had finished and written something down on the board at the end of his bed and moved on, Miss Pollock drew the chair nearer and touched his arm. He opened his eyes.

'They think I'm your wife,' she whispered.

'Eh?'

She had forgotten that he was deaf. The nurse was taking the pulse of the man in the next bed, so she leaned close.

'They think I'm your wife,' she whispered again, and then, as the nurse moved on, she added, 'I never said I wasn't, or they might not have let me stay.'

She couldn't help laughing a little, and he smiled at her.

'Don't you go nowhere,' he said.

She saw that he was drifting away again, and took his hand so as to have something to hold on to while he was gone.

When the nurses brought the lunch in, one of them put a tray down on the table across his bed and roused him.

'Come along, Mr Charrington,' she said. 'You ought to have something to eat – build your strength up.'

He had a bite or two, and then pushed the

263

plate towards Miss Pollock.

'You have a bit,' he said. 'I can't seem to fancy it.'

'Ooh, I couldn't!' she said.

'Go on,' he said. 'It'll only go to waste.'

So, after a nervous look round, she did eat some of his white fish and mashed potato and cabbage, and then shared a bowl of blancmange with him, although she felt rather guilty when the nurse came to take the tray away and said, 'Well done, Mr Charrington.' What's more, when they brought him a cup of tea, they brought one for her, too.

'This ain't bad, is it?' said Mr Charrington. 'At this rate, we shan't want to go home.'

It occurred to Miss Pollock that they hadn't actually got a home to go to, except for their little place on the beach – and that might not be safe any more, now that the policeman had seen it – but she said, 'I'm glad I done right.'

'You always do right,' he said.

To hear him say that gave Miss Pollock the strangest feeling, especially when he looked at her with that smile which she felt was hers and no one else's. She took his hand and felt it close on hers.

Miss Pollock had said that she never had an afternoon nap, but she did nod off in the chair that afternoon. When she woke up, she realised that she needed to go to the toilet. Luckily, when she had been waiting earlier, she had seen where it was, and had gone there, although it wasn't nearly as nice as their own public toilets with the flowers outside. As she went out of the ward, the sister said, 'Are you going home for a little while, Mrs Charrington?'

'Oh ... no,' replied Miss Pollock. 'I thought I'd stay for a bit longer.'

'I'm afraid you won't be able to stay after visiting hours,' said the sister, sharply, but Miss Pollock kept moving and pretended that she hadn't heard.

As she was returning, she saw the nurse speaking on a telephone on the wall at the end of the corridor and a man in pyjamas and dressing gown coming out of the ward. Everything was very calm and peaceful. Then a bell rang, and everything changed. The nurse dropped the telephone receiver and left it dangling. A doctor in a white coat came from nowhere, and he and the nurse ran towards the ward. Through the glass door Miss Pollock saw the sister on her feet and running.

'Hullo,' said the man in the dressing gown. 'Someone's in trouble.'

'What?'

'Heart failure, most like,' he said.

She was suddenly sure that it was Mr Charrington, and began to move towards the

265

ward, but the man put a hand out to stop her.

'I shouldn't, love,' he said. 'They won't want you in there now.'

Miss Pollock didn't know how long she sat on the chair in the corridor. Her heart was beating as though she had been running. She saw doctors and nurses hurrying about, and machinery being wheeled into the ward, but it was as though she was shut up inside herself – just herself holding Mr Charrington, not the old gentleman in the hospital bed, but the Mr Charrington she knew, and loved.

She had crept to the door and seen the curtains drawn round his bed, so she knew that it was his life which they were trying to save. She felt that she ought to pray, but she hadn't really prayed since Sunday school when she had been taught to put her hands together and say, 'Pray God bless dear Mummy and Daddy and Granny and Grandpa and my brothers and sisters and friends and relations and pray God bless me and make me a good little girl amen,' but that didn't seem quite suitable. As a matter of fact, it never had been, which was probably why she had never really prayed after she became too old for Sunday school. Of course, she had gone to church, but that wasn't praying. She thought of the Lord's

Prayer, but that began, 'Our Father which art in Heaven,' and she didn't want him to be in Heaven. She wanted him down here, helping Mr Charrington. In the end, she just sat clutching her handbag and whispered, 'Please, God. Please, God,' over and over again.

It was the sister who came and stood beside her.

'You can go in now, Mrs Charrington,' she said.

As Miss Pollock followed her into the ward, she looked towards the far bed, but the man lying in it was a stranger.

'We've moved him to a bed near the door,' said the sister, 'where we can keep an eye on him.'

Miss Pollock saw, dismayed, that Mr Charrington had something which looked like a glass mask over his face, and that there was an iron cylinder on wheels beside the bed. She sat down, afraid to touch him, afraid of doing the wrong thing, feeling that the hospital had taken him over. But after a little while he opened his eyes and turned his head slightly so that he could see her. He pulled the mask off.

'There you are,' he said. 'I thought you'd gone.'

He moved his hand, and she knew what he wanted and took hold of it. She remembered what he had said.

'I ain't going nowhere,' she said, stoutly.

He smiled at her, and she smiled back.

'Now, Mr Charrington,' said Sister Payne, 'you must keep that oxygen mask on, or I shall have to ask your wife to leave.'

She came to put it on, adjusting the elastic behind his head, and then went away. Mr Charrington winked at Miss Pollock above the mask, and his hand closed on hers.

Forty-Two

Taking photographs for the *Brightlesea Gazette* was not Pete's sole or even his primary work. Wedding groups, winsome children, lifeboat crews, Rotary members, gold-watched businessmen, and wrecked cars from fatal road accidents were all observed through his viewfinder with the same dispassionate professionalism, and, it appeared, forgotten as soon as he had packed up his gear and departed, as though they had no life outside his camera except for the carefully but unemotionally selected glossy prints subsequently appearing in the paper or put on display in the window of his shop.

'I thought we could have a picture of Ed

outside the café,' suggested Julian, 'with the door open so that we can see the tables inside.'

'Mm,' said Pete. *Better to be either inside or out*, he thought.

'And this is Norman Taylor. He carried him here from the beach.'

Pete nodded, eyeing Norman's black face dubiously. He really needed special lighting for that. Always a danger of overexposure.

'Want to take him on the beach?'

'Oh, that's a good idea!' said Julian. He always tried to flatter Pete into some kind of friendly relationship, and it never worked. He turned to Norman. 'Can you show me where you picked the old man up?'

Norman hesitated.

'Well, I...'

'One bit of beach looks much like another,' Ed intervened hastily. 'Much better take it outside the café.'

'We'll take a couple here,' replied Julian, remembering that he wanted to make some more telephone calls, 'and then go down to the beach.'

As he led the way past the shelter and down the slope, Norman still hoped to keep the secret of the little house.

'He was collapsed on the beach, was he?' said Julian. 'Where exactly was that?'

'Well...'

But Pete was wandering about. Ed was

right. One bit of beach did look just like another.

'Might use a boat as background,' he said.

After that, it was only a matter of time.

Norman felt very uneasy as he watched Pete taking flash photographs of every detail of the absurd little home.

'You're not going to put those pictures in the paper?' he asked, as Julian began to climb up the steps to the boat.

'Of course. Why not?'

'She may come back.'

'What, *here?*'

Julian glanced round, amused. Norman thought of little houses which he had seen back home – tarpaulin shelters, sagging shacks roofed with corrugated iron – and felt a sudden hatred for this young man. Always well fed, well housed – what did he know?

'He's left his jacket here,' said Julian, picking it up. 'This looks like his wallet. I'd better take it to the office.'

'No!' said Norman. He knew that Julian wanted to search through it to find out more and print it in the paper. 'I'll take it.'

'No, it's all right...'

'I'll take it,' said Norman, and took it from him. 'I'll take it to the café. If she comes back and misses it, that's where she'll go.'

'Fine,' said Julian, after a longing look at the jacket now firmly held in Norman's grasp. 'There are some other things here – clothes, a case...'

'I'll take the cases to the café,' said Norman. 'Ed'll look after them.'

'Right,' said Julian, yielding his place on the ladder.

'I'm off, then,' said Pete.

'Oh, just a minute,' said Julian, seeing Norman reaching over the boat. 'Can you get a picture of Norman up there? Lean over, Norman, as if you're lifting him up.'

'No!' said Norman, and instinctively put a hand up to shield himself from the camera. 'No, don't take that! I don't want it.'

Pete lowered his camera and shrugged, but as he walked out with Julian, he said quietly, 'I got a shot of him outside the café.'

'Good,' said Julian, and suddenly had to share his growing surge of excitement, even if it was only with Pete. 'It's a great story. We'll get a two-page spread out of this.'

'I dare say,' said Pete, and yawned. 'See you.'

He crunched away up the beach, as Norman emerged carrying the suitcase and holdall and glanced back at the little house.

'If you print those pictures,' he said, 'everyone will come poking around here, taking their things.'

'Don't worry,' answered Julian. 'The paper doesn't come out till Tuesday. I'm just going to ring the Council. They'll sort it out.'

Forty-Three

Mr Harper always left for lunch early on Fridays. It was as though he had run out of energy – or perhaps it was courage. Towards the end of the week, his in-tray was full of papers, many of which needed decisions. It wasn't so much that he wasn't able to deal with them, but rather that he was tired of keeping up the pretence that he was always sure he was right, and, anyway, didn't give a damn whether he was right or wrong.

'Need to recharge the batteries, eh?' he would say cheerily, as he arranged a game of golf for the afternoon. And, to his secretary, 'I think I'll take that file home. See you Monday.'

So when Julian telephoned the Council Offices and was put through to Mr Harper's office, it was his secretary who answered. Mrs Hamilton had a rather low opinion of Mr Harper, feeling that she could do the job a great deal better herself. However, instead of betraying what she considered to be his inadequacies or undermining his authority, she gratified herself by extending her duties to cover those which, in her opinion, he failed to perform satisfactorily, or which, indeed, he failed to perform at all.

'I'm afraid Mr Harper isn't in the office at the moment,' she said. 'I am his secretary. Can I help you?'

'This is Julian Brown of the *Brightlesea Gazette.*'

'Oh yes?'

Mr Harper would probably have heard a warning bell at that moment, but Mrs Hamilton had never had to deal with the Press and treated all callers alike, eager only to show her own mastery of the workings of the Housing Department.

'I wonder if you could give me some information about the eviction of a Council tenant.'

'Oh yes?'

Never mind warning bells. Alarm bells would have been ringing now.

'If you could give me the name...'

'It's Mr Charrington.'

'I don't think ... No, I mean the name of the property.'

'Oh, right. It's ... er ... just a minute. It's Number Six, Hampton Row.'

'Ah!' exclaimed Mrs Hamilton, triumphantly, remembering the file which she had just stowed safely away after the last meeting. 'Yes, of course. Hampton Row. You need to speak to the Old People's Welfare Department. Miss Waterlow.'

'Right,' said Julian, leaning on the counter in Ed's Café. 'Could you give me the number?'

'Certainly,' responded Mrs Hamilton, delighted to display her efficiency.

'I hope you're going to pay for those calls,' said Ed.

Miss Waterlow wasn't in her office either, but her secretary instantly made it clear that she had no intention of giving him any information.

'When do you expect her back?'

'I'm afraid I can't say,' replied Mrs Price, in a tone reminiscent of Mrs Micawber declaring that she would never, never desert Mr Micawber. 'But if you would care to give me a message for her, I will make sure that she receives it.'

'Thanks very much,' said Julian, with ferocious irony. 'Perhaps you would tell her that it relates to aged Council tenants who have been made homeless. Perhaps you would *care* to ask her to call me at the *Brightlesea Gazette* as soon as possible.'

'I will give her your message when she returns,' said Mrs Price, frostily.

If Mrs Price had not been so busy being defensive, she might have realised that it would have been a better idea to disclose that Miss Waterlow had left the office to attend the funeral of one of her clients. The old lady who had been so painfully ejected from the Pavilion Hotel – formerly Bayview – and whose increasing infirmity and incontinence had caused such difficulties at Pinelea Old People's Home, had solved all their problems by dying, quietly and all alone, having no living relatives and no one to care what became of her except the distressed but despairing staff at Pinelea and Miss Waterlow herself.

The funeral had taken place very quickly. There was no doubt about the cause of death, which was old age and heart failure, and there were no relatives to be informed or invited to attend. Tears were shed by the lumpish, ignorant, kind-hearted girls who had cared for her to the end, but Miss Waterlow was dry-eyed. She felt that she had failed – but how, and what more could she have done?

'Hullo, darling!' cried her mother, delightedly. 'You're home early. I'm so glad. There's a lovely film on television tonight. Trevor Howard.'

Julian put a generous two bob down on the counter for the phone calls.

'That should cover it,' he said.

He was delighted that Miss Waterlow had not been in her office. If the Council Housing Department and the Old People's Welfare were unavailable, his story would have an extra, immensely popular element of heartless bureaucracy.

Quietly satisfied, Julian went off to his lodgings to write the article.

Forty-Four

After all the excitement of the past week, Miss Pollock found the ward nice and peaceful. Some of the men in the other beds had headphones on, and she worked out that they were listening to the radio, especially when she saw one man beating time to the music. Now and then, one of them would call 'Nurse!' and the nurse would get up from behind the desk where she sat just inside the door and go to him. They came to check on Mr Charrington quite often, and sometimes they would draw the curtains round his bed and ask her to wait outside. Once she heard the sister say to a doctor, 'He's holding his own,' and Miss Pollock thought that was good. It did occur to her to wonder what would happen if he didn't hold his own, but she decided not to think about that.

It was quite a shock when strange people started to stream into the ward. She looked at them, puzzled, and frowned, as though they were invading her territory, and, glancing instinctively back at Mr Charrington, found that his eyes were open. He briefly pulled the mask off to say, 'Visiting time.' 'Oh,' said Miss Pollock, without really knowing what that meant, and it was a surprise when the nurse came to her and said, 'There's someone here to see you, Mrs Charrington.' She made sure that Mr Charrington had closed his eyes again before she went outside.

She was even more surprised to see the black man.

'Oh, Mr Sambo!' she said.

He hesitated.

'That ... that isn't really my name, Madam,' he said.

'Oh. I thought the policeman...'

'It was a joke.'

(Here Norman was mistaken. Arthur Whitehead had called him 'Sambo' just as he would call a Scotsman 'Jock' or an Irishman 'Mick' or a red-headed man 'Ginger', because if you didn't know his name it was more polite than saying, 'Here, you!')

Norman saw the old lady's puzzled look and added, 'My name is Taylor, Norman Taylor.'

He was unprepared for the smile of pure pleasure which lit up her face.

'*Taylor?*' she repeated. 'Well, I never! That was my uncle's name. Uncle Alfie. His name was Alfred Taylor. Well, I never!'

Norman found himself smiling back.

'I don't think we're related,' he said.

'We might be,' she protested, and then saw the twinkle in his eyes, just like Mr Charrington's.

'Oh!' she said, and clicked her teeth.

Norman realised that it was the first time since he came to England that he had made a joke to someone about his being black.

'I came to see the old gentleman,' he said, 'but they say he's not well enough for visitors. How is he?'

Miss Pollock paused to think. She really didn't know how he was. At last she said, carefully, 'He's holding his own.'

'That's good!' exclaimed Norman, heartily.

Miss Pollock was delighted. That was what *she* thought.

Norman reached into his pocket.

'I wanted to tell him that we found his jacket,' he said, 'and I thought he might need these.'

He produced Mr Charrington's wallet and pension book. Miss Pollock received them rather doubtfully.

'I took the jacket to Ed's Café,' said Norman, 'and the two cases. He'll keep them safe until you go back.'

Miss Pollock nearly told him that she didn't think she could ever go back, because if she did the Council might catch her, but she was afraid that would make her sound like a criminal, so she just nodded. She was very relieved to know about the cases with all their clothes in them, and rather hoped he'd put her vests in as well. She wanted to say thank you, but she wasn't very good at that, and even scowled a little instead, but he seemed to understand, and smiled at her very kindly.

'I'd better be going,' he said, and added, 'Ed sends his best.'

'Ed?'

'From the café.'

'Oh yes.'

He turned to go but then paused.

'There was a man from the newspaper asking questions,' he said. 'The *Brightlesea Gazette*.'

'Oh?'

'He said his name was Julian Brown.'

'Oh,' said Miss Pollock, pleased. 'I like him.'

Norman took a moment before replying.

'That's good,' he said. 'I hope the old gentleman's better soon. Well, goodbye.'

'Goodbye, Mr Taylor,' said Miss Pollock, and watched him walk along the corridor until he was out of sight.

She hoped he would come again soon. It was almost like having a visit from Uncle Alfie.

Forty-Five

Julian actually felt nervous when he gave the editor his article and spread the photographs out on the desk. The trouble was, he cared too much about it, feeling that it was the best thing he had ever written, the first real piece of journalism instead of just local tittle-tattle.

'Mm,' said the editor. 'I like the headline.'

Julian drew a deep breath of satisfaction. His eyes followed the words as the editor silently read them: 'Old Couple on Heartbreak Beach – Mr and Mrs Charrington, evicted by Brightlesea Council from their home in Hampton Row...'

The editor looked up.

'Have you talked to the Council Housing people?'

'I rang them before lunch yesterday, and they'd all gone home for the weekend.'

'Had they, indeed?' said the editor, and allowed himself a rare grin.

He read on to the end.

'No interview with the old couple,' he said.

'No,' answered Julian. 'The ambulance had just left. I went to the hospital, but they said the old man was too ill, and the wife was with him.'

'Mm,' said the editor again, but this time with a note of undisguised enthusiasm. He looked up at Julian with the wolfish smile of a journalist happy in the face of disaster. 'If he dies, that really *will* be a story!'

He moved the photographs about on the desk as if he was playing Pelmanism.

'It's not bad as it is.'

He paused on the set which showed the little beach home.

'We should get some good captions for these. Something about Brightlesea Council's way of housing its old people.'

The telephone rang and he answered it, still looking at the photographs.

'*Brightlesea Gazette* ... Just a minute.' He handed the receiver to Julian. 'Miss Waterlow for you.'

Julian felt another little surge of triumph. The editor might well have followed it up himself, but instead had trusted Julian, treating it as his story.

'Mr Julian Brown?' said a cold female voice.

'Speaking.'

'This is Miss Waterlow, Old People's Welfare Department. I found your message when I came into my office this morning. Something about Council tenants?'

'Mr and Mrs Charrington,' said Julian.

'Evicted by the Council. Made homeless. Were sleeping on the beach. And he is now critically ill in Brightlesea Hospital.'

He could hear the silence at the other end of the telephone, and winked at the editor, who grinned appreciatively.

'What was the name again?'

'Charrington. Like the beer.' The editor shook his head at him, and Julian continued quickly, 'I've spoken to the Housing Department, and they confirmed that the Council house from which they were evicted was Number Six, Hampton Row.'

The voice at the other end sharpened.

'Hampton Row? Did you say you spoke to Mr Harper at the Housing Department?'

'No,' replied Julian. 'He'd gone home for the weekend. I spoke to his secretary, who—'

'Oh, well, that explains it!' broke in Miss Waterlow, with a note of triumph. 'Mr Harper, or his deputy, Mr Simmonds, could have told you that Mr Charrington was not the tenant of Number Six, Hampton Row.'

Julian's mouth fell open in dismay, and he saw a look of mild enquiry on the editor's face.

'So, who was?'

'I'm afraid I can't tell you that.'

'You mean you don't know?'

'I mean it really is none of your business.'

'Presumably it is *your* business if an elderly

couple is homeless, and he is now danger-ously ill in hospital.'

'Yes, certainly, and I will look into it, but all I can tell you at the moment is that they were not living at Number Six, Hampton Row.'

Julian began to feel increasingly desperate. If they had *not* been evicted by the Council, the sharp edge of the story would be lost.

'Perhaps we could meet and talk about it,' he said.

'I shall be in my office on Monday,' said Miss Waterlow, briskly, and rang off.

Julian looked at the editor.

'She says the Charringtons were not living at Hampton Row.'

'So why did they say they were?'

Julian shrugged helplessly.

'It'd be worth looking for Charrington in the Electoral Register,' said the editor, suddenly. 'You probably won't be able to get hold of it until Monday, but if you can find their address, then you can get back to the Housing people and see if they were evicted, too.'

He began to put the photographs together.

'Don't be too depressed,' he said. 'It's still a good story. You may be able to talk to them on Monday – talk to her, anyway, and get a picture with any luck.'

'Ye-es,' said Julian. 'And I think this after-noon I might go to Hampton Row – see if I can pick anything up there.'

283

★ ★ ★

Miss Waterlow had come in to her office that morning to clear up the final formalities after the death of the old lady in Pinelea, and her mother had not been best pleased. She almost seemed to feel jealous of Miss Waterlow's elderly clients, and would be getting impatient. She and her daughter always did their shopping on Saturday morning, and then they would have lunch at the Wooden Spoon before going to a matinee at the Odeon.

In spite of her cool tone to Julian Brown, she did feel some concern. Was it possible that it was Miss Pollock who was in hospital? She almost left it until Monday, but she didn't want to have that niggling worry at the back of her mind over the weekend. The almoner, a conscientious woman, often went to the hospital on Saturday.

'One phone call,' said Miss Waterlow, aloud, as though to pacify her mother.

Forty-Six

By Saturday morning, it was as though the life of the hospital, at first so strange, had closed round Miss Pollock. The routine of the ward became her routine. She even gave a hand with the bed-making now and then.

She had taken her coat off, and one of the nurses had hung it up for her in their sitting room. Of course she had kept her hat on, as you did in someone else's house, but there were times when that space with the bed and the locker and her chair and the curtains which could be drawn round it did feel like a little home, hers and Mr Charrington's.

After the visitors had all left on the evening before, a very tall, upright lady in a navy-blue dress came and walked round the ward with the sister and a nurse.

'Who is that?' she demanded, when she saw Miss Pollock.

'Mr Charrington's wife,' replied Sister Payne, and then, dropping her voice, 'Open order, Matron.'

'I see,' replied the matron, severely. 'Tidy that bed.'

'Nurse,' said the sister, and the nurse

smoothed the bedcover where Miss Pollock had leaned on it to take hold of Mr Charrington's hand.

When the matron had left and supper was being brought round, one of the nurses, who had an Irish accent, took Miss Pollock into the small sitting room, where there was a tray on the table.

'I thought you might like a bite to eat,' she said.

'You'll be in trouble, O' Neill, if Sister sees you!' said another nurse, who was looking in a mirror as she tucked her hair severely behind her cap.

'Ah, sure, it'd only go to waste!'

'I don't want to get you into no trouble,' said Miss Pollock, nervously, feeling that Sister was almost as frightening as Matron.

'Don't you be worrying yourself, Mrs Charrington,' said Nurse O' Neill, cheerfully. 'Sister never comes in here. You sit down and enjoy it. You have to keep your strength up.'

Miss Pollock was a bit worried later when she saw the sister look in through the round glass window in the door, but she didn't say anything, just went away. It was lucky, thought Miss Pollock, that Sister Payne hadn't noticed her sitting at the table eating her meal. And she didn't say anything, either, when she was back in the ward and the other nurse gave her a nice cup of tea.

She was upset when Nurse O' Neill came to her and said that she was going off duty.

'Don't worry, Mrs Charrington,' she said, seeing Miss Pollock's dismay. 'The night staff will look after him. And I'll be saying a prayer for the both of you.'

Miss Pollock didn't quite know what to say. Nurse O' Neill was Irish, and that probably meant that she was a Catholic. Miss Pollock's father always used to say that he didn't like Catholics because they wanted the Pope to rule the country. Miss Pollock wasn't quite sure who the Pope was, and she felt rather disloyal to her father in thinking that she didn't really care, anyway.

'Will you be here tomorrow?' she asked.

'I certainly will,' replied Nurse O' Neill. 'Now, you get some sleep tonight, and I'll see you in the morning.'

It was a comfort to Miss Pollock to find that after all the lights were put out in the ward, there was still a shaded light on the table inside the door, and that either a nurse or the night sister sat there all night, answering faint calls from the restless men and coming often to check on Mr Charrington. She knew that he was very ill. It seemed a long time since he had opened his eyes and smiled at her, although when she took his hand and pressed it, she thought she felt a little tightening of his fingers in return.

287

The night nurse insisted that Miss Pollock should go and have a sleep in the nurses' sitting room. She didn't want to leave him, but they promised to call her if there was any change. A nurse put two armchairs together and persuaded her to take her hat off, and even brought a pillow and put a blanket over her. After a while, she fell into a deep sleep, and awoke with a start to find that it was daylight. As she came out of the sitting room, a young doctor was speaking to the night nurse, looking at the papers he had in his hand.

'How is he?' he asked.

'Still with us,' answered the night nurse, and gave a funny sort of smile and shook her head.

'It's only a matter of time,' said the young doctor.

'Oh, Mrs Charrington!' exclaimed the night nurse, hastily. 'I hope you had a nice sleep. Your husband is still holding his own.'

It seemed to Miss Pollock that Mr Charrington was a little better. He opened his eyes and said, 'There you are.' When Nurse O' Neill came on duty, she managed to persuade him to take a little porridge for breakfast and a whole cup of tea. He did have one bad turn when someone had taken the oxygen cylinder away for another man, but Miss Pollock called, 'Nurse! Nurse!' and they came running to bring it back again.

She was surprised at herself afterwards, but at the time she did it without thinking, only knowing that nothing and no one mattered to her as long as he was all right.

It was in the afternoon, when the ward was quiet, that a nurse came to say that the almoner would like to see her. Miss Pollock was rather pleased. She knew that the almoner made sure that patients and their families had somewhere to live and someone to look after them when they left the hospital. Perhaps she had found a place for Mr Charrington.

The almoner was a middle-aged woman, very plainly dressed in a tweed skirt and an ugly, coffee-coloured blouse, and she had straight, salt-and-pepper hair. She was standing by the office talking to Sister Payne as Miss Pollock came out of the ward, and she didn't waste any time in, as Miss Pollock's mother would have remarked, 'how are you, how's your father?'

'Ah,' she said. 'Sister tells me that you came in the ambulance with Mr Charrington, who was admitted yesterday. That is his name? Mr George Charrington?'

Miss Pollock didn't much like the way she spoke to her, but that certainly was his name, so she nodded.

'And you gave his address as Number Six, Hampton Row. That is not correct, is it?'

A mulish look descended on Miss Pollock's

face. The almoner glanced at Sister Payne.

'Do you know his proper address?'

He was living with his son and his daughter-in-law and they weren't a bit nice to him, and if he never sees them again it will be too soon, and I don't know the address, and if I did, I wouldn't tell you. She didn't say that, but as she closed her mouth tightly, the almoner seemed to understand at least the last part, because she glanced at the sister again and then spoke very sternly.

'Are you Miss Pollock?' she enquired.

They had caught her, thought Miss Pollock, but there was nothing she could do about it, so the less said the better. She nodded.

'I expect you would like Miss Waterlow of the Welfare Department to get in touch with you,' suggested the almoner.

'No,' said Miss Pollock. 'I wouldn't.'

And she turned to go back inside the ward.

'Miss Pollock!' called the almoner, but she pretended not to hear.

'She's rather deaf,' she heard Sister Payne say, and couldn't help smiling to herself.

'You look cheerful,' remarked Mr Charrington.

'It's being so cheerful as keeps me going,' said Miss Pollock.

It was something they used to say on the wireless, somebody's catchphrase, and it had always made her mother laugh. She was glad to see that it made Mr Charrington smile. She didn't want him to know that, as she sat down, cold terror was creeping up inside her. He didn't smile for long, and she was afraid he was going to close his eyes and drift away. She wasn't sure how long it would be before they came and took her away, and she wanted him to stay with her as long as possible.

People began to come into the ward and she said, quite loudly, 'They're early!'

'They let them in early on Saturdays,' he replied.

They hadn't expected to have any visitors, so it was quite a surprise when the large lady in the navy-blue coat and hat trod firmly in, looked round the ward and stopped by Mr Charrington's bed.

'Good afternoon,' she said.

Miss Pollock saw Mr Charrington's frown and realised that he wouldn't know who she was. It was funny to find herself introducing them, just as if she was in her own house.

'This is the lady that made them bring me in the ambulance,' she said, and to her, 'This is Mr Charrington.'

'I'm Mrs Harrison,' said the lady, as though that explained everything.

'Pleased to meet you,' said Mr Charrington, but his voice was very faint.

Seeing that the man in the next bed didn't

have any visitors, Mrs Harrison said a polite, 'Excuse me,' turned the chair round and firmly sat down.

'I just came to see how you were,' she said to Mr Charrington.

She saw that he was slipping out of awareness, and her eyes met Miss Pollock's, as though her enquiry was for both of them. She had a handbag so large that it was more like the black bag the doctor used to bring on house calls. She opened it and took out a brown paper bag and produced a bunch of grapes.

'I brought these for him,' she said. 'I always think black grapes have more flavour than white ones.'

'Oh,' said Miss Pollock. It occurred to her that if Mrs Harrison thought that she was Mr Charrington's wife, she ought to thank her on his behalf. She tried to think what her mother would have said. 'Very kind of you, I'm sure,' she said, carefully.

'Not at all,' replied Mrs Harrison, graciously. She glanced round. 'Nurse!' she called. 'Would you kindly find a bowl for these?'

Miss Pollock was impressed. She would never have dared to ask a nurse to do something like that, but the bowl was brought in a moment, and as she took it and stood up to arrange the grapes in it, she felt more than ever as though this was her home, hers and

Mr Charrington's, and Mrs Harrison was their first visitor. As she sat down, she took his hand again, wanting to share it with him.

Mrs Harrison wasn't quite sure why she had come – at least she told herself that she wasn't quite sure. She had never met the old gentleman, and she was pretty sure that his wife didn't remember her. The old lady looked different without her hat. Her hair was grey but naturally curly, so it made her look younger. Her hand, as she moved to take Mr Charrington's, was as small as a child's. Accustomed as she was to checking the marital state of unknown couples arriving at her door at Crestview in search of bed and breakfast, Mrs Harrison's eyes rested instinctively on the third finger. There was no wedding ring. They were not married.

Mrs Harrison felt like getting up, taking her grapes and going home. They'd been living in sin. That was probably why they'd been thrown out. All the time she'd been a nanny, she had done her best to teach the children right from wrong, and the thing she felt most strongly about was not breaking marriage vows – and getting married in the first place. Mrs Harrison was not really an orphan, although she always said she was, and for all she knew, she might have been, because the truth was that she had been a foundling. She had been left by the gates of the hospital, she presumed by an unmarried mother, and brought up in an orphanage. The Master and Madam had been like her adopted parents from the day she came into their household as an ignorant nursemaid, but it wasn't the same. Every child needed a mother and a father, and marriage was the only way to make sure of that. She didn't know why the so-called Mr and Mrs Charrington weren't married, and she didn't want to know. As she used to say in her nursery, 'I don't want to hear any excuses. There's no excuse for bad behaviour.'

Mrs Harrison picked up her handbag.

'Well,' she said, 'I'd better be going.'

It was at that moment that Sister Payne came into the ward and straight up to the bed.

'Miss Pollock,' she said, 'I'm afraid you'll have to leave now.'

Mrs Harrison looked at her, startled. Miss Pollock instinctively tightened her grasp of Mr Charrington's hand.

'I ... I want to stay until he's better,' she said.

'Only close relatives are allowed to remain out of visiting hours, and that's in very special circumstances.'

'Well,' said Miss Pollock, obstinately, 'then I'll wait until the visitors go.'

'I think it would be best if you left now,'

294

said the sister, in a tone which had scarified many an unwary probationer. 'Nurse has your coat and hat.'

Miss Pollock saw the dismayed face of Nurse O' Neill as she stood in the open door, and began to withdraw her hand. Mr Charrington became aware that something was happening.

'What? What's going on?'

'I've got to leave now,' said Miss Pollock.

'What? Why?'

'They know I'm not...' She leaned close. 'They know I'm not your wife.'

'It's all right, Mr Charrington,' said Sister Payne, in the mild and comforting voice she reserved for really sick patients. 'Your friend can come back during visiting hours if she wants to.'

Mr Charrington's agitation increased.

'No!' he gasped. 'No. She ain't got no-where to go.'

'Don't worry, George,' said Miss Pollock, more distressed by his distress than by her own. 'I'll be all right.'

'No, no!' he said, and clung to her hand more desperately than ever.

'Now, don't upset yourself, Mr Charrington,' said Sister Payne. 'Everything is arranged. Miss Pollock, the almoner has had to go and see another patient, but if you go downstairs, she will meet you there. She has managed to find a temporary place for you in an old people's home.'

'No!' said Miss Pollock. 'No!'

Mrs Harrison saw the look of blind terror in her face and acted as instinctively as if she had seen a child in danger. She stood up.

'There's no need for that,' she said, brusquely. 'She can come and stay with me.'

Forty-Seven

Mrs Bickstead was usually alone in the shop on Saturday afternoons. Donald always went to watch Brightlesea play. Like his father, he was not in the least sporty, and she sometimes wondered, as she gave him the money for the ticket, whether in fact he intended to go at all. But, as always, she didn't want to confront him, being afraid of what she might find out.

Business was slow, and she sometimes thought that it was hardly worth opening at all. But she really didn't know what she would do with herself otherwise, so she caught up with a bit of stocktaking and began to do the week's accounts.

When Julian came in, she had just discovered a discrepancy – not a slight discrepancy but quite a serious one of at least twenty pounds and probably more. It was Donald, of course, but it couldn't be simply filching from the till, because she had taken care lately to cash up at lunchtime as well as in the evening. The stock didn't quite tally, either, and she reckoned that he had been charging customers above the proper price and putting the difference in his pocket, but, typically and carelessly, getting it wrong. She was wondering what she was going to do about it when the shop bell rang and she saw Julian. She put on her shopkeeper's smile.

'Good afternoon,' she said.

'I wonder if you can help me,' he said.

Oh, damn! she thought. Not a customer, and the last thing she wanted to do at the moment was to help anyone, especially some idiot who'd managed to get lost.

'I'm interested in Hampton Row,' he added.

'Oh yes?'

That sounded better. Perhaps he was a property developer. There were a lot of young property developers about. Perhaps he was going to knock those old houses down and build flats. Maybe luxury flats. Why not? Build them high enough and they could have a view of the sea. She'd get their custom – a better class of customer, too. Then, if the shop was more prosperous, if it made more money, then she could give Donald a bigger allowance, and he wouldn't need to steal.

'You don't by any chance know who lives at Number Six?'

'Miss Pollock?' exclaimed Mrs Bickstead.

'Ah,' said Julian, gratified, and fished out his notebook and wrote it down. 'Miss Pollock.'

'Are you from the Council?' enquired Mrs Bickstead, suspiciously.

He shook his head.

'Julian Brown, *Brightlesea Gazette*.'

She looked at him in horror. Miss Pollock must have had an accident – might even be dead. She remembered the evening – which evening was it? – when she had seen the little figure hurrying by in the rain. She had been going to call out to her, hurry after her, but then Donald had suggested cashing up, and she had done nothing. And then, last Saturday, she remembered her own irritation when the old lady had come into the shop, and – it was like a memory brought from the subconscious by hypnotism – the look of dismay on Miss Pollock's face when Donald had come to serve her instead.

All this flashed in random, cinematic images across her mind before she said, 'Is she ... Has she had an accident?'

'I'm not sure,' said Julian. 'Do you know a Mr Charrington, George Charrington?'

'No.'

'Mm.'

'What is it? What's happened?'

'I'm not sure,' said Julian. 'A Mr Charrington was taken into Brightlesea Hospital on Friday, and his wife gave their address as Number Six, Hampton Row, but—'

'Oh no!' interrupted Mrs Bickstead. 'Miss Pollock's lived there for, well, all her life, I believe, and her parents before her.'

'Perhaps she took lodgers.'

'No,' replied Mrs Bickstead, decidedly. 'I'd've seen them. Besides, she's not the sort. Kept herself to herself.'

'Perhaps they lived in one of the other houses.'

'The others are all empty.'

'They certainly look empty,' said Julian.

He had walked along the desolate, shabby little row, with the overgrown front gardens and the windows bare or half covered with torn netting, and he had stopped outside Number Six. He remembered the treasures in the makeshift dwelling on the beach, and had the strangest feeling that they belonged in this little house.

'When did you last see Miss Pollock?' asked Julian.

'She came in for her shopping last Saturday, as usual.'

'But not this morning?' he said, quickly.

She shook her head, and the image of the little figure hurrying past in the darkness and the rain flashed again across her mind. She had a sudden thought.

'A woman from the Council was round here last week, asking for her. She said she couldn't get any answer from the house. There was a policeman here, and I think they broke in.'

'*Really*? What happened?'

'Nothing.' She actually had to pause and think back. She had been so engrossed in her worries about Donald that she hadn't walked down to the house but had just waited outside the shop until the policeman returned to collect his biscuits.

'Was she all right?' she had asked him.

'Oh yes,' the policeman had answered, with a strange note in his voice almost like contempt. 'She'd gone away.'

'She'd gone away,' Mrs Bickstead repeated now to Julian, 'but...'

'But?'

'It just wasn't like her. She never went away – *and* she left half a pint of milk on the doorstep.'

They were both silent for a moment.

'Well,' said Julian, 'thank you for your help. And' – in the first flush of triumph at his acquisition of 'Julian's Corner', he had had some cards printed at his own expense – 'if you hear any more news of Miss Pollock, perhaps you'd let me know.'

Julian's sense of achievement at having obtained Miss Pollock's name soon subsided. Walking past the Crestview Bed and Breakfast and the Pavilion Hotel, he wondered gloomily how he could possibly rewrite his article. The pictures were still fine, and the headline 'Old Couple on Heartbreak Beach' still worked, but he had no idea who the Charringtons were. For all he knew, they could be a pair of down-and-outs from London. What was fatally lacking, as the editor had pointed out, was an interview with them. Julian suddenly made up his mind. He would try the hospital again.

He arrived just before the end of visiting hours and asked casually for Mr Charrington. As the receptionist turned to check her list of patients, a very trim dark-haired nurse who was standing by the desk looked at him quickly and said, 'He's in Princess Alice Ward. But I don't think he's well enough for visitors.'

'I was hoping to speak to Mrs Charrington,' said Julian. He saw an odd expression on her face and, in a sudden flash of inspiration, he added, 'Or Miss Pollock.'

'I'm afraid she's just left,' said the nurse.

She turned towards the door, but Julian said, quickly, 'Could you spare me a few minutes? How about a cup of tea?'

'Oh ... I'm just going off duty.'

'Have a cup of tea with me first. And a toasted teacake?'

301

Nurses were always hungry and always hard up.

'Well, I...'

'Oh, come on. You're Irish. You can't refuse a cup of tea.'

He was right. Nurse O' Neill couldn't.

Forty-Eight

When Mr Fanshaw agreed to become hospital chaplain quite soon after he came to Brightlesea, he looked upon it as a privilege, but also a challenge. He would be communicating with people in their times of greatest crisis, when they were facing sickness and death. That was what religion was *for*, and he would be there, not offering platitudes but genuinely making a difference, bringing them close to God in their hour of need.

But it didn't quite work out like that. The patients were more concerned with the minutiae of hospital life than anything else. He soon knew better than to come at meal times, but it was not uncommon for him to arrive prepared to offer spiritual uplift only to have the patient greet him with the words, 'Would you ask Nurse to bring me a bedpan?' The older patients, however firmly they

302

had declared their religion to be Church of England, clearly felt that it was not something to be talked about *except* in platitudes, whereas the younger ones were embarrassed to have it talked about at all. It was true that just occasionally, in times of extreme grief and fear, he knew that he had brought a few moments of comfort, but there was nothing dramatic about it, nothing to match the ecstasy of those early days when he was first ordained and knew that he had the God-given gift to inspire others with that faith which meant so much to him. Still, he did his best, even if it did feel more like soldiering on than fighting the good fight.

That Sunday he was visiting one of his parishioners and bringing him Holy Communion. He was a good Christian man and it was gratifying to be able to give him comfort, even though he was not *in extremis*, but visiting him was like visiting the Elder Brother rather than the more satisfying Prodigal Son. Returning between the beds down the ward, he heard a voice say weakly, 'Nurse! I want to see the padre.' It was the old man in the bed by the door. Mr Fanshaw approached him. He was clearly very ill.

'I am the hospital chaplain,' said Mr Fanshaw. 'Can I do anything for you? Would you like me to say a prayer?'

'No,' replied the old gentleman, with unexpected emphasis. 'I want to get married.'

Well, thought Mr Fanshaw, at least that makes a change from a bedpan.

It took a little while to establish that this was not a generalised desire, but that he actually had someone in mind.

'Miss Pollock,' he said. 'Ellen Pollock.'

'Right,' said Mr Fanshaw. 'And when did you...? That is, how soon were you thinking of...?'

'Now,' said Mr Charrington. 'Here. Now. Today.'

'Ah,' said Mr Fanshaw, smiling. 'I'm afraid that wouldn't be possible.'

The old gentleman's flesh might be weak, but there was no doubting his spirit, and his voice, though feeble, still managed to be sharp.

'Why not? You're a vicar. You're allowed to marry people.'

'Yes, but, strangely enough, not here in hospital,' said Mr Fanshaw.

'There's a chapel.'

'Yes, but it's not licensed for weddings. And even if it were, you'd need a special licence. No, I'm afraid—'

Mr Fanshaw's kindly and perhaps slightly condescending voice was cut short, as Mr Charrington struggled to sit up, struggled for breath, struggled to talk.

'She ... I must ... I must marry her. She ... you...!'

304

The nurse came running to put the oxygen mask on and lay him back on the pillows. She looked at Mr Fanshaw reproachfully.

'You really mustn't upset the patient.'

'I'm sorry,' said Mr Fanshaw, and patted Mr Charrington's arm. 'I'll come back tomorrow. We'll talk about it then.'

'No!'

He managed to grab Mr Fanshaw's hand, and held it with surprising strength.

'I'm all right,' he said.

Mr Fanshaw looked anxiously at the nurse. 'I think it would upset him more...'

'Very well,' said the nurse. 'But you must try not to agitate him.'

As Mr Charrington released his hand and closed his eyes, Mr Fanshaw sat down. He felt obscurely ashamed of himself, not so much for having upset the old man, but because he knew that he had not really treated him with proper respect. If a younger man had said he wanted to get married, he would have taken it more seriously, just as he would have spoken differently to a better-educated man. He had always disliked people who used a patronising tone when speaking to children, as though they didn't deserve adult consideration. But perhaps, he thought, it was even worse to treat old people as if they were children. And then, of course, he was uncomfortably aware that he had felt a certain impatience because he wanted to get home to his lunch.

Mr Charrington opened his eyes and was about to pull the oxygen mask off, but Mr Fanshaw stopped him.

'Mr Charrington,' he said, 'there's no hurry. When you feel up to it, please tell me all about it.'

He was dismayed to learn that they had known each other for less than a week. In any other circumstances, that would have ended the matter. As it was...

'Wouldn't it be better to wait a little while?' he suggested.

'No,' said Mr Charrington, decidedly. 'She can't manage on her own. She's as brave as a little lion, but she can't manage on her own. Besides, how long've I got?'

'Well...'

He had never indulged in the 'You'll be fine, old chap' response, and he had learned long ago to avoid all comment on medical conditions beyond a discreet note of sympathy.

'Whatever it is,' said Mr Charrington, 'I want her with me. Now they know she's not my wife, they won't let her stay.'

'I'm sure I could speak to Matron ... arrange something.'

'Don't make no difference. I want us to be married. I ain't got much to leave – well, nothing, really. Just my pension. But I want her to know we're together. Even after I'm gone, I want her to know.'

His voice was fading fast. Mr Fanshaw looked at the nurse and stood up. He leaned over Mr Charrington.

'You rest now. I'll come back this afternoon. I need to see her ... to talk to her.'

'You got a treat coming,' said Mr Charrington, faintly.

Forty-Nine

Being looked after by Mrs Harrison was rather like being taken in charge by a large but benevolent policeman. As soon as she and Miss Pollock got back to Crestview, Mr Harrison was dispatched to fetch the suitcases from Ed's Café. Mrs Harrison was there when Miss Pollock opened her suitcase, just as she would have supervised the opening of the children's trunks when they returned from boarding school. Miss Pollock was dismayed to find that her vests and nightdresses weren't there.

'I put them behind his head,' she said, 'to make a piller.'

Mrs Harrison had by now mastered, or rather, made herself mistress of the situation, which was entirely respectable. Respectable bore no relation to 'what will the

307

neighbours think?' – the gentry didn't care in the least what the neighbours thought. But to be respectable meant being worthy of respect, doing what was right, for yourself and for those you cared about. Mr Charrington and Miss Pollock, she was now assured, were perfectly respectable, and so were Miss Pollock's vests and nightdresses.

'Perhaps they're in his case,' she said.

Thanks to Norman, indeed they were.

'I expect you'd like a nice, hot bath,' said Mrs Harrison, in exactly the tone in which she used to say, 'Bathtime, children!'

Miss Pollock was amazed by Mrs Harrison's bathroom. It had a great big white bath standing on big legs like claws, and a cylindrical metal machine above it.

'Where's the copper?' enquired Miss Pollock.

'Don't need a copper,' replied Mrs Harrison, tolerantly. 'Just turn the tap on, and the hot water will come through the geyser.' She saw Miss Pollock's look of alarm.

'You go and get undressed and I'll run your bath. You can have your supper in your dressing gown.'

She knew that Miss Pollock had a dressing gown because she had seen it in the suitcase.

Miss Pollock would have felt very uneasy if she had had to eat in the front room where small tables were set out for bed and breakfast guests with spotless white tablecloths

308

and shiny cruets and bottles of HP sauce, but instead she was allowed to have supper with Mr and Mrs Harrison in front of the kitchen fire. They even had television, which she had never seen before. She thought that Mrs Harrison didn't quite approve of it, especially the girls who were dancing and kicking their legs up in the air with very little on, but there was a man with a funny hat who did magic tricks which kept going wrong, and he made Mr Harrison laugh a lot, and Miss Pollock laughed, too.

When Mrs Harrison said it was bedtime, Miss Pollock found that the embroidered sheet was turned back over the pink eiderdown, and that there was a hot-water bottle in the bed. She lay and thought about Mr Charrington and wished that she could be with him.

Fifty

Mr Fanshaw made a few enquiries before he returned to the hospital, and his wife brought him coffee and sandwiches in his study.

Arriving at the hospital, he went straight to Princess Alice Ward with a sense of anticipation and saw through the glass doors that Mr Charrington already had a visitor. 'You got a treat coming,' Mr Charrington had said, and he realised that he had somehow expected that the love of Mr Charrington's life, however old, would have a sort of pre-Raphaelite spiritual beauty, but instead this was a little old lady in a shabby coat and a terrible felt hat with a feather in it. He drew a deep breath and went in.

'Hello, Padre,' said Mr Charrington. 'This is Miss Pollock, Miss Ellen Pollock.'

'Pleased to meet you,' said Miss Pollock.

She recognised him at once. He was the nice young man from the church who had taken the place of old Mr Treadgold.

'I waited till you came,' said Mr Charrington, and then turned his face towards Miss

310

Pollock as she sat holding his hand. 'Here,' he said, 'what would you say if you and me was to get married?'

Mr Fanshaw was unprepared for the radiant smile which transformed the commonplace little face.

'Oh, yes!' she exclaimed. 'Then I could stay with you. Then we could always be together.'

'That's what *I* thought,' said Mr Charrington, gratified.

'You do understand,' said Mr Fanshaw, 'that I can't marry you myself, not here. It will have to be the registrar.'

Mr Charrington looked at Miss Pollock.

'What do you say?'

She scowled in incomprehension.

'As long as we're properly married?' he suggested.

'Oh, certainly,' said Mr Fanshaw. 'And I could give the marriage a blessing afterwards, if you'd like that.'

He looked towards Miss Pollock, and so did Mr Charrington. She smiled and nodded.

'Very nice,' she said.

Sister Payne did not take kindly to the idea of the marriage taking place in her ward. As a matter of fact, she did not take kindly to the marriage at all.

'I'm surprised that you can even consider

it,' she said. 'Miss Pollock was very sly.'

'*Sly?*'

'Saying that she was his wife when she wasn't.'

'Did she actually say that?' asked Mr Fanshaw, startled.

'Huh!' said Sister Payne. 'We all called her Mrs Charrington, and she didn't put us right. My nurses gave her the patients' meals and allowed her to sleep in the nurses' sitting room, and I turned a blind eye. She made a fool of me.'

Mr Fanshaw knew from experience that no one made a fool of Sister Payne and got away with it, and he faced another battle when he insisted on her summoning a doctor.

Needless to say, since it was Sunday, there was no consultant on duty, and the houseman was young and inexperienced. Mr Fanshaw had more than half an idea that the declaration should be signed by a more senior medical man, but he knew the local superintendent registrar, having had occasion to liaise with him over various wedding arrangements in the past, and he didn't think that he would give him any trouble.

'This is really intended for someone with a terminal illness like cancer,' said Sister Payne.

'Can you guarantee that Mr Charrington won't die?'

'Certainly not,' said Sister Payne, and

looked at the doctor. 'I wouldn't say that about any patient, but that's quite different from saying—'

'I agree with the sister,' said the young doctor, who knew which side his bread was buttered. 'I'm not prepared to say that he *will* die.'

'So why have you moved him to the bed by the door?' enquired Mr Fanshaw of the sister. 'We all know what that means. The patients certainly do.'

'He's lasted longer than we expected,' said the sister, coldly.

'Yes,' said the doctor, 'he's surprised us all, and he may continue to do so.'

'But if he doesn't?'

'He's not what I would describe as terminally ill,' said the doctor obstinately, his determination strengthened by a sense of medical solidarity with the more experienced Sister Payne.

Mr Fanshaw realised with alarm that he was going to lose the argument. He thought of that radiant smile, and how the old man had wanted them to be together for the rest of his life, long or short. Mr Fanshaw seemed to spend much of his time preparing for marriage people whose plans appeared to extend no further than decorating the church and dressing the page boys like miniature Nelsons, and he couldn't bear it. Suddenly it was as though this wedding meant more to him than anything had for the past twenty years. He had no hope of the sister changing her mind, and turned his attention entirely upon the young houseman.

'Mr Charrington wants to marry Miss Pollock before he dies because he loves her,' he said, 'and because they want to be together while they can. But you refuse to sign a declaration that he is, or is likely to be, terminally ill. God forgive you if you are wrong.'

The young doctor looked at him, startled. People didn't often mention God these days, thought Mr Fanshaw. Come to think of it, he didn't often mention God himself. The doctor picked up the pen, looked at the sister, glanced towards the ward, looked back at Mr Fanshaw and signed. Whether he signed from a superstitious and vestigial fear of God or merely from an instinctive disinclination to take a chance, Mr Fanshaw neither knew nor cared. He hoped God didn't, either.

Fifty-One

Julian took considerable pleasure in telephoning Miss Waterlow on Monday morning.

'I'm glad to say that I have discovered who was the tenant of Number Six, Hampton Row. It was Miss Pollock.'

'She still is the tenant,' replied Miss Waterlow, coldly, 'although I really don't know what it has to do with you.'

'But she's not living there now, is she?'

There was a silence.

'Perhaps you know where she is living now?'

There was another silence. Julian clenched his fist in triumph. She didn't know.

'If you'd care to meet me,' he said, 'I'll be happy to take you there.'

'It would be a great deal easier,' said Miss Waterlow, coolly unengaged, 'if you were to give me her address.'

'That's not possible. I'll meet you at the shelter on the front near the public toilets and opposite Ed's Café. In half an hour?'

He rang off, pleased with himself. That'd give her something to think about. Let her

315

sweat a little, the disagreeable woman. She might even think that the old lady had topped herself. He'd teach her to be unco-operative with the Press – and especially with Julian Brown!

Miss Waterlow told Mrs Price that she had to go out.

'You do remember that you have a meeting with Mr Simmonds at eleven?'

'I should be back by then,' said Miss Water-low, at her most businesslike. 'It's that tire-some man from the *Gazette*, but I hope I can get rid of him once and for all.'

Watching Miss Waterlow approach at a brisk walk, Julian was startled to see that she was a lot younger than he had thought, and really rather good-looking, in spite of being severe-ly dressed.

'Glad you could make it,' he said, but not quite as ironically as he had intended. 'This way.'

'What on earth do you mean?'

'This is where Miss Pollock lives,' said Julian, leading the way down the slope.

At the foot of the slope, he turned and offered his hand, but she ignored it, and had no difficulty in walking on the stones in her sensible shoes. Her face was expressionless, but she was full of foreboding. He had said it was where Miss Pollock was living now, so obviously she wasn't dead, but as she followed him past the decaying boards and rubbish-strewn cave, she dreaded finding a pathetic old figure wrapped in a blanket.

'In here,' said Julian. 'It's all right. She's not here.'

He stood back with a feeling of triumph, and she went past him, and stood still, gazing round. She saw the little stove and the kettle, and the tins and saucepan, and the makeshift bed, and beside it the donkey and basket, the photograph and the jug which said 'A present from Southend'. And then she saw the coronation mug. To Julian's horror and astonishment she sat down on a nearby fisherman's box and burst into tears.

'I can't bear it!' she said. 'I can't bear it!'

Julian stared at her helplessly.

'She's all right,' he said, and came and squatted down beside her, hesitating to put a comforting hand on her. 'She's been visiting Mr Charrington in hospital, but she's all right.'

'I tried,' she gasped through her sobs. 'I really tried. And then, I was so afraid she was dead.'

This time he did put his arm round her.

'She's fine,' he repeated. 'Don't worry.'

Miss Waterlow got out her handkerchief and began to pull herself together.

'I'm sorry,' she said. 'It was just ... all her little treasures.'

'I understand,' said Julian, and looked at

them properly for the first time.

'Is she living here now?' asked Miss Waterlow.

'I don't think so. I talked to one of the nurses at the hospital, and she said Miss Pollock went off with someone.'

'But who?'

'The nurse didn't know. She thought it might be a relative.'

'We can't leave all her things here. Anyone could ... And if I have them taken back to her house ... It's going to be demolished, and...' She broke down again. 'I don't know what to do!'

'I've got an idea,' said Julian.

He had seen Norman Taylor sitting in the shelter, and, going a few steps up the slope, was relieved to see that he was still there.

'Norman!' he called. 'Can you help us?'

Norman came readily, still enduring his compulsory and lonely holiday.

'Is everything all right? I haven't seen anyone hanging round here.'

'No, it all seems to be in order, but ... This is Miss Waterlow from the Welfare Department. She thinks we ought to put the rest of the things in a safe place. Do you think Ed would put them with the suitcases?'

'Suitcases aren't there any more,' said Norman. 'Someone came and took them away.'

'What? Who?'

Ann Waterlow and Julian spoke together.

318

Norman thought for a moment.

'Mr Harrison. He said the old lady was staying with him and his wife.'

'Harrison!' exclaimed Julian, suddenly. 'Mrs Harrison. Crestview Bed and Breakfast. That's where she is!'

Norman fetched a large box from Ed's and they packed everything in it, and then Julian and Ann Waterlow left him to carry it to the café while they set out to walk to Crestview. On the way there, Julian heard the story of Hampton Row and the elusive Miss Pollock, who never opened any letters and who was so determined to preserve her independence.

'What about Mr Charrington?'

'I don't know. He's not a Council tenant, and I don't know anything about him.'

'We'll be able to ask Miss Pollock,' said Julian.

But when they arrived at Crestview and rang the shiny brass doorbell, there was no reply, and the spotless lace curtains were motionless.

'She's probably at the hospital,' said Julian.

Fifty-Two

Mr Charrington had had a bad night, and when Mr Fanshaw arrived with the superintendent registrar, Sister Payne said at first that she didn't think he'd be well enough. But at the sight of Miss Pollock, Mr Charrington, breathless as he was, gave a broad smile and gasped, 'Here comes the bride!'

'Oh, you!' said Miss Pollock, and sat down beside the bed and took his hand.

'They have to say the words of declaration and the words of contract,' said the superintendent registrar quietly to Mr Fanshaw. 'Do you think he's up to it?'

'I think so,' said Mr Fanshaw, and looked at Sister Payne.

She shook her head disapprovingly, but said, 'Yes. He knows what he's doing.'

Mr and Mrs Harrison had come as witnesses and at the last minute Nurse O' Neill darted in with a large bouquet of flowers for Miss Pollock, which made Sister Payne look more disapproving than ever.

'Are we ready?' enquired the registrar, and Mrs Harrison, seeing that Miss Pollock was rather hampered by the flowers, stepped forward and took them, and then stood behind holding them like a stout, elderly bridesmaid.

It would all have seemed terribly strange and unreal to Miss Pollock, except that she was holding Mr Charrington's hand and he was looking at her all the time and smiling. She didn't have any trouble saying the words, because he said them first.

'I do solemnly declare that I know not of any lawful impediment why I, George Albert Charrington, may not be joined together in matrimony to Ellen Mary Pollock.'

Then she had to say it, only the other way round. The next bit was more difficult, and she might not have managed it, except that when he had done it, he gave her an encouraging nod and a wink.

'I call upon these persons here present to witness that I, Ellen Mary Pollock, do take thee, George Albert Charrington, to be my lawful wedded husband.'

Mr Charrington put his gold signet ring on her finger – only it was really too big – and the registrar said that they were man and wife and that Mr Charrington could kiss her, but of course she wouldn't have dreamed of kissing him in front of all those people, so she just pressed his hand, and the vicar said a nice blessing, and then it was all over.

'That went off all right, didn't it?' said Mr Charrington, when everyone else had gone and they were alone.

'I'm glad I wore my best hat,' she said.

'Good idea of mine, weren't it, getting married?'

She nodded, but frowned.

'George, they said ... they said we could get married because ... because you...'

'Don't worry,' he said. 'I ain't going no-where.'

Fifty-Three

Julian got Mr George Charrington's address from the Electoral Register and noted that Mr Kenneth Charrington and Mrs Gwen Charrington also lived there. He took the bus out. (If only he had a car!) It was a sort of seaside suburb, except that it was two miles from the sea, a hinterland of indistin-guishable trim lawns and hanging baskets. Mr Charrington's house was untidier than the others, and there was a battered child's bicycle lying on the grass outside. Grand-children, thought Julian as he rang the door-bell.

The woman who came to the door was not exactly welcoming, but Julian put on his friendly smile.

'I'm looking for Mr George Charrington,' he said.

'He doesn't live here any more.'

She was almost shutting the door before he managed to say, 'Do you have a new address for him?'

'No.'

He didn't quite put his foot in the door, but he leaned forward.

'You're not his daughter?'

'No.'

But there was a flicker in her eyes.

'Daughter-in-law? Mrs Kenneth Charrington?'

'That's none of your business.'

Julian took out his card and held it out to her.

'Julian Brown, *Brightlesea Gazette*. Did you know that Mr George Charrington has been sleeping rough on the beach, and that he is now in Brightlesea Hospital?'

He saw that she was alarmed by his words.

'Perhaps you could tell me—' he said.

'Nothing to say,' she said, and this time she did slam the door shut, leaving him with the card in his hand.

Rewriting the article took him a long time, and he wasn't at all satisfied with it when he realised that he was beaten by the approaching deadline and must deliver it to the office. The editor read it through and looked surprised.

'A bit mild, isn't it?' he said. 'What happened to them being evicted by the Council?'

'Well,' answered Julian, with a touch of nervousness, 'they weren't exactly evicted. The Council Welfare people did their best, but Miss Pollock wouldn't cooperate and sort of slipped through the net.'

'Mm,' said the editor. 'What about George Charrington?'

'I think he's fallen out with his son and daughter-in-law, but I can't be sure.'

'Mm,' said the editor. 'Trouble is, it makes it all a bit flabby.'

'Yes, I know,' agreed Julian, and reached for the typescript. 'I'll try to sharpen it up.'

'No,' said the editor, putting it aside. 'There's not time. I'll have a go at it.'

Fifty-Four

Arthur Whitehead had a day off, so he came down to breakfast after the children had left for school. He saw the *Brightlesea Gazette* on the mat and picked it up.

'Well, I never!' he said, turning towards the kitchen as he studied the front page. 'This is interesting, Joyce.'

He heard his mother-in-law's voice saying, 'What's he talking about?' as he advanced into the kitchen.

'There's a piece here about the old gentleman I picked up on the beach. And the old lady who was with him ... Wait a minute. Where's my notebook?'

He went out quickly and got his notebook out of his uniform jacket where it hung on a hook in the hall, and returned, looking at it.

'Here it is. Number Six, Hampton Row. I wrote it down. Dear, oh dear! I should have known who she was. I went to her house – even heard her name – but my mind wasn't on my job.'

'I hope you're not going to talk about your nasty police work all morning!'

Arthur looked up from the paper. His mother-in-law was sitting at the end of the table in the place which used to be his, and Joyce was at the stove.

'That's not a very nice thing to say,' he remarked, conversationally.

She looked slightly startled, and he was aware of Joyce being very still, not looking round.

'I suppose I can say what I like!'

'You can, but it's still not very nice.' He sat down at the table. 'Now, see here, Mother,' he said, 'you and me are going to have a little talk.'

She ignored that.

'May I have my paper, please,' she said.

'It's not your paper. It's my paper, mine

and Joyce's. Same as this house is ours, mine and Joyce's and the children's.'

'I suppose you want me to leave!'

'No. I don't want you to leave. We're very happy to have you here, but it's not your house. You're a visitor, and you have to try to fit in a bit. I *have* got a funny sort of job, and it means I come and go at odd times, but that never worried Joyce until you came here, did it, love?'

He looked towards Joyce. Her back was still turned. This was make-or-break time. Her mother looked at her, too. Joyce looked round.

' 'Course it didn't. You were a policeman when I married you.'

Arthur looked back at his mother-in-law and saw in her face that she knew she was beaten. She would always be an unpleasant old lady because that was in her nature.

She had been an unpleasant woman, and probably had been an unpleasant child. But the truth was that she was just as helpless as that old lady who had clutched him with tiny hands on the seafront, saying, 'Help me!' He suddenly smiled.

'Come on, Enid,' he said, 'live and let live, eh? I tell you what. I'm going to have a cooked breakfast, if Joyce doesn't mind cooking it for me. Why don't you join me?'

'Not for me, thank you!'

'Oh, go on, have a boiled egg. That won't

hurt you.'

She saw that he was teasing her. He had never teased her before.

'Oh, all right!' she said, crossly. 'I'll have a boiled egg!'

And he could just see a tiny twitch at the corner of her mouth which could almost have been a suppressed smile.

Fifty-Five

'Here, Norm, we're in the paper,' said Ed, as Norman arrived for breakfast.

Norman came to join him at the counter where he was studying the two-page picture spread.

'Good one of you,' said Ed. 'Can't see much of the café.'

'They haven't got any of the old lady and gentleman,' said Norman. 'They seem to think he's pretty ill.'

'Ah, that's newspapers for you. Always make things sound bad. One knockout and they say you're finished. You ever been a boxer?'

'Who, me? No. My cousin was.'

'What was his name?'

'Thaddeus Taylor.'

'What, Toughie Taylor? I fought him once.

327

Cor, his head was hard! Hard as a cocoanut. I'd've beaten him if we hadn't clashed heads. Opened a cut over my eye. Mind, it wasn't his fault. He didn't mean to do it. Where is he now?'

'Somewhere up north,' said Norman. 'He got into a bit of trouble – couldn't stand the aggro.'

'Oh, yeah.'

'He married a white woman.'

'Oh.' Ed nodded wisely. 'Yeah.'

'They couldn't find anywhere to live in London. Whites wouldn't have them, nor would the blacks.'

'I don't know why people can't live and let live,' said Ed. 'Where are you living, then, Norm?'

'I've got a room just round the corner.'

'Why do you come here for all your meals? Not but what I'm glad to have you, but—'

'My landlady won't let me cook.'

'Don't she do bed and breakfast?'

'Not for me,' said Norman.

'How much do you pay?'

'Two pounds a week.'

'Cor blimey!' said Ed. 'Two quid a week for one room and no food? You'd better come and lodge here. I've got a spare room you can have. Quid a week, throw in the breakfast, and all other meals you pay for.' He saw Norman's startled look. 'Why not?'

'You don't want a black man.'

'Huh!' said Ed. 'I'd sooner have you than your cousin. His head! Hard as a cocoanut! Do you want sausages? Where's that bloody woman?'

On the way to the kitchen, he suddenly stopped.

'You know something? I'm fed up with her always arriving late and stealing me blind. I've got half a mind to write to Doris.'

'Doris?'

'A woman I knew. I got on really well with her. I wonder if she'd come back and live here.'

Norman's face didn't change, but inside he felt stiff and empty. Regretting it already, was he? Well, better now than later. At least he hadn't given notice to his landlady.

'You won't want me here, then,' he said.

'What, because of Doris? You'd like her. I reckon you and her would get on really well. And' – he gave his gap-toothed grin – 'I wasn't thinking of putting her in the spare room!'

Fifty-Six

John Weatherfield didn't go down Hampton Row now, but he still left a crate of milk at Mrs Bickstead's shop. She was looking at the *Brightlesea Gazette* when he arrived.

'Have you seen this?' she asked. 'Miss Pollock.'

'What about her?'

'Sleeping rough on the beach. Oh, dear!'

He looked at her vacantly.

'I feel badly about that,' said Mrs Bickstead. 'She came here for help, and I didn't give it to her.'

It was a relief to say it to someone, get it off her conscience, but John Weatherfield was already going out of the door and she heard his cart start up just as Donald came through from the back.

'Donald,' she said, 'if you ever steal from me again, I shall call the police. You'll work in the shop every Saturday, morning and afternoon, until you've paid back what you owe me. Now, smarten yourself up and get off to school.'

John Weatherfield bought a copy of the

Gazette and read it in his cart during his milk round.

He studied the photographs of the place on the beach with the makeshift bed and the stores and said, 'Huh!' aloud. So the old girl had finally moved out, but it was too late for him. His wife had moved out, too, taking the children. She left a scrawled note saying, 'Can't stand this life any more. Gone to London. Don't worry about the children. I'll write when I have a job and somewhere to live.'

He knew none of it was true. She'd gone off with the other man, otherwise she'd've taken the money from the drawer. She'd left it all behind because she knew the other man would look after her, and that John was a failure whose family had to live in one room.

When he'd finished his deliveries, he left the milk cart at the depot and the bag of cash in it.

'John!' called the cashier as he began to walk out. 'You haven't checked in.'

No, he thought. *I'm checking out.*

He walked home, and trudged up the stairs and let himself into the room. It was just as it had been when he got back from work the day before. She had left most of the children's toys behind. The other man would buy new ones, and a house and garden to put them in.

The note was still on the table, and he put

the newspaper down beside it. She had left an old scarf over the back of a chair. He picked it up, but decided that it wasn't strong enough. The belt from his best trousers was hanging beside it. He put the scarf back and picked up the belt and went out on to the landing above the stairwell.

Fifty-Seven

Julian Brown arrived at Miss Waterlow's house before the milkman had returned to the depot, and Mrs Waterlow answered the door in her dressing gown. She always got the breakfast and then had her bath after Ann had left for work. Unlike Mr Charrington's daughter-in-law, she greeted Julian with a welcoming, enquiring smile.

'I'm sorry to come so early,' he said. 'I'm Julian Brown. Could I possibly see Miss Waterlow?'

'Oh,' she said, brightly. 'Do come in. I'll just see if she ... Do come in.'

She showed him into the sitting room with its log-effect electric fire and colour television set.

'Do sit down. Would you like a cup of coffee?'

It was meant to sound like Judy Garland's

mother making the boy next door feel at ease, but Julian felt rather smothered by such enthusiastic hospitality.

'No, thank you.'

Mrs Waterlow smiled charmingly (Fay Bainton?) and withdrew, leaving the door ajar.

'Darling!' she trilled. 'A visitor for you.'

Ann Waterlow looked at first astonished and then indignant.

'What on earth? How did you get this address?'

'From the telephone book. I'm sorry. I had to see you before...'

She saw the copy of the *Brightlesea Gazette* in his hand.

'It's not what I wrote,' he said. 'At least, it's more or less what I wrote originally, but when I knew what had really happened, I rewrote it. Only ... only the editor has changed it back ... well, made it much worse ... He...'

As he floundered, she held out her hand for the paper and he gave it to her. He watched as she read the headline, 'Old Couple on Heartbreak Beach', which was followed by the text: 'Evicted from her home by a heartless Council and failed by an uncaring Old People's Welfare Department...'

She looked up at him.

'I'm so sorry,' he said. 'He just saw it as a good sensational story.'

333

'I'm surprised you didn't say, "Guilty Head of Old People's Welfare burst into tears." '

'Don't!' he said. 'Please don't!'

He briefly put his hand on hers. Mrs Waterlow, tiptoeing to the half open door, smiled to herself and withdrew. Miss Waterlow read on.

' "Ellen Pollock met George Charrington, made homeless by his unfeeling family ..." Is that true?'

'I don't know, but I imagine so. I saw his daughter-in-law and she certainly didn't want to know.'

She turned the page and saw the full spread of photographs.

'Oh no! All her things! How *could* you?'

'I know. I didn't see her as a person, just as a story. Same as I saw you, until I met you.'

His eyes met hers.

'Well...' she said.

She closed the paper and was about to give it back to him.

'You'd better keep it,' he said.

'Hm. Yes.'

They exchanged a rueful smile. It was strange but enjoyable for her to share a confidential anxiety about her work with him.

'I'd better get along to my office,' she said.

'I'll walk with you.'

She hesitated.

'All right, but don't let Mrs Price see you.'

'I'll buy a false moustache on the way.'

Then, amazingly, she laughed outright, and he laughed, too.

Well, he's not Ronald Colman, thought Mrs Waterlow, watching them walk away together, *but he seems to be a nice young man.*

Fifty-Eight

When Miss Pollock arrived at the hospital, she found that Mr Charrington's bed had been moved again, and it was quite a surprise to find him sitting up in an armchair. Sister Payne had insisted that she should go home overnight with Mrs Harrison, promising to telephone if he showed any signs of taking a turn for the worse. But instead he had taken a turn for the better.

'We're quite pleased with him,' said Sister Payne, grimly, 'but he mustn't be excited.'

Miss Pollock saw the *Brightlesea Gazette* tucked away under a folder in the sister's office and nearly asked if she could have a read of it while she was sitting with Mr Charrington, but didn't quite like to, and, after all, she was quite happy just to be with him and to talk when he wanted to talk and to be quiet when he didn't.

'They've moved your bed again,' she said,

335

and he grinned.

'I told you I wasn't going nowhere,' he said.

But after a while she saw that he was getting tired, and, although timidly, she asked Nurse O' Neill if it wouldn't be a good idea for him to get back to bed.

'I think you're right, Mrs Charrington,' said Nurse O' Neill.

Miss Pollock looked at him and giggled.

'I keep forgetting,' she said.

'I don't.' He leaned back against the pillows with a sigh of relief. 'It ain't half good to have you here.'

It was a shock when, as the first visitors began to arrive, a man walked in and straight up to Mr Charrington and said, 'Dad, what the hell is all this about?'

'Eh?' said Mr Charrington, waking up with a start.

The man was carrying a folded newspaper and banged the bed table with it.

'What's all this rubbish in the paper about us throwing you out? Gwen is really upset.'

'Oh, is she?' said Mr Charrington, calmly. 'Hullo, Ken. This is Ellen.'

But he didn't look calm and comfortable any more, and felt for her hand.

'I'd like to speak to you alone,' said Ken.

'You can say what you like in front of Ellen.'

Ken gave her an unfriendly glance, looked round for another chair and took one from the next bed without apology and sat down.

'I suppose you came to see how I was,' said Mr Charrington, with a touch of sarcasm. 'How did you know I was here?'

'Said so in the paper. And all this junk about "made homeless by an unfeeling family". How could you say that? It was you that walked out.'

'I never said nothing. Never even saw them.'

'Well, then, this chap, Julian Brown, how did he know you were sleeping on the beach?'

'Dunno. Never heard of him.'

Miss Pollock took a breath, but then let it go. Ken was aware of it.

'I suppose it was you. Did you go blabbing to the paper?'

'Don't you have a go at her!' said Mr Charrington, struggling to sit up.

There was a time when she would have been frightened by Ken, but now she was much more concerned about Mr Charrington.

'Don't you upset yourself, George,' she said. 'You lean back, now.' She looked across at Ken. 'I never saw him, neither. I just know his name from the paper. Julian's Corner.'

'I think you owe this lady an apology,' said Mr Charrington.

337

'Yes, all right,' said Ken, perfunctorily. 'No offence. Well, I don't know where he got it all from, but, come on, Dad, you can imagine how it made me feel, reading that, me and Gwen.'

'Hm, well, sorry if you're upset, but it's nothing to do with me,' said Mr Charrington.

Ken seemed to decide to accept this as an apology.

'Well, we'll try to put it behind us, eh? Sister says you'll be able to come out soon. We've no objection to you coming back. Your room's still there, and Gwen doesn't bear any malice.'

'Very good of her, I'm sure,' said Mr Charrington.

'That's settled, then,' said Ken, standing up. 'Get them to give Gwen a ring when you're coming out, and I'll come and pick you up.'

'Right,' said Mr Charrington. 'Can I have that paper?'

'Oh ... very well,' said Ken, and gave it to him reluctantly. 'I can buy another one. And if that reporter gets in touch with you, mind you set him right.'

He nodded to Miss Pollock and went out.

When Mr Charrington took the paper, Miss Pollock had unobtrusively withdrawn her hand. He hadn't told Ken that he was married. And when Ken suggested him going back to them, he had said, 'Right.' Ken didn't seem like a very nice man, but he was his son, and her mother always used to say that, come what may, blood was thicker than water. Maybe after all he felt it would be best for him to go home to his family. That's what everyone wanted. She wouldn't stand in his way. They'd only got married so she could stay in the hospital with him. Maybe an old people's home wouldn't be so bad. But that cold terror crept back again.

Mr Charrington was looking at the paper.

'Here,' he said, 'there's a picture of our café. And that black feller.'

'Norman,' said Miss Pollock, struggling to speak naturally. 'Norman Taylor.'

He looked at her, surprised.

'Wassermatter?'

'Nothing.' She struggled again. 'It might be best ... when you get out ... it might be best for you to go ... go with Ken. They could look after you better.'

He looked at her in astonishment.

'What, go back *there*? I should ko-ko! They're just upset 'cause they've got a bit of bad publicity. Me go back with me tail between me legs to that hard-face bitch...'

'Oh!' She clicked her teeth.

'And Ken under her thumb as usual, and Johnny putting his tongue out at me? I don't think so! Why, did you think I might?'

'When he said about it, you said "right".'

'Didn't feel up to arguing about it.'

'Oh.' She hesitated. 'And you never said nothing about...' She put her hand to the signet ring which Mrs Harrison had stuffed with tissue paper.

'What, about us being married? None of their business!' said Mr Charrington.

She was delighted. That was how *she* felt about it, but ... She was his wife, and it was up to her to be practical. Her mother had always said, men weren't practical.

'George,' she said, 'we still ain't got nowhere to live.'

'Never mind,' he said. 'Something'll turn up.' He rested his head back against the pillow. Ken's visit had tired him out. 'Maybe we'll go back to our little house on the beach.'

He smiled at her before closing his eyes, and she smiled and nodded, but she still felt that chill of fear. Would they have to go into an old people's home? And did they have an old people's home for married people?

Fifty-Nine

'The owner rang to congratulate you,' said the editor, when Julian arrived in the office. 'Luckily, he doesn't like the housing manager – thinks he's a pompous pratt.'

'Miss Waterlow wasn't too happy,' said Julian. All the way there, he had been wondering what he would say, intending to make some high-principled protest, but in the end it came out rather mildly. 'She felt we hadn't been very fair to her.'

'Got to know her, did you?' enquired the editor. 'I thought so. Never want to get too close. I always say, if you're a local newspaperman, don't get too pally with the councillors, and if it's a national, don't get too friendly with members of the Government.'

Julian was silent. Perhaps, he thought, he wasn't really cut out to be a journalist after all. Too honest. Too much concern for other people's feelings.

'It's come out well, though,' said the editor. 'We can follow it up next week. He may pull through or he may not. Make a good story either way.'

Had the man no feeling? Luckily the

341

telephone rang then.

'Yes? Who? Kathleen O' Neill? Yes, he's here.'

He put his hand over the mouthpiece.

'I can't keep up with your girlfriends,' he said. 'Miss Waterlow one minute, Kathleen O' Neill the next.'

'Kathleen? She's the nurse from the hospital. Hullo? Hullo, Kathleen. Yes. *Really?* And is he...? Right. Thanks for telling me.'

He put the telephone down and met the editor's quizzical gaze with triumph.

'She's the one who tipped me off about Miss Pollock. They've got married.'

'Who have?'

'Miss Pollock and the old man. In hospital. Yesterday afternoon. Damn! If only she'd told me sooner! What a story!'

'We can get something out of it next week,' said the more philosophical editor. 'Meanwhile...'

He scribbled on a piece of paper and passed it over to Julian.

'Old friend of mine. *News Chronicle*. Sleeping on the beach, deathbed wedding – should be good enough for a para or two, and a quid or two. I should ask for your own byline. Mention my name. You might get it.'

'Thanks!' said Julian.

'I owe you something,' said the editor, amused. 'No one likes being rewritten, even if it is an improvement.'

Julian grinned and set off for the hospital. His short-lived career as an oversensitive journalist was over.

Sixty

Mr Harper had first heard the expression 'when the shit hit the fan' from a Canadian officer just after the Dieppe raid, and had thought it rather coarse, especially when used over drinks in the anteroom, but it struck him now as all too appropriate.

Mrs Hamilton, of course, had a copy of the *Brightlesea Gazette* to thrust at him as soon as he reached the Housing Department, and also had a long list of telephone calls, mostly from councillors, all demanding an instant response. Mr Simmonds was lurking miserably outside, clutching a file.

'See you in a minute, Simmonds,' said Mr Harper, quite forgetting to call him Bill.

'Yes, Sir,' said Mr Simmonds.

Mr Harper spread the newspaper out on his desk. He looked at the photographs and made an exasperated noise. Sleeping on the beach! Where the hell were the police, and why the hell didn't they pick them up and bung them in a hostel? Then he read the text

343

and groaned, underlining the worst bits in red ink. Then he called Mr Simmonds in.

'Who's this man, Charrington?' he demanded, 'and what was he doing on the beach?'

'I don't know, S– ... Tom. It seems that he was living with his son, but they had a quarrel or something and he got thrown out. I rang the hospital, and they say he's getting better. He'll probably be back with his family in a day or two.'

'Silly old bugger!' said Mr Harper, irritably. 'Anyway, he's not a Council tenant – that's the main thing. How about Hampton Row?'

'Miss Pollock? We ... You handed her case over to Miss Waterlow.'

Mr Simmonds felt rather treacherous, but his wife always said he was too soft, and at this stage of the game it was every man for himself.

'Ah, yes,' said Mr Harper. 'I'll have a word with her.'

But at that moment, Mrs Hamilton put her head round the door.

'A call from the chairman of the Council, Mr Harper. He would like to see you as soon as possible.'

The meeting with the chairman of the Council did not begin particularly well. Mr Bigelow and Mr Harper had played golf together, and were accustomed to meet on equal terms, but banging his fist on the copy of the *Brightlesea Gazette* and demanding, 'What's all this about, Harper?' did not exactly fulfil the usual social niceties.

Mr Harper decided to respond with unconcerned high-handedness.

'The Press getting the whole thing wrong, as usual,' he said, cheerfully. 'This man, Charrington, isn't even a Council tenant.'

'And the old lady?' Mr Bigelow, too vain to wear the glasses he needed, peered at the newspaper. 'Miss ... What's her name?'

Mr Harper couldn't remember.

'Ah, yes,' he said. 'Miss Waterlow.'

'Is that her name?' said the chairman, surprised.

'No, no, I'm just saying that Miss Waterlow of Old People's Welfare has been looking after her. She's usually very efficient. I'm sure it's just a misunderstanding.'

'Well, sort it out, will you? Don't want it to get out of hand. I've had the local BBC Radio chap on the phone, and the news editor of the *County Times*, so I've called a Press conference for this afternoon.'

Mr Harper felt his mouth fall open.

'You...?' He closed his mouth and managed a smile. 'Right,' he said, cheerily. 'Right.'

'Press conference' was rather a grand term, but the news editor from the *County Times* was there, and an admittedly minor representative of BBC Radio, as well as, for no apparent reason, the man who ran the local trade journal. Last to arrive was that fellow from the *Gazette* who had caused all the trouble in the first place.

Three chairs had been set out facing them, and another had to be hastily added for Mr Simmonds, whom Mr Harper had decided to bring with him at the last minute 'to remind him of details', as he said. He hadn't managed to reach Miss Waterlow beforehand, but greeted her with a *bonhomie* which he hoped would conceal considerable unease.

'I hope you'll sit beside me,' he said, 'and we'll face the enemy together!'

She smiled, which made a pleasant change. It had sometimes seemed to Mr Harper that she didn't respond very warmly to his friendly advances. But it was a very uncertain smile, and Mr Harper had a nasty feeling that she was no more confident in facing the Press over this matter than he was.

After the chairman's introductions, it was the BBC Radio man who began, with all the enthusiasm of a junior reporter eager to make his mark.

'Were you embarrassed, Mr Harper, to discover that two of your evicted Council tenants had been sleeping on the beach?'

Mr Harper drew a mental breath of relief.

There is no more welcome gift than an opening question from a journalist who hasn't mastered the subject under scrutiny.

'I'm afraid I must put you right. Neither of the people concerned had been evicted by the Council, and Mr ... Mr...'

'Charrington,' muttered Mr Simmonds.

'Mr Charrington is not a Council tenant. Although,' he added, hastily, 'we have, of course, every sympathy with anyone who has housing problems, and we will do our best to assist them.'

There was a brief silence, during which the other representatives of the Press showed a tendency to glance at Julian Brown. They think he got his facts wrong, thought Mr Harper with satisfaction. Storm in a teacup. All go home. Julian got his notebook out and pretended to study it.

'Would it be true to say, Mr Harper, that the Hampton Row tenant was under an eviction order?'

'Since the whole property was due for demolition and redevelopment, that was inevitable,' said Mr Harper, feeling better every minute. 'But the lady in question was treated with every consideration. My colleague, Mr Simmonds, called on her to explain the matter and promise alternative accommodation...'

'Are you going to offer Mr Charrington alternative accommodation,' enquired the

BBC man, who had got his second wind, 'or when he comes out of hospital, will he have to go back to the beach?'

Mr Harper put on his thoroughly responsible look and shook his head reprovingly.

'As I am sure you are aware, housing is very limited – which is one reason for redeveloping properties like Hampton Row – but we will certainly try to find somewhere suitable for him, although he may prefer to return to his family.'

There was another brief silence. Mr Harper glanced at the chairman, who, preparing to rise, said, 'Well, I think—' but Julian cut across him.

'Is the "suitable accommodation" you are offering Miss Pollock the same as you offered her before?'

Mr Harper glanced at Mr Simmonds.

'A place in an old people's home, yes.'

'But that wouldn't be suitable, would it?'

Mr Harper frowned, puzzled.

'In view of the fact,' said Julian, 'that Mr Charrington and Miss Pollock were married yesterday?'

Mr Harper looked at Miss Waterlow and saw her gazing in astonishment at Julian, and saw his tiny, apologetic shrug in return.

'I hope they won't have to set up house on the beach again,' said the *County Times* news editor to the BBC man.

The chairman was seeing headlines reading 'Heartless Council Separates Heartbreak Couple'. He looked at Mr Harper. So did everyone else.

And then Mr Harper had the inspiration of a lifetime.

'I'm glad to say that the Council's flats for newly-weds are just completed,' he said, 'and we shall be delighted to offer the first one to Mr and Mrs Charrington.'

Sixty-One

Everyone was very kind. Mrs Harrison told her that when Mr Charrington came out of hospital, they could stay there together until their flat was ready. She had never before slept in the same bed as someone else, but she found that it seemed quite natural to share the big double bed with Mr Charrington. After all that had happened, it was nice to have a cuddle and to go to sleep with his arms round her, and she didn't mind his snoring, although if it got too loud, she would think of the Harrisons and give him a little push and say, 'George, you're snoring!'

Mrs Harrison did them a bed and breakfast at a special rate, and she threw in supper as well because she said they didn't eat much and she and Mr Harrison enjoyed their company.

Mrs Sparkes arranged what she called a 'wedding reception' for them at the Pavilion Hotel, and said it was a wedding present from her, and Mrs Harrison insisted on buying her a new hat for it, but she really liked her own hat better, and flatly refused to have a new coat when the other one was perfectly good.

The man from the *Gazette* came and took photographs, and Julian Brown interviewed them sitting on a sofa holding hands.

'Will we be in "Julian's Corner"?' she asked.

'Of course. And a picture, too.'

'I don't much care about having my picture in the paper,' she said, 'but I'd like to have a picture of Mr Charrington.'

When the flat was ready for them to move in, there were quite a lot of people there as well. Mr Harper seemed to be in charge, and Mr Simmonds was there, and Miss Waterlow, and, of course, Julian Brown, and the chairman of the Council, whose wife cut a ribbon across the front door while the photographer took more pictures, and a little crowd outside all cheered.

But at last everyone had gone, and they had a chance to look round on their own. It was a really nice flat. There was a toilet and bath and washbasin all in the same room and quite as nice as the public toilets, and in the kitchen, although there was no grate for cooking, Mr Charrington said she'd soon get used to the gas, and there was a gas fire in the sitting room which he said was much easier than having to light it with paper and wood and fetching coal from outside.

'Huh!' she said.

She knew which *she* preferred.

She stood and looked round the sitting room. There was the photograph of her father in uniform, and the coronation mug and the donkey with a basket on its back and Uncle Alfie's jug with 'A present from Southend' on it, and on the wall was the *Little Sweetheart* picture. It looked nice, she thought, really nice.

She saw that Mr Charrington was watching her with that special amusement in his brown eyes.

'Well,' he said, 'are we going to put the kettle on, or aren't we having any tea today?'